Abraham's Bones

by

Joe Prentis

Abraham's Bones

Abraham's Bones
All rights reserved
Copyright 2007 by Joe Prentis

Reproduction in any manner, in whole or in part,
In English or in any other language, or otherwise
Without written permission of the author is prohibited.

This is a work of fiction.
All characters and events portrayed in this book are fictional,
And any resemblance to real people or incidents is purely coincidental.

PRINTING HISTORY
First printing 2007

ISBN 978-1-4357-0080-2

PRINTED IN THE UNITED STATES OF AMERICA
10 9 8 7 6 5 4 3 2 1

If you purchased this book without a cover, you should be aware that this book might have been stolen property and reporter as 'unsold and destroyed' to the publisher. In this event, neither the author of the publisher has received payment for this stripped book.

Joe Prentis

To the wonderful men of God, both past and present, who have served and shepherded the congregation of First Baptist Church.

Abraham's Bones

I wish to thank the many people who helped and encouraged me with this project. A special thanks to my wife who endured the long hours I spent in front of my keyboard and for her help as first reader. Also to my brother Fred and to Irma who read portions of the manuscript. I also want to thank the wonderful group at Crimescene Writers for the thoughtful way in which they answered my questions and gave me technical advice whenever I had a difficult problem. A special thanks to fellow writer Susan Fleet, who always had an encouraging word when my spirit lagged.

Chapter One

As the Vatican limousine approached the service entrance of the *Porta Sant' Anna*, John Christopher leaned forward in the soft comfort of the rear seat, examining the view spread out before him. He had attended mass here on several occasions, but like most of the other visitors, he had always arrived on foot. This magnificent enclave was even more impressive, he decided, when seen from the rear seat of this luxurious automobile. As he waited, expectantly, the driver swung the car across the busy thoroughfare and rolled to a stop in front of the wrought iron gateway. Two Swiss Guards emerged from their glassed enclosure and swung the gate, causing a crowd of tourists to scurry toward the safety of the pedestrian walkway. The powerful engine purred softly as the car moved down the length of the cobbled drive and drew to a halt in front of the Apostolic Palace. Christopher stood for a moment on the walk gazing upward at the magnificent structure, then followed his escort up the steps to the entranceway where he was greeted by a papal aid with a youthful, cherubic face.

"I'm Father Salviati," he said, as Christopher shook the soft, animated hand. "If you will come with me, His Eminence is waiting."

Christopher followed his escort down a wide corridor, their footsteps echoing loudly on the smooth marble floors. Climbing three flights of stairs and passing through a series of chambers, they stopped in front of an elaborately carved door. Just inside the en-

Abraham's Bones

trance was a tall, stately official he had met almost five years before, Albert Louis Mason, the former Cardinal Archbishop of New York. It had been three years since their last meeting, and he saw that Mason had aged somewhat, although he still had the carriage and vigor of a much younger man. The warmth of Mason's smile dispelled any hesitancy he had in coming here.

"I'm grateful you were able to come so promptly, Mason said, indicating a chair with a wave of his hand.

Crossing in front of the oversized desk, Christopher sank gratefully into the softness of a rose damask settee. As he waited for the cardinal to explain his reason for summoning him here, he glanced through the tall windows overlooking the square. He decided he was somewhere to the right of the third floor balcony where the Pope made his Sunday appearances. A large crowd filled Saint Peter's Square, and he would have liked nothing better than to stand in front of the windows and watch the ceremony that would be unfolding at a few minutes after eleven o'clock. This momentous event would start when an open-topped Fiat Jeep bearing the Pope would pass through the Acro delle Campane and move slowly through the waiting crowd. Most of the Vatican was off limits to visitors and few people outside the priesthood had seen a Papal Mass from this lofty perch.

Christopher turned away from the window as an attendant entered the chamber with a silver tray and coffee service. He presented a cup that looked as fragile as an eggshell with the thoughtful deliberation of a bishop at High Mass. Christopher raised it to his lips and felt the warmth spread through the cold numbness in his chest. Mason continued to search through the clutter on his desk until he found the file he was looking for underneath a neatly folded copy of the *L'Osservatore Romano*.

"I'm sorry to have pulled you away from your conference, Dr. Christopher. I would have waited until the afternoon session was over, but I have some important business I wish to discuss with you."

"No problem, Your Eminence. I'm glad to be of service."

Christopher had come to Rome to attend an archeological conference at the prestigious Gregorian University. As he thought about the tense atmosphere at the morning session, he could not help wondering if Mason's problems had any connection with his own.

"Your conference is going well?" the cardinal inquired politely, bringing Christopher's thoughts back to the present.

"We have experienced some of the same infighting you would expect at a political convention. I'll be amazed if it continues past today."

Mason's shaggy eyebrows lifted, revealing a pair of eyes as blue as a leprechaun's. "The representatives are concerned about what, specifically?"

"Some of them are objecting because the western nations are conducting most of the archeological work in the Middle East. Until recently, everyone has been content to leave archeology in the hands of the most qualified personnel."

Mason opened a folder, examining a thick report for a moment, and then leaned forward and passed it across his desk. Attached to the top sheet was a photograph of a tall, skeletal figure peering into the lens of the camera. The vacant look in his eyes gave him the appearance of a corpse.

"His name is Father Sangallo," Mason said. "He made an effort to enter the morning session at your conference yesterday but was detained by the Carabinieri."

Christopher frowned at the scrawled message above the Papal seal. "I wasn't aware of the incident. Do you happen to know what he wanted?"

"Actually, he wanted to see you."

Christopher glanced up from the photograph to find Mason studying him intently. "Do you happen to know what he wanted? I've never heard of this man."

"He's evidently heard of you. He has also demanded an audience with the Holy Father." When Christopher did not say anything in response, Mason sighed and looked uncomfortable. "These rural priests can sometimes be distressing. Dozens of them petition the Vatican each year expecting some unknown village personage to be elevated to sainthood."

"I'm sure there's nothing to worry about. If he returns to the conference, someone in security will deal with it."

"Appearances can sometimes be deceiving. During the last world war, he was only a boy, but he was deeply involved with the resistance movement. For the last fifty years, he has been content to sit in his quaint little village and minister to his congregation. For no apparent reason, he has suddenly turned into a dangerous zealot."

Christopher was now thoroughly confused. He had assumed Mason's desire to see him had something to do with the conference, but the difficulty obviously involved something of a more serious nature.

"Has he made threats?"

Mason lifted his hands outward causing the light from the chandelier to glint brightly from the gold ring on his finger. "For the moment, let's just say it has something to do with faith."

"If this has anything to do with miracles, I might not be able to help you. My experience lies in the opposite direction. Every area of my profession requires scientific proof and careful documentation."

"Am I to assume you've never seen a miracle?"

Christopher paused, not knowing where Mason was going with this. "I've seen things I couldn't explain under the rules of scientific experimentation," he answered carefully.

"But no burning bushes in the deserts you've wandered across?"

"Nothing dramatic, I'm afraid."

Mason's face crinkled but the smile did not reach his eyes.

"I'm also assuming you no longer have any official connection with the State Department in Washington."

Christopher wondered how much Mason already knew about his decision to leave government service and decided to keep his explanation simple. "I accepted the position in Washington with the understanding I would only serve until the crisis in the Middle East was over, or until suitable personnel could be recruited to fill my position. I resigned last year in order to return to archeology."

Before Mason could reply, there was a knock on the outer door of the office. His forehead creased in annoyance as the door opened cautiously.

"Yes?" Mason inquired without turning all the way around. A papal aid entered the office and leaned toward Mason's ear. He whispered rather urgently, looking mildly unhappy all the while, and then presented a folded sheet of paper before withdrawing from the chamber. Mason read the message in silence, and then ejected himself from his chair with a surprising amount of agility and crossed to a window overlooking the plaza. He stood for a moment in silence, and then lifted his head and gazed at the cross on top of the obelisk.

"God works in mysterious ways," Mason mused in a distant voice. Then turning quickly around, he fixed him with a penetrating stare. "Are you acquainted with Congressman Nick Danville?"

"I've never met Congressman Danville, although I know of his accomplishments."

"Accomplishments," Mason repeated with the faintest touch of humor. "No wonder you were such a good negotiator, Dr. Christopher. Some of his critics have characterized him in less flattering terms. He has been in Israel for the last week on what he has described as a fact-finding tour. A terrorist's bomb killed him and his entire delegation."

"Has anyone claimed credit for the incident?" Christopher asked.

"The only explanation is in reference to the political climate—as if that explains anything. The authorities accused him of trying to smuggle an artifact out of Israel that has a great deal of significance to the Muslims. Is there such a thing as a coffin case?" Mason moved away from the window, walking slowly and looking down at the floor like someone picking his way through a minefield.

"Coffin cases were Canaanite in origin, dating from around 2000 BC. The Egyptians used something similar to bury their dead, although the ones they used were a lot more elaborate. You may recall the one containing the body of King Tut."

"What would be the significance of this relic to the Muslims?"

"No real connection except for it being a part of the area's early history. The Shepherd Kings who ruled Egypt during Abraham's era were probably Canaanites, and possibly from Ashkelon."

"Do you know a reporter named Keith Maitland?" Cardinal Mason asked, abruptly changing the subject.

"We are acquainted," he admitted reluctantly. "He worked for one of the major news services in Washington. There were some questions about his ethics. He was transferred to their European bureau as a result."

"Maitland has flooded our Public Relations Office with inquiries on a number of subjects. Your own name has come up."

Christopher nodded his appreciation for the information, but decided to keep his thoughts to himself.

Mason was toying with the note the messenger had given to him a few minutes before. He opened it and peered cautiously inside. "According to the information I have received, the Palestinians have rejected General Zecori's appointment as the chief negotiator. Some of my friends in Washington suggested it might be useful to have you contact some of the leaders in the area. We won't be able to make any progress until someone persuades the interested parties to return to the bargaining table. I'm prepared to offer you a position which would make this possible."

"And this would involve what?" Christopher asked cautiously.

"The Vatican does not have diplomatic relations with Israel, so we cannot officially appoint you as our ambassador. I am prepared to offer you an appointment as ambassador-at-large to the Middle East. Your contacts with world leaders will give you unlimited opportunities to accomplish what formal diplomacy hasn't been able to bring about. Tempers have been heating up again all over the region, and some of it has spilled over into the streets. I am especially interested in any suggestions you might have in reducing the level of tension. Suicide bombings and riots seem to be increasing by the hour."

"I appreciate the seriousness of what you are saying, but you seem to be implying the reaction in the streets is a byproduct of the political situation, when it is really the other way around. There is nothing spontaneous about any of it."

Mason sighed. "It is hard to realize we have a whole generation obsessed with conducting a holy war."

"If the only tool you have is a hammer, every problem begins to look like a nail. Pounding on the problem produces a steady supply of victims and nothing else."

Mason had become still in his chair. "Are you suggesting we have an irresolvable situation in the Middle East?"

"Let's just say too many of our solutions have been short-sighted. While the Zionists had uncontested control of the government, there were fewer problems from a diplomatic standpoint. In recent years, the power of the ultra-Orthodox Jews has been steadily increasing. Many of them believe the present political state is not the one foretold by the prophets."

"Which is precisely the reason I think you are the right man for the job. Your experience in Middle Eastern affairs will be invaluable."

"If I were to decide to accept your appointment, what would be the extent of my responsibilities?" Christopher asked.

"Will your normal duties require you to travel to areas outside of Israel?"

"I will be visiting archeological sites in Egypt and Jordan in the next few weeks."

"Will you be speaking with any of the government leaders while you are there?"

"Not directly, but you have to realize most of the mid-level positions are held by family members of the persons in authority. It would be relatively easy to convey any message to the proper individuals."

Mason gave a relaxed smile as he leaned back in his chair. "This is a remarkable turn of events. I think our people will agree it was an opportunity created in heaven."

Although he was hopeful, Christopher did not share Cardinal Mason's bright optimism. "If the proposals are unacceptable, they might argue it was a plot hatched in hell."

Mason looked sober for a moment, but did not comment, as if failure was not an option.

"Friendship, Dr. Christopher, can go a lot further than diplomacy. Our actions and our doctrine must show some coherence. We must not abandon the principals of the church for the prospect of a temporary peace. I am prepared to supply you with a small but competent staff to handle any contingency. The most difficult problems might come from another quarter," he said, gesturing toward the report Christopher had returned to the corner of the desk.

"And this priest of yours is a part of the problem."

"Let's say he is a small manifestation of the problem. It is a lot broader than one priest."

"Do you have any idea why he wanted to see me?" Christopher said.

"It has something to do with some artifacts in his possession. He seems to believe there is a spiritual significance attached to those objects. A number of persons in his village claim to have been healed."

"Has anyone examined them?"

"Father Ricci is one of our leading experts on Middle Eastern antiquities. He has made a preliminary examination but has not reported his findings. I understand there is an inscription in an unknown language Father Ricci has been unable to decipher. He has suddenly taken ill. His doctor reports he slept better during the night, but he seems to have become delusional. He has reported voices speaking to him out of the darkness and he has seen a strange light. I hope it is a reaction to his medication rather than the onset of Alzheimer's."

Before Christopher could reply, Mason climbed abruptly to his feet.

"If you can spare the time, I would like to show you something remarkable. It's the perfect example of what can happen when scientific method isn't followed."

Without waiting for Christopher's reply, Mason came briskly around the corner of his desk and headed for the door. Christopher followed him down the corridor to a flight of stairs and descended to the ground floor. They passed through a courtyard and across an expanse of well-manicured lawn. He was surprised when they came around the corner of the building and discovered they were approaching the basilica from the north side.

Mason allowed him to stop inside the doorway and look up at the dome towering high above them. Sunlight spilling through the windows in the lantern tower was illuminating the richly decorated interior. Someone had once told him the walls of this huge building were 26 feet thick, which was necessary to support a dome over 400 feet high. Mason let him stand for a few seconds examining the soaring columns and then beckoned him on with a wave of his hand. They passed in front of the Papal Altar to the giant statue of St. Andrew, then through another door into a narrow passageway leading down into the grotto. Mason stopped with his hand on the door and started speaking in the monotone of a tour guide.

"In Roman times, the Trastevere region was a sparsely settled area outside of the city proper. At the time Constantine was preparing to build this church, the Circus Nero was unused. It would have been an easy matter to locate the building there. Instead, he leveled this spot which was an enormous engineering feat, requiring the removal of a million cubic feet of earth."

They descended a flight of stairs and passed through a doorway into an area having the appearance of an alleyway in some ancient village. The walls of these small buildings abutted directly against the neighboring structures.

"We are standing underneath the dome of the basilica," Mason said. "Before the area was leveled, this was a necropolis and these structures were above-ground tombs. Most of them can be dated from before the time of Christ."

Christopher peered through one of the open doorways and saw a room about twelve feet square. There were several pots setting at the rear of the room. Mason shined his flashlight into the mouth of a jar.

"Most of these contain human remains," he said as he reached inside. Something rattled as he stirred around in the contents.

They continued along the passageway until they came to an open area. The stones in this section were red and the walls were considerably higher. Mason gestured toward the ceiling.

"If you were to drop a plumb-bob through the floor from the top of the dome, it would pass through the altar and point directly at this spot. They found an inscription reading, *Petros eni.*"

Peter is within! Christopher turned sharply around. He had read of this but had never expected to see it firsthand.

Mason began pacing back and forth like a caged lion. Christopher knew he had brought him here to see the grave, but there was another reason compelling him to do so. Mason stopped in the shadows, moving his flashlight along the top of the foundation stones. There were probably electric lights here, but for some reason, Mason had not switched them on. He lowered the flashlight, illuminating a small circle around his feet. The pale glow reflected from the stones left his body shrouded in darkness, his face a dim apparition.

When Mason spoke, his voice was scarcely above a whisper. "Constantine believed this was the tomb of Simon Peter and located the church here to fulfill the prophecy. The bones were subjected to scientific tests and it was proven to be the body of a large male who died somewhere near the end of the first century."

Christopher glanced around at the walls and saw several inscriptions he guessed to be the names of Simon Peter's successors. Before he could ask his question, Mason interrupted.

Abraham's Bones

"Have you seen the movie about the dropping of the atomic bomb on Japan?" Mason asked. "I've often wondered if the scene in the Oval Office really happened, or was it the invention of some Hollywood writer? President Truman was in the process of selecting a pilot to lead the squadron. He handed the soldier a button and asked if he could end the war by pushing it, would he do so. There was a dramatic pause while the camera panned forward showing only his hand and the button. His thumb remained motionless for what seemed like eternity and then plunged downward. It was one of Hollywood's most suspenseful moments."

"I'm not sure if I understand the question, Your Eminence. Was the soldier allowed to ask for clarification?"

The flashlight moved, tracing a jagged pattern along the ground. "There are some things in life you don't question, my son. Before this is over, it might test the extent of your Christian commitment."

Mason took a step closer and Christopher found himself staring directly into the cardinal's eyes.

"Do you see the inscription on the stone where you're standing?" Mason asked, directing the beam of light downward where it illuminated a small circle around his feet. Dirt covered most of the writing, but Christopher could make out an inscription on the polished stone. When he looked up, the piercing gaze had not shifted even a millimeter.

"After the crucifixion, a Christian friend placed a stone there to mark the grave. You are standing on Simon Peter's tombstone."

Christopher had a sudden, almost overpowering desire, to leave this place and get as far as he could from this soft-spoken cleric. As if he were sensing his uncertainty, Mason inched closer where there was no more than a hand's breadth separating them.

"It's imperative for us to arrange informal discussions no later than the end of this month. Will you accept the assignment, Dr. Christopher?"

He hesitated, and then after a moment of wondering if he was the worse kind of a fool, gave a brief nod of his head.

"Then raise your right hand," Mason commanded. "I would like to administer your oath of office before God and these witnesses."

Christopher glanced around at the shadows where the other Popes had joined the bones of Simon Peter throughout the ages. As he lifted his hand to take the oath of office, he could not help wondering where such a momentous decision might take him.

Chapter 2

Senator Amos Cauldfield looked up in annoyance as his secretary entered his office unannounced. She hovered just inside the doorway until he dropped his pen and placed the thick report in his out basket. Six other bills urgently required his attention, and at this rate, he would be here until after midnight. He knew he had a luncheon scheduled with someone, but he could not remember whom it was with or the nature of the business.

"There's someone named Siedman from the Department of State to see you," Kelly said in a tentative voice, laying a cream-colored business card in front of him. "No one bothered to make an appointment, but evidently it's urgent. The request came directly from the Oval Office."

None of this made any sense to him, but before he could put her through the third degree, she jerked the door open and retreated to the outer office. Cauldfield swiveled his chair away from the clutter on his desk and walked to a window overlooking the Mall. The incessant downpour made the Washington Monument almost invisible in the distance. Behind him, the door closed softly. He took his time in turning around.

Siedman was not what he had expected. The suit she was wearing could easily have been mistaken for a military uniform, although there was nothing military about the attractive young woman facing him across the corner of his desk. He waved a hand toward the green leather chair in front of the desk and returned to his own seat.

"I'm here at the president's request," she said as he scooted some files around and leaned back in his chair.

Kelly was an expert at running interference, but somehow this woman had wormed her way through the outer defenses and was sitting in his office as calmly as Joan of Arc had sat before Henry the VII.

"How may I help you?" he asked.

She waited for a few seconds as if she could not decide if he was being deliberately tiresome, and then her eyebrows ruffled in a way he found wonderfully attractive.

"Didn't the president call you?" she asked in a lovely soprano voice.

"I have no idea," he said, not bothering to explain that he would not have taken the call even if he had known the president was on the line. When he did not elaborate, she glanced down at her lap for a few seconds before her chin came up, revealing a pair of eyes as green and unblinking as those of a cat.

"The White House should have briefed you," she said.

"In this case they didn't."

"It would have saved both of us a lot of time."

"I don't have a lot of time as you can see by looking at my desk. Why don't you just tell me as briefly as possible?"

"There's no way I can be brief about this. It's far too complex to explain in a few words."

"Try," he suggested, watching her face carefully.

She took a quick breath and shook her hair away from her collar. Her hair was shoulder length, a glistening shade of black. It curved inward just below her earlobes with the ends tucked inside the collar of her blouse.

"We may be on the brink of a diplomatic crisis in Israel if we attempt . . ."

"I believe those problems have been resolved," he interrupted before she could finish. "Negotiations should be resuming within a matter of days."

"This has nothing to do with negotiations. We've been asked to turn off the spy satellites covering the Israeli sector of the Middle East."

He stared at her for a moment, but when she did not attempt to clarify her statement, he said, "It's completely out of the question. Every nation in the region benefits as much as Israel does. We've discussed this before."

"This time it is Israel who is asking us to turn them off."

He stared at her for a moment, not sure he had heard correctly. "Do you have any information which would clarify this request? What could their military hope to gain? I'm afraid I don't understand."

"It didn't come from the military. It came from the Prime Minister's office. This request came immediately after the government announced the discovery of a Roman road skirting the southern wall of Ashkelon. It was more than thirty feet beneath the soil, but they were able to see it clearly after processing the imagery from the satellite. The technology is called Thermal Infrared Multispectral Scanning."

"Am I correct in assuming this is similar to the radar scanning our planetary probes have done on Mars?"

"All of it wasn't radar," she said, and launched into a detailed explanation of how the technology worked. After a minute of listening, he held up his hand and stopped her.

"I wasn't aware anyone at the State Department was an expert in space technology?"

"I am an archeologist. We use some of the same technology."

Cauldfield examined her face for a few seconds and then turned her business card around. Her name was Julia Siedman and the job description identified her as assistant to the director of Middle Eastern Affairs at the State Department. "You're Alexandra Siedman's daughter."

"Yes, I am," she said, and he noted the pleased smile softening her features.

Alexandra Siedman was legal counsel for the Republican National Committee and had helped shape the careers of many of her party's hopefuls. She was attractive and intelligent but could sometimes be ruthless. This young woman was softer in appearance, but was probably no less of a formidable opponent.

"I believe we met last year at the President's Christmas Program," he said. "You were with John Christopher."

"I was, yes."

There had been a brief but significant pause before she answered his last question. Her expression had not changed, but he could not help noticing her small, delicate ears had reddening slightly. After studying her reaction to this question, he decided to ask another.

"I've often wondered why Christopher didn't stay with the State Department until the present crisis was over. His contacts with the leaders in the Middle East have been invaluable."

"I'm . . . not completely sure. He didn't confide in me."

"And what is your relationship with him now?"

This time he got the full impact of her green eyes.

"I don't have a relationship with him now, and I didn't come here to discuss my private affairs. I came at the president's request."

The abrupt way in which she had answered made him pause for a few seconds before he replied. "I didn't ask the question to antagonize you."

"I'm sure you didn't, but I don't like questions about my personal life." Her lips parted slightly, and were softer looking, as if she was focusing on some inward pain.

"It wasn't about your personal life. I was asking about your working relationship," he said, attempting to moderate the tone of his voice, but even as he was speaking, he realized he had not succeeded very well.

She tossed her hair in a gesture that was becoming familiar. "Dr. Christopher and I were employed in the Middle Eastern section of the State Department until his resignation. I have known him for most of my life. When we were in school, we spent our summers together in Israel. My grandparents were in charge of the archeological site where we worked."

He searched through the clutter on his desk and extracted a thin folder with a half dozen sheets stapled together. Turning to the second page, he circled a paragraph and slid it across the desk. She read it in silence and then looked up.

"I'm familiar with the problem in general terms."

"How serious is it?"

Her shoulders lifted slightly. "Very serious, and it has become worse in the last few months."

"Could you clarify the situation? I have read the reports my staff prepared, but none of it seems to make any sense. I can understand why Arab terrorists might want to blow up religious sites having nothing to do with Islam, but these people are apparently Jews."

"Israel has immigrants from 80 nations represented in a population of six and one-half million people. An organization calling itself Shiva has raised a great deal of controversy within the government over immigration issues."

"I don't think I'm familiar with them. Is this a political organization?"

"We aren't exactly sure what they are, but they are on our watch list. So far, no violence has been attributed to them."

"Do you happen to know what the name means? I seem to have heard the word, but I can't recall at the moment."

"It means seven."

"Seven what?"

Her shoulders lifted slightly. "Shiva is the Hebrew numeral for seven, but it is used in countless ways just as it is in English."

"Do you have any idea why anyone would want to bomb these religious sites? The existence of Israel depends on the preservation of its heritage. It's the only element binding them together as a nation."

"If you are a European Jew, and your family has not had any contact with the homeland for two thousand years, you look at things differently than a Jewish person who grew up in the Middle East. To say someone is a Jew is almost as ambiguous as saying someone is an American."

"These conditions have existed for most of my lifetime," he said. "Why they are trying to blow the country out from under each other now?"

"The differences are in numbers and this is what most of our people fail to understand. When some of the more vocal groups were relatively small, the Zionists ran the government and ignored the opposition. A growing percentage of emigrants are members of ultra conservative factions. It's changing the whole structure of the country."

"None of this explains why they would want us to turn off the surveillance satellites when they pass over Israel," he said. "It has to be a government decision made at the insistence of the military."

"Most Israelis would rather see religious sites destroyed than to have the spiritual side of their faith overshadowed by brick and stone. I believe this request is purely political because of what the imaging revealed. Evidently, another Roman road was one too many."

"Or it could be a ruse by the military," Cauldfield suggested. "A weapons' system could be hidden in the ground they don't want our satellites to detect. The latest technology makes it possible to see more than a hundred feet into the soil."

"I'm not sure we understand everything about their motivation, but the president believes we should humor them. Rather than fighting this through a half dozen committees, we were wondering if you could get everyone's cooperation in an expedient manner."

"I have a better suggestion. The Vatican has appointed John Christopher as ambassador-at-large to try to bring the leaders of the area back to the conference table. I would like to send you to the area as Washington's representative. You seem to be very knowledgeable regarding the political situation."

"I was born in America but I have spent most of my life in Israel. I still consider it to be my home."

"Then you *are* Jewish."

She hesitated. "Actually, I'm a Christian."

Her answer brought several questions to mind, but he could not think of an appropriate way in which to phrase them. Instead, he said, "The first meeting will be no later than the end of the month. Would you have any objections to working with him on this assignment?"

Her green eyes blinked once as she considered the implications. "No," she said after a moment. "I have no objections."

Cauldfield pressed a button on his intercom. The office door opened immediately as if Kelly had been hovering with her ear to the door.

"Get Dr. Erlich on the telephone," he commanded. "I want to talk to him as soon as a meeting can be arranged, and then call Al Jazeera and see if they know how to reach Sanura."

Julia was immediately on her feet. "Did . . . Are you talking about Richard Erlich and Sanura Hamada?"

He looked up in surprise. "Yes, I've consulted both of them on numerous occasions when I have a question about the Middle East. Do you know them?"

Her lips parted as she gazed at him through narrowed eyes. "Yes, in a manner of speaking."

Cauldfield leaned back in his chair and regarded her thoughtfully. "Is this problem similar to the one between you and Christopher, or is it something different?"

Julia lifted her hand and waved it vaguely around before letting it drop back to her side. "I'm sorry," she said. "My remark was inappropriate."

"Bring us some coffee, Kelly," he said into the intercom without taking his eyes from her face. Her eyes moved randomly around the office as if she was trying to find a way to escape, and then she seated herself cautiously on the edge of her chair. Almost immediately, Kelly came hurrying through the door with two steaming cups and placed one of them in her hands. She took a tentative sip and then sat the cup on the edge of his desk. Her embarrassment had softened her features and he realized this young woman wasn't simply pretty—she was beautiful.

"Tell me," he invited as gently as he could.

She took a deep breath and studied him silently for a moment before she replied. "My grandparents worked in the Middle East for over forty years. My grandmother wrote twenty-seven books about their archeological discoveries. Erlich was her publisher. After she was diagnosed with Alzheimer's, Erlich produced a television documentary in which he made it appear as if my grandparents were minor employees of his publishing company. Sanura was the director and narrator of the documentary. She is very knowledgeable about the Middle East, but she is also a radical Muslim. People tend to overlook the outrageous things she says because she was a world-class tennis player and still has a tremendous following among sports fans around the world. During the years she has worked for Al Jazeera, she has interviewed almost every radical revolutionary in the Middle East. My grandmother has signed a contract with Erlich to write a historical novel, and he has hired Sanura to help her. My grandfather is dead because of Erlich, and I will have to go through all of this unpleasantness again."

Cauldfield had seen the same look on the faces of demonstrators as they rushed the police lines. "And how was Christopher involved in this?"

She took a quick little breath and focused her eyes in the general direction of his face. "After Erlich's documentary appeared on television, some documents disappeared in a very mysterious manner. John could have given us some support, but for reasons of his own he chose not to do so."

"Did this have anything to do with his decision to resign from the State Department?"

She closed her eyes for a second and then opened them slowly, blinking against the light. "No," she breathed, in a voice so low it was barely audible above the pounding of the rain against his window. "It had absolutely nothing to do with it. It was entirely his decision."

She climbed abruptly to her feet, and he did the same, coming around the corner of his desk. He brought her to a halt by touching her arm and then gathered her cold hands between his own.

"You don't have to accept this assignment," he told her. "I'm sure the department will have another expert who will be satisfactory." Her chin lifted suddenly and he found himself looking into her eyes.

"I see no problem," she said. "Thank you for seeing me."

"I'll see what I can do about your request," Cauldfield said. She squeezed his hand in reply and turned toward the door of the outer office. Cauldfield stood where he was until the door had closed behind her, wondering what had caused this lovely young woman so much pain.

Chapter 3

Maitland had first become aware he was being followed when he had left *da Benito* restaurant almost an hour before. One of the men was walking almost a hundred meters behind him, while the other was sauntering along the opposite side of the street with an air of nonchalance as improbable as the broad-brimmed hat he had placed squarely on the crown of his head. Both of them seemed to think they could become invisible by keeping their eyes focused on the cracks in the sidewalk.

Amateurs, he thought contemptuously as he continued along the avenue toward a tour group gathered in the Piazza di Santa Maria. Judging by the suits these two men were wearing, they were plainclothes policemen from the Carabinieri, probably snatched from their boring desk jobs by some autocratic supervisor who thought they needed some experience in the field. If they were seeking experience, they could not accuse him of failing to give them a good workout, although they were probably annoyed because he had kept them waiting in the cold while he had enjoyed a sumptuous meal and a bottle of the restaurant's finest wine. The man across the street had exceptionally small feet for someone with such a large girth, and his legs did not seem to be moving with the steady pace of almost an hour before. Without giving any warning of his intentions, Maitland turned abruptly and jogged across the street in front of an oncoming car. Behind him, he could hear hard leather slapping against the surface of the pavement as both of the men broke into a sprint.

As Maitland drew near the idling bus, he saw an elderly woman reading aloud from a pamphlet while the members of her tour group were busy snapping pictures. When each of them returned home, these pictures would be indistinguishable from the hundreds of others from previous trips, and no one would be able to remember exactly what each photograph represented. He had never been able to understand the fascination tourists had with Roman churches, and could not understand their willingness to tramp through countless grottos and nameless courtyards. Churches filled the entire city, and you could not walk anywhere in the *Trastevere* without hearing the annoying clamor of their bells. He skirted the church and started up the street toward the hill. Behind him, he could hear the woman describing the *Tempietto* by Bramante, commemorating the spot where St. Peter was martyred, blah, blah, and blah.

There was no traffic here and he could hear the labored breathing as the two men struggled to keep up. Turning to his left, he circled the small, round edifice, and then cut through the park, stopping by the statue where Anita Garibaldi remained frozen in time atop her noble steed. For a brief moment, he gazed across the rooftops toward the Vatican, frowning thoughtfully to himself. He suppressed the desire to break into a run, knowing if he outdistanced these two, they would summon help with their cell phones. He wanted them to continue following him until Giulietta had time to pick up the package and return safely to their apartment.

The wind was not blowing as strongly as it had earlier, and he imagined he could feel a touch of spring in the air. After a few more minutes of brisk walking, he turned down a familiar street and saw the glimmer of sunlight on the slowly moving waters of the Tiber. Going quickly up the steps of his apartment, he unlocked the door without looking behind him. The apartment was quiet and he did not see Giulietta anywhere, although he could hear soft music playing from the bedroom on the floor above. He imagined she was soaking in his tub as she did on infrequent occasions.

He removed his jacket and draped it across the back of his favorite chair. He was desperately in need of a drink. Instead of mounting the stairs as he first intended, he went down the hallway and into the kitchen. Opening one of the cabinets, he found the bottle of Jack Daniels where he had hidden it almost two hours before. The ice tray refused to move until he slammed it with the palm of his hand. He dropped three cubes into the bottom of a thick tumbler, and then dashed a couple of inches of 90-proof into the glass. He emptied it quickly, then tilted the bottle and filled it again. This time he took a slow sip and ran the amber liquid around on his tongue, savoring the biting, smoky taste.

"Giulietta!" He called again, but did not receive a reply. He listened for a moment wondering if she had followed his instructions, or if she had done something stupid. He called her name again, this time more sharply. When he received no response, he slammed his glass on the bar top and went quickly toward the stairs.

"*I'll kill her,*" he threatened under his breath.

He rounded the newel post in a rush and went quickly up the stairs. The music had grown louder and he realized it was coming from the television, rather than from the entertainment center he had bought the previous month. Following the sound of the music, he found her stretched out on the mattress with the contents of the package spilled across his side of the bed. The only movement of her body was the rhythmic rise and fall of her breast. He bent toward her, seeing the smooth perfection of her small, compact body. It always left him breathless despite the three months they had been together. She had the face of a Madonna and the grubby, unkempt body of a street urchin. He had hoped he would find her soaking in the tub, but he could see her feet were dirty. They were always dirty, the soles as black as the cobbles in the Piazza Bella. His hand closed around her hair and he yanked her from the bed. Her voice was pitched high, a mixture of anger and pain.

"Have you lost your mind?" she shouted at him. "What do you think you are doing? Turn me loose!"

Instead of answering, he swung her around where she was facing the torn envelope and the pile of documents he had removed from the bed.

"Can you explain this to me?"

"Someone tried to take it from me! He tore the end of the envelope when he snatched at it, but I turned and I ran."

He grabbed her shoulders and gave her a hard shake. "Who was it? Was it a policeman?"

Her mouth was open now, and he could see the whiteness of her teeth and the anger smoldering in her eyes.

"Don't tell me you have gotten me in trouble with the authorities. I did everything I could do to save your precious package! You have no reason to be angry with me."

He lifted his hands from her shoulders, knowing she was telling the truth. She was beautiful, so beautiful, when she was angry.

"Okay," he said. "*Va bene*," but this enraged her even more.

"*Non va bene!*" You are crazy, evil, a dirty old man!"

He looked at her angry, startled expression, then threw back his head and laughed. "You are right! I am dirty. I think dirty, I live dirty, and I think you are the most beautiful child I have ever seen."

"*Ti detesto!*" she cried and whirled toward the stairs. A few seconds later, he heard the slamming of the front door. There were times in the last few months when he had thought he loved this precocious child with her simple taste and unpredictable moods. He realized he was not likely to see her again. As he gathered the contents of the package and seated himself with his back against the headboard of the bed, he decided it really didn't matter. By tomorrow night, he would be in Tel Aviv.

He flipped slowly through the papers, examining a picture showing John Christopher standing next to a young woman he recognized as Julia Siedman. A hand-lettered sign in the background told him this had been a fund-raising event for an African charity organization at the National Gallery of Art. Separating this picture from the others, he leafed slowly through the rest of the file, then stopped and examined a photograph clipped to a thick report.

Even without the sticky note attached to the photograph, he would have known the girl standing at the opposite end of the tennis court was Julia's sister. She was staring expectantly into the distance as she waited for the serve. Her body was trim, athletic, the perfect example of little rich white girls who played the sport. The note said her name was Daniella. She was fourteen, the same age as Giulietta. He closed his eyes and realized he was holding his breath. This story could be the most important event in his career. It could earn him a Pulitzer!

Chapter 4

Julia looked up at the stranger blocking her view through the sixth floor window overlooking the Mall. It was not easy to get a window reservation in this fashionable restaurant, and she had managed to do so only once before when she had booked a table several weeks in advance. A last minute cancellation had occurred just as she had arrived at the reservationist's desk and Giorgio had been gracious enough to escort her to this window seat. If she was not mistaken, this was the same table Rachel Ray had occupied only a few months before when they had filmed an episode for the Food Channel. She had thought this stranger was going to take a seat at the adjoining table, but he was gazing directly at her.

"You're Julia Siedman," the man said, more as a statement of fact than as a question.

After studying his face for a few seconds, she was sure she had never seen him before. He reminded her of someone she had seen in the Olympics, or had it been one of the tennis players at the U.S. Open. Before she had time to speculate any further, he indicated the empty chair with a wave of his hand.

"May I?" He asked, and was already in the act of seating himself when she said, "Actually, I'm expecting someone."

If he heard her protest, he gave no indication as he folded his lean frame into the chair.

"Have we met?" Julia asked. There were dozens of people she could have had lunch with, but she had wanted to be alone where she could go over the events of the past hour and assure herself she had not made a mistake in accepting Senator Cauldfield's appointment. As she tried to think of some way short of rudeness to drive him away, his mouth widened, displaying a set of perfectly aligned teeth and a smile he had probably practiced in front of a mirror. He did not seem to be bothered in the least by the direct way in which she had confronted him.

"We haven't actually met, but when I couldn't reach you at your office I decided to catch you here," he explained.

As Giorgio unfolded the menu and presented it to her, she suddenly realized no one at her office knew where she would be having lunch. This stranger could not have known unless he had followed her from Senator Cauldfield's office. As she gazed at his pleased expression, she could not decide if he was delighted with her appearance, or if he was pleased with his own.

"Order anything you want," he said. "Lunch is on me."

As a waiter passed the table carrying a tray laden with sweet smelling pastries, she had a perverse impulse she did not have the power to suppress. "I think I will have the lobster and one of those large salads with . . ."

"Lobster isn't on the luncheon menu, and even if it was, I doubt if my employer would go that far to make you happy."

A vase of freshly cut flowers was setting in the center of the table. He picked it up, looking doubtfully at the small, delicate petals, and then deposited it on a cart laden with dirty dishes. Julia decided it would be amusing to see if she could make him as uncomfortable as he had made her.

"And who might your employer be?"

"Congressman Nick Danville."

During the last year, Danville had been involved in an ongoing dispute with the State Department on a variety of issues. She resisted an urge to fold her menu and walk out.

"You followed me here," she said, and was surprised when he nodded rather eagerly in agreement.

"Guilty as charged. I followed you when you left Capitol Hill. My name is Gary Maser. You forgot to ask."

"What do you want from me, Mr. Maser?"

"Gary."

"I think I will stick with Mr. Maser for the moment. You have ten seconds to tell me what you want."

"I couldn't possibly in ten seconds, and we haven't ordered yet."

"You have already wasted half of your time." This time she did fold her menu, but he stopped her by placing his hand gently on the back of her wrist. She looked past Maser's shoulder and caught Giorgio's eye. She was relieved when he moved forward with the grace of a jungle cat and stopped only a few paces away.

"Why don't you tell me what you want?" she invited. Maser's attention was focused on the strap of her sandal as if he had forgotten his purpose in being here. She changed her position in the chair and placed both of her feet flat on the floor.

"You may not have heard, but Congressman Danville has been kidnapped."

Julia hesitated for a moment, unable to determine what this unexpected event could have to do with her. "I'm not acquainted with Congressman Danville."

"I didn't suppose you were, but what I have to tell you is confidential. I wonder if you could meet me somewhere so we could discuss this in private?"

Julia felt a stirring of alarm at this unexpected request. "You should have called my office and ask for an appointment? If you will excuse me, I have to go."

Maser scooted his chair back a few inches. "I'm terribly sorry to sound so mysterious, but this isn't the place to discuss something of a confidential nature."

"You're back on the clock, Mr. Maser. You have another ten seconds to start making some sense."

Maser seemed to have only two modes. Either his eyes were focused intently on hers, or they were darting rapidly around the restaurant.

"Congressman Danville has been kidnapped."

"And what makes you think I can help you?"

"The kidnapping occurred in Israel. The first report we received led us to believe the terrorists had killed him. Then we received word he is alive and they are demanding one million dollars for his safe return."

"Am I to assume you will be in charge of trying to secure his release?"

The way in which Maser was chewing at the cuticle on his thumb, reminded her of a laboratory rat locked in a cage.

"Actually, I'm only a go-between."

"Mr. Maser, if what you are telling me is the truth, a man's life is at stake. My job description identifies me as a trained negotiator, but what I do is in the field of international politics. The last thing you need is someone meddling in a situation they don't understands. It could have a disastrous result."

"The communication we received was straightforward and to the point. I have every reason to believe they will uphold their end of the bargain."

"I hope your assumptions are correct for Congressman Danville's sake."

"I'm hoping they will give us a time and a place to deliver the ransom where we can settle this as quickly as possible."

"Then why do you think you need my help?"

"As soon as we received the communication, I spoke to someone who is very knowledgeable about terrorism in the Middle East. He knows you quite well and he says you have contacts with certain individuals who are members of this organization."

Julia frowned at him, not completely sure she understood what he was suggesting. "And who is our mutual friend?"

"A newspaper reporter named Keith Maitland."

"I would hardly call Keith Maitland a friend, and I have no idea what he means by contacts."

Maser looked quickly around, but when it appeared no one at the nearby tables was interested in what they were discussing, he leaned forward and spoke in a soothing voice hardly above a whisper.

"The organization holding Congressman Danville is known as Shiva."

Julia tried to keep her astonishment from showing. According to the information she had received, Shiva's existence was a carefully guarded secret. Could someone have leaked this information to the press? Then she realized it was not what Maser had meant. He had suggested she actually knew someone inside the organization.

Abraham's Bones

"And who am I supposed to know in Shiva?"

Maser placed the tips of his fingers together and looked down at his carefully manicured nails. "My informant tells me your sister is a member."

Julia felt a rush of anger surge through her body with the intensity of an electrical shock. "My sister is not a member of any terrorists organization! If you know anything about Keith Maitland, you must know he is an accomplished liar. He has been in legal trouble countless times because of his unsubstantiated allegations."

"I have reason to believe Mr. Maitland's information is correct. At his suggestion, I spoke to Sanura Hamada. While she refused to confirm my suspicions, she could not deny them either. She is very knowledgeable about the Middle East and she seems to think . . ."

Julia was immediately out of her chair and was barely able to restrain herself from swinging her purse at his head.

"My sister is little more than a child, Mr. Maser. Suggesting she could have a connection with this kidnapping is preposterous. Stay away from me in the future or I will have you thrown in jail."

Maser climbed quickly to his feet but she easily evaded the fingers plucking at her sleeve. When he attempted to follow, Giorgio stepped into his path, blocking the passageway toward the exit.

"Is there a problem?" she heard the waiter ask politely. She could not hear Maser's reply for she was already winding her way between the tables.

Ignoring the group of rain soaked tourists huddled under the protection of their rain gear, Christopher ran up the steps and pushed through the doors leading into the lobby of his hotel. He had intended to call some of his colleges and arrange to meet them for dinner, but with this unexpected rain, he had changed his plans. He would call the concierge and have something sent up from the ABC Grill. Turning toward the elevator, he heard someone calling his name. He waited as a blue uniformed messenger approached from the direction of the desk.

"I have a package for you, *signore*," the messenger said as he extended a clipboard. Christopher signed his name and received an envelope containing several sheets of thick paper. He glanced at the upper left-hand corner and saw the word, Sangallo, written in a spidery script. The name sounded vaguely familiar, and then he remembered this was the name of the priest who had tried to reach him at the conference. He turned quickly around but the messenger had already crossed the lobby. Christopher started to call after him, but instead, tucked the envelope under his arm and walked toward the elevator.

As the elevator lumbered upward, he dug his address book from his pocket and glanced at his watch, trying to determine the time in Washington. He could hear the telephone as he unlocked his door. He ignored the incessant ringing and went to the windows overlooking the street. Traffic on the Via Veneto had slowed to a crawl. Lightning flashed, filling the room with a blinding light. He let the curtain fall back in place and clicked on a floor lamp beside the couch. The telephone had continued to ring.

"Christopher," he said as he scooped up the receiver and placed it against his ear.

"This is Andre Havran, Dr. Christopher. I wonder if we might get together this evening to discuss an important item of business."

After sitting in meetings all day, business was the last thing he wanted to discuss. A list of the convention's officials was lying on the table where he had dropped it before leaving for the morning conference. Flipping quickly through the booklet, he found the page listing the telephone numbers of the committee members. He located Wilmington's name and the phone number of his hotel.

"You might try Neal Wilmington, Mr. Havran. I'm not on the board this year."

"This doesn't have anything to do with the convention, Dr. Christopher. It was another matter I wanted to discuss with you."

"Could you tell me the nature of your business? I have some important things I need to take care of this evening."

There was a pause and for a brief moment, Christopher wondered if the connection had been broken. Then the voice came back, this time with a distant sound as if the caller had moved away from the telephone. "We met last year in Washington at Roger Chaffre's retirement dinner."

Chaffre's retirement dinner had been the last function he had attended before leaving his job at the State Department.

The wind outside was now gusting, driving rain across the balcony. He pulled the curtain back a couple of inches and saw two men standing in the cloudburst looking at the bumpers of their automobiles. Someone on a Vespa swung recklessly toward the sidewalk, charging past with the exhaust popping like the firing of an automatic weapon.

"Tonight is completely out of the question. I have some work to do and I don't want to go out again in this rain."

"I'm across the street from you, Dr. Christopher. I could come over and meet you downstairs at the Grill. It has some of the finest food in Rome."

Christopher lifted his head and looked across the Via Veneto at the walls of the American Embassy gleaming wetly in the glare of a dozen or more spotlights. His room was directly in line with the *Palazzo Margherita*, the fortress-like building housing the embassy offices. Something in this cautious, well-modulated voice had aroused his curiosity.

"Very well, Mr. Havran, would one hour from now be convenient?"

"One hour from now would be perfect. I'll arrange for a table."

Christopher placed the telephone back on its cradle and went to the attache case he had dropped just inside the entrance. Thumbing quickly through though the thick bundle of papers Cardinal Mason had give to him, he found a booklet containing a summary of the offices of the Curia and the relationship between each. He read this section of the booklet, making a few notes for future reference, and then flipped to the last page containing a list of telephone numbers. There was one for the American Embassy, but this number was for the American Embassy to the Holy See. Havran had called him from the building across the street housing the offices of the American Embassy to Italy. The Vatican was a sovereign nation and had its own consular representatives. Any official contact between his office and the American government would be through the Consulate to the Holy See located near the Vatican. They would not be trying to reach him through the embassy across the street.

Who was Andre Havran and what did he want?

He remembered the package he had signed for in the lobby. He went to the coffee table and picked it up, looking first at the address before thrusting his finger underneath the flap. A stack of photographs slid into the palm of his hand.

Christopher angled the top photograph toward the light and saw the object in the picture had the color and appearance of a roofing tile. Focusing on the first line of text, he realized he had never seen anything like this before. Scanning quickly to the bottom of the first photograph, he did not see any words he recognized. There were seven tablets, all of them intact with only a few blemishes on their surface. At the bottom of the last one was a small sketch drawn in exquisite detail, showing two kneeling figures with their outstretched wings almost touching in the center. Beside the sketch, were several bird-like figures enclosed in an oblong frame that looked like an Egyptian cartouch. As he studied these figures, he realized each of them contained seven straight lines, cleverly constructed by someone who was a talented artisan. The letter seven was the perfect number, often used in ancient inscriptions to represent the deity. He studied the pictures for another minute and then looked at his watch. It was time to meet Havran in the grill.

Chapter 5

The ABC Grill had always been one of Christopher's favorite restaurants. His last occasion to dine there had been during the previous year when he and Julia had been in Rome on business for the State Department. They had stayed across the street at the American Embassy, eating hasty meals at the conference table while they worked. On their last evening, they had slipped away and spent a long and pleasant evening dining on some of the best cuisine Rome had to offer. It had been an occasion to remember, for they had discussed the future and their desire to get back into archeology full time. Back in Washington a week later, he had made an appearance on Fox News to promote a documentary Dr. Erlich had produced on archeology in the Middle East. When he returned to his office, Julia had told him Erlich had stolen her grandmother's research. Trying to reason with her had been an impossible task and the discussion had become heated. She had stormed out of his office and refused to see him again.

He pushed these haunting memories aside as the waiter seated him by a window overlooking the street. It was early to be dining by Roman standards, but there were already a respectable number of tables filled. He saw someone approaching and looked up as the man drew a chair out on the opposite side of the table.

"I'm Andre Havran," he said, pointing at the wine list. "If you haven't already ordered, I might suggest the *Brunello di Montalcino*. It's the equal of the best Bordeaux."

Christopher studied the man's features, noting a head of closely cropped hair, graying at the temples, and a tasteful but nondescript suit. At any political event in Washington, there would be men like him standing on the fringe of the crowd with a cord dangling from one ear. Havran had suggested they had met at Roger Chaffre's retirement dinner, but he was certain he had never seen this man before. Rather than challenging him openly, he decided to wait and see how this little drama would play itself out.

The waiter appeared at their table and they placed their orders, engaging in small talk about the city and the various points of interest along the broad avenues of this upscale neighborhood. Havran kept the conversation light until the waiter placed the steaming plates of antipasto in front of them, then unfolded his napkin and began eating with a surprising appetite.

"I regretted your decision to leave government service, Dr. Christopher. There are a number of people who know their way around a conference table, but you're acquainted with most of the diplomats and you speak the languages like a native."

"I stayed longer than I intended. I am an archeologist, not a bureaucrat."

"In your situation, I think the word *patriot* fits better than bureaucrat."

"I don't think of myself in those terms, Mr. Havran. Archeological work in the Middle East depends upon the political stability of the region. I thought anything I could do to promote world peace would compensate for the time I spent away from my career."

"The position you've accepted with the Vatican is prestigious, but you're likely to find yourself in the same situation you gave up when you left Washington. I can't help wondering why you considered it in the first place."

"My role will be to bring the delegates back to the bargaining table. It shouldn't take more than a week or two at the most."

"What will be your first step when you return to Israel?"

"My first step?" Christopher said.

"Well, you seem to be suggesting you aren't going to be entering immediately into negotiations. I naturally wondered what your approach might be."

"I will continue with what I am doing now. If tensions continue to build, they will probably shut down all of the archeological work in the region. I have been evaluating everything currently underway and trying to help the various teams make intelligent decisions in the time they have left. My duties will bring me in contact with various government leaders all over the Middle East. It will be easy to steer the conversation into the proper channels."

"I seem to recall reading an article in *National Geographic* about the work at Ashkelon. I assumed most of it had already been dug up."

"Less than two percent of it has been excavated."

Havran looked surprised. "Maybe I'm showing my ignorance, but I've never understood how those ancient cities were buried in the first place. Where does the dirt come from? Is it from sandstorms?"

"Most of the deposits are the natural process of human existence. Ancient civilizations used the streets for a sewer and there were animal droppings, wood, garbage, and potsherds thrown out of the doorways on a daily basis. Every few centuries invading armies knocked the buildings down and built on top of the ruins. There is no way you could dig up all of Ashkelon. The mound is over 50 feet high and covers 150 acres."

Havran's eyes had a faraway look as he contemplated the immensity of what Christopher was describing. "I can imagine 50 feet high, but I'm a city boy and I have no idea how large 150 acres would be."

"We are talking about a pile of rubble ten times the area of the World Trade Center collapse. They used power equipment to clear the wreckage away and it took over seven months. Archeologists use small hand tools. Anything larger would destroy most of the artifacts."

"This is interesting. I would like to see it firsthand."

The waiter arrived at that moment with the *secondo*, a steaming platter of *brasato al Barolo*—the braised short ribs that were a specialty of the house—and a *contorno of scorzanera alla romana*. Havran had not yet explained his mission, but Christopher decided to contain his curiosity until they had finished their meal and the attentive waiter was content to leave them in peace.

"Getting back to the political side of your job," Havran said as he dropped his napkin on the corner of the table. "As you are already aware, political conditions have taken a nasty turn in recent months. Fighting could break out almost anywhere."

"I'm optimistic, but it's obvious we need to proceed with caution."

"Then I wish you luck, Dr. Christopher. My main concern is the possibility of open warfare breaking out along the border the Muslim world shares with China. It would be a serious mistake on the part of the terrorists. Many of these radical groups have grown accustomed to having the governments of the Middle East look the other way. Ideology is driving the unrest now. It can be dangerously unpredictable where China is concerned."

"I'm well aware of the dangers we will be facing in the coming weeks."

On the other side of the table, the dark eyes came up to examine him carefully. "I wasn't just speaking of the dangers in the Middle East. I'm speaking of Rome as well."

Havran had apparently been talking with someone in government and was overreacting to the priest's attempt to force his way into the conference.

"I really don't think there's anything to be concerned with."

"I wasn't referring to the trouble at the conference, Dr. Christopher. Are you aware you are being followed?"

Christopher sat his glass carefully on the tablecloth and studied the troubled expression on the other man's face. "Who would be interested in me? I'm just barely interested in myself."

"I suspect they have some connection with al-Qaeda, but at this point we don't know."

"Who are we?"

Havran blinked as if he was surprised at the question. "Who do you think I represent?"

"A while ago I thought you might be with the military."

Havran gave him a startled look. "I resigned from the military almost ten years ago. I should have explained everything, but I thought you knew."

"Knew what?"

"I have a personal interest in this as well as a business arrangement. I am the administrator of Julia and Daniella's trust funds. We like to think of our investors as being a part of our family."

"What company do you represent, Mr. Havran?"

"Marshall Wurman Associates."

"And who is Marshall Wurman?"

"The investment banker."

Christopher thought for a moment but drew a complete blank. "I'm afraid I don't understand. What is Mr. Wurman's interest in the peace process?"

"Most of his family perished in the holocaust. He wants to make sure this particular episode isn't repeated."

"And what is your position with Mr. Wurman?"

"I'm a research associate. In the past couple of years, Mr. Wurman has provided over half of the funds for archeological work in Egypt. I have just arranged a grant to the University of Cairo to provide financial assistance for the work at Tel el Amarna."

"I would have expected a Jewish philanthropist to spend his money in Israel, considering the political climate in the Middle East," Christopher said.

"Mr. Wurman has spent a substantial amount in Israel, but an investigation of the historical problems has to start in Egypt. He is determined to establish the identity of the Pharaoh of the Exodus."

For a moment, Christopher was not sure Havran was serious. "There isn't enough proof to establish the correct date to everyone's satisfaction."

"I would have thought the dates of most Biblical events would have been established a long time ago."

"It isn't from a lack of trying, but anytime you question the traditional dates of any biblical event, you are fighting an uphill battle. Many of those dates were little more than guesswork by people who knew nothing about history or science. Finding the answer to those questions might be an interesting undertaking, but the same money spent elsewhere might prove to be worth far more."

Havran's eyebrows drew together. "I'm afraid I don't follow you."

"Archeological projects intended to prove some biblical fact are always doomed to failure. Some of our early archeologists manipulated data in an attempt to make their findings fit the prevalent theories. It cast suspicion on everything they did. We are better off sticking to scientific method and letting the discoveries speak for themselves."

"Mr. Wurman has a substantial amount of proof in his possession to back up his claims."

"What kind of proof?"

"Some artifacts came into his possession in recent weeks. I would like for you to examine them."

"The possession of illegal artifacts can be a criminal offense," Christopher said.

"Mr. Wurman is not a collector, Dr. Christopher. He intends to build a museum where he can display all of his artifacts. It will be available to the scholar for research and for viewing by the public. Mr. Wurman has no desire to keep anything for himself."

"The current procedure is for archeologists to make everything available to the authorities in the nations where they are working. Where did Mr. Wurman obtain these artifacts?"

Havran's eyes went quickly around the room, and then he leaned forward and spoke in a quiet but somewhat defensive manner. "He obtained them from Congressman Nick Danville."

Despite his efforts to maintain a neutral expression, he found himself blinking under the steady gaze. "I'm more than aware of Congressman Danville's contribution to the arts, but the buying and selling of illegally obtained artifacts is a criminal matter. It's viewed very seriously in the Middle East."

"When you hear the circumstances under which they were obtained, I think you will agree with what he did."

"Once an artifact is moved without proper documentation, its historical value diminishes dramatically," Christopher said.

"A lot of artifacts have been destroyed when the looters are in danger of being caught. If we hadn't acted quickly, they could have been lost forever."

"Congressman Danville was killed this morning," Christopher said. "A terrorist planted a bomb in his SUV. It killed him and his entire delegation."

Havran hesitated. "According to a report I received only an hour ago, he was taken hostage. The kidnappers are asking for one million dollars for his safe return. Mr. Wurman is prepared to pay the ransom as soon as details of his release can be arranged."

"Kidnapping for ransom isn't the usual pattern in the Middle East. Are you sure your source is reliable?" Christopher asked.

"We are very sure, but there are some problems concerning his release."

"What problems?"

"The terrorists have informed us they will only work through a reliable intermediary. Certain officials in Washington are suggesting it might be useful if you would make the arrangements."

During their discussion of archeology and history, Christopher had started to relax, but he drew back now as he examined the expression on the other man's face. "Whom do you really work for, Mr. Havran? The CIA?"

"I thought I explained my role in this. Surely you don't think I am misrepresenting myself."

"You called me from the embassy compound across the street," Christopher said. "It is unlikely you would have been there unless you were a government employee." He scooted his chair back, prepared to rise from his seat when Havran leaned toward him again.

"Hear me out, Dr. Christopher. This is a lot more complicated than you might imagine."

"I am sure it is, but I am not the man for the job, whatever it might be. I'm sorry I can't help you." He had started to rise when Havran lifted his hand and indicated the unfinished bottle of wine. Against his better judgment, Christopher settled back in his seat, prepared to hear whatever argument he cared to present.

"You have been involved in government service for a number of years. I don't understand your reluctance."

"I was employed by the State Department."

"The State Department has close ties with all of our intelligence services, plus a lot of others around the world. Surely you don't think I'm suggesting something unlawful?"

"This is the point I'm trying to make. Something legal in Washington might not be viewed in the same way in the Middle East."

"I think if you knew the whole story you would view it differently."

"Try me."

Havran pinched his lower lip between his thumb and forefinger. "I was in and out of the Middle East for a number of years while I was with the Pentagon. In the years I have worked for Mr. Wurman, he has never asked me to do anything illegal or disloyal to my country. In fact, this is the reason I am here. It is my understanding you received a package containing information about some recently discovered artifacts."

"I haven't had time to evaluate them properly."

"Do you know where the artifacts were discovered?" Havran asked.

"There was nothing to indicate their source," he said.

"It is my understanding they were found in the harbor at Alexandra more than fifty years ago. There is a strong possibility they came from the museum of ancient history destroyed by the Romans. They are believed to date back many thousands of years."

This information was interesting considering what he had learned from Cardinal Mason, but as he thought about the implications of Havran's information, he sat upright in his chair.

"Does this have any connection with Congressman Danville's kidnapping?"

"You might say so—in an indirect way."

"And what is Marshall Wurman's role in this?"

Havran sat completely still, his eyes focused on the far corner of the room. Christopher was suddenly aware the faint sound he was hearing was not traffic noise, but was emanating from a small device attached to the back of the other man's ear. A small flesh-colored wire disappeared into the collar of his shirt. *Was some unseen person listening to their conversation and giving instructions to Havran?* He resisted the urge to take a careful look around the room.

"Actually, I was sent to Rome to try to recruit you for this mission. We desperately need someone with your qualifications."

"To what end?"

Havran set his wineglass carefully on the table. "I cannot overstate the importance of this undertaking, Dr. Christopher. Mr. Wurman's interest goes far beyond archeology. He is involved in a lot of government contracts, and as a result, he is prepared to provide financial assistance to help in the peace process."

Despite his better judgment, Christopher remained in his seat. "Why do you think outside financing is needed?"

"Mr. Wurman is a billionaire recluse in the tradition of Howard Hughes. Three years ago, he established a foundation for bringing about a lasting world peace. He is willing to place billions at the government's disposal if necessary. He offered to compensate the government for some of the expenses incurred during the Iraqi war, but his offer was rejected by some of our more liberal politicians."

This offer represented a lot bigger cookie jar than the Iran-Contra affair, without any accountability to congress or the oversight of some governing agency.

"I'm afraid I'm not interested, Mr. Havran. Cardinal Mason would take a very dim view of this whole affair."

Havran sat for a moment toying with his wineglass, and then tilted his head at an angle where Christopher could see the brightly-lit American flag from across the street reflected in the lens of his glasses.

"Actually, it was Cardinal Mason who suggested this meeting," he said.

Christopher stared back at Havran without blinking. What had started out as a challenge, had taken on a new and disturbing dimension.

Chapter 6

Julia saw the blinking light on her answering machine as she went rushing through the door of her apartment. She punched the button as she ran past, knowing she would not have time to do everything she needed to do before her flight to Israel. On her previous assignments she had been given a full week to prepare, but the president's Chief of Staff had given her an absentminded shake of his head when she had told him she simply could not be ready to leave on such short notice.

"I'm sure you can work something out," he told her with a little gesture of dismissal as he turned to the group of minions hovering at his side.

The answering machine beeped as she kicked off her shoes. She was halfway to her bedroom when she heard her mother launching into a message as if she was dictating a memo to her secretary.

"Gavin will let you in. You will find the package in the kitchen. Give your grandmother my best and tell Daniella I will call her soon."

Julia continued to stare at the answering machine after the message had stopped. She had not seen her mother in almost three months, although she had left message after message on her answering machine. On her birthday she had received an expensive pair of earrings and a greeting card, although it was obvious it was not her mother's signature on the card.

She whirled away, trying to think. There wasn't time to make a list, but it was obvious she needed her passport and her clothes. Rushing toward her closet, she grabbed an armload of dresses and skirts from her closet—letting the hangers drop to the floor—shoved everything inside and slammed the suitcases shut as she began punching numbers on the keypad of her phone.

Light rain was falling as she ran down the steps to a taxi waiting at the curb. The damp air produced an astringent smell unique to Washington as to no other place on earth. It reminded her of the smell of toner emanating from a copy machine, while others had described it as the odor of power and money. She gave the driver her mother's address in Georgetown as she jerked the door closed.

"But you said the airport," the driver protested as she punched in her secretary's number.

"Georgetown first," she said, settling back in the seat as the office phone was picked up. She explained the problem to her secretary and told her to call Jamison Kearney and explain the situation to him. By the time she had finished the call, the driver had rocked to a stop in front of her mother's apartment. She rang the apartment manager's bell and was escorted to the elevator by the manager's assistant.

The young man stopped in the doorway as she continued down the hallway flipping on lights. She found the package wrapped in plain brown paper on the kitchen cabinet beside the telephone. She picked it up, and without thinking, pressed the button on her mother's answering machine. She heard a beep and then her sister's voice explaining she was disappointed, but understood the reasons why their mother had not been able to attend the banquet, then said goodbye with a little catch in her voice.

Julia looked around the richly furnished apartment where two presidents had lived before moving into the White House. From where she was standing, she could see into the formal dining room and the chair near the foot of the table where she sat the last time her mother had entertained guests. She had never been invited here just to visit, had never had a mother-daughter conversation in this house, nor had she spent a night here since she had been shunted off to her first year at Andover.

She looked at the wastebasket as she weighted the package in her hand, but instead, placed it back where she had found it and went quickly down the hallway where the manager's assistant was staning by the door jingling his keys.

Springtime in Rome had always been a pleasant experience for Christopher, despite the unseasonable weather for most of the week. Shop owners along the thoroughfare had set pots of flowers in front of their windows, but the weak spring sunshine did little to highlight their colors. Rain from the previous night had stopped, although there was still a steady drip of icy water from each rooftop. Underneath the awning of a small bookshop, he glanced through the window and was surprised to see his picture on the front cover of a magazine. He retraced his steps and pushed through the entrance where a tinkling bell announced his visit. The proprietor accepted his money and went back to his crossword puzzle. He pocketed the change as he scanned the front cover, then flipped through the pages until he found the pictures of a half-dozen Washington politicians credited with some cautious statements about the upcoming peace talks. On the opposite page was a photograph of a man being shoved against the side of a van. The headline read: *Ambassador Christopher refuses to talk to the press. Injured reporters threaten to sue!*

The picture looked vaguely familiar, and after studying it for a moment, he realized where he had seen it before. A well-known singer and actress had been leaving a New York bistro when her bodyguards had become involved in a shoving match with a group of over-aggressive paparazzi. The man in the foreground was about his own height, and the resemblance was close enough to fool almost anyone. He had started to throw the magazine away when another story caught his eye. This one quoted an unnamed official in the Pentagon.

Are there unknown links between John Christopher and Middle-Eastern terrorists groups?

The article went on to mention the frequency in which his name occurred in intercepted messages from al-Qaeda. When he saw Keith Maitland's name, he threw the magazine into a trash container without reading any further. Cardinal Mason had warned him of Maitland's inquiries at the Public Relations Office at the Vatican. Maitland's assignment to the European bureau of his network had resulted from reporting information he knew to be false. Julia's mother had played a role in Maitland's banishment from Washington's political scene. If Maitland was aware of this, he would not relax until he had received retribution from everyone connected with his downfall.

A strong gust of wind tugged at his coat as he reached the Piazza Barberina. Crossing the cobblestone promenade, he pushed his way through the entrance of the La Baita Cafe. This was one of the preferred meeting places for tourists, where many of them ate a sandwich while standing in the narrow space in front of the bar. The smell of food was heavy in the air, and binding all of these fragrances together was the tart odor of apple wood from the wood-burning stove in the kitchen. The maître d' escorted him to a table by the front windows, affording him an unobstructed view of the piazza. He ordered a bottle of wine while waiting. It had no more than arrived when he saw Havran on the far side of the fountain peering across the plaza toward the Quattro Fontane. Christopher wondered what Havran was waiting for, when he realized there was someone with him. The stream of water cascading from the upper basin of the fountain obscured his companion from view. The two men remained hidden for a moment longer, and then came toward the restaurant at a moderate pace as if they were making an effort to blend in with the tourists. As they drew closer, he could see the elderly man was limping slightly.

As Havran escorted his guest to the table, Christopher noticed how out of place this man looked in his drab worker's clothing. A Greek fisherman's cap covered his forehead concealing most of his features. He dropped wearily into his seat, hiding his face from view. Havran continued to stand beside the table examining the crowd before he took his own seat.

"Someone was following us," Havran said, without bothering to introducing the man he had brought with him.

Christopher scanned the piazza but did not see anyone looking suspicious. Turning his attention to the man seated across the table, he realized he looked vaguely familiar, and then he noticed the top of a clerical collar peeking through the open lapels of a threadbare coat.

"This is Father Sangallo," Havran said, confirming his suspicion. Christopher tried to hide his surprise as he reached across the table and grasped a thin, trembling hand, wondering what Sangallo could want with him now.

"I'm afraid I haven't had time to evaluate your photographs," he explained.

When Sangallo leaned forward, Christopher could see a row of widely spaced teeth the color of old ivory.

"Do you have the pictures locked safely away? You can't imagine how important they are now that I no longer have the artifacts."

"I mailed them to my office in Israel after I learned someone had searched my room. How did you come into possession of them?"

"Are you a spiritual man, Dr. Christopher?"

Judging from Cardinal Mason's remarks, this priest was a devout mystic, interested in generating a miracle for the populace of his provincial village. He hesitated, sensing Sangallo would be disappointed if he gave him a truthful reply, yet not wanting to be misleading.

"In religious matters I am a moderate, although I don't deny the miraculous nature of God or the power of prayer," Christopher said.

Some of the tension seemed to have gone out of the priest. "I assumed as much after reading your most recent book."

"From what Cardinal Mason told me, I understand several miracles have been associated with the artifacts and a number of persons have been healed."

Sangallo's eyes narrowed. "My village is a poor one, Dr. Christopher. If there are any miracles, they came from the money my friend left me on his death. The money might have been dishonestly obtained, but it mended the roof of our church and bought a supply of medicine we desperately needed."

"Are you offering the artifacts for sale?"

"Certainly not," Sangallo said, looking offended.

"Then I'm afraid I don't understand my role in this."

Sangallo's eyes darted back and forth for a few seconds as if he did not know what to make of Christopher's remark. "I thought it would be obvious. The text is written in an unknown tongue."

Abraham's Bones

Sangallo had made an interesting choice of words when he referred to the inscription as a 'tongue' rather than simply saying it was an unknown language. This immediately brought up images of first century Christians and the linguistic miracles attributed to them.

"I wouldn't go so far as to say it is an unknown language. We have found examples where someone borrowed an alphabet from another culture. Is there anything you can tell me about the location where the artifacts were found?"

Sangallo was darting glances toward the window as if he was still trying to locate his mysterious pursuer. He seemed rational enough, but Cardinal Mason obviously thought differently. Sangallo waited until a man in a dark suit passed the window, and then directed his attention back to the two men seated with him at the table.

"The artifacts were among a number of art objects taken from the Jews during World War Two."

"And how did they come into your possession?"

"I received them from one of my parishioners. As he lay dying, he told a rather interesting story. He said he was helping move some contraband across the border near the end of the war. Partisans attacked the convoy and stole most of the treasure. He had an opportunity to grab something, so he took an ammunition box. He was rather disappointed when he saw the contents of the box. He hid it away in his barn, afraid someone might connect him to the attack. Some of the people involved were in the German High Command. They didn't want any witnesses who could implicate them when they took up their lives again under new identities."

Christopher suddenly wondered if this priest might have had an active role beyond confessor. Had he been one of the *bandire* who carried out the raid? "Why did you send the photographs to me?"

The lines in Sangallo's face deepened and he looked saddened and older, as if the weight of this sin was an actual, physical presence. "Because I want them returned to their rightful owner."

"I understand there are several government agencies empowered to handle those matters. Why didn't you go directly to them?"

Sangallo's watery eyes blinked and for an instant, Christopher thought he would refuse to answer. He dropped his gaze and ran his thumb across the tips of his fingers as if he could feel the remainder of his life slipping through his hands.

"I decided to trust you after I saw the name on the container inside the ammunition box."

"The name?"

"The label on the box said, Pearlman. I understand you are associated with his granddaughter, Dr. Audrey Siedman."

Christopher leaned back in his chair and looked at this frail priest with his nervous mannerisms and evasive answers. He thought back, trying to remember what he knew of Dr. Siedman's family and their history. He knew they had lived in Switzerland during the war and had been involved in the banking profession. Where had Dr. Siedman's family obtained these artifacts, and what was the significance of their discovery? These were not the kind of items a collector would acquire as art objects, and then another question occurred to him.

Who were these dangerous people following Sangallo and to what lengths would they go to get their artifacts back.

Chapter 7

Julia settled into her seat and fastened the seatbelt, wondering if there could be any further problems with her already hectic schedule. The day had started out impossibly rushed—an Amtrak into New York after the closure of Washington International when they had detected nitrates on the shoes of a landscape contractor—and now the lights were flickering ominously as the plane was getting ready to taxi on the runway.

"I say . . . are you Michaela Harris?" the young man seated next to her asked. He had an erratic smile, strangely in phase with the flickering lights, and a shock of unruly hair growing low over his forehead.

"No, sorry," she said and shifted her body slightly away after focusing for a second on his hopeful expression. Her repeated efforts to reach Christopher had been unsuccessful, and when she had tried to call her sister, there had been no answer. After thinking about this for a moment, she decided Christopher and Daniella were probably dining together in some fashionable restaurant, which would account for her problem of being unable to reach either of them. The thought of them being together and enjoying themselves, while she had to endure hours of boredom on this crowded flight, was more than she could stand.

The lights had stopped flickering and the plane was now rolling steadily forward. "Who is Michaela Harris?" she asked when the young man continued to focus intently on her face.

"On the early morning news on Fox Network."

Julia vaguely remembered having seen someone on one of the networks named Harris, but did not think it had been on Fox. This Harris, if she remembered correctly, was a willowy blonde with blue eyes, while her own hair was black and her eyes were green. Harris had been the subject of a prolonged manhunt in Pakistan, having disappeared while she was on assignment to interview a tribal chieftain.

"I understand Harris is missing and presumed to be dead," she said as the plane started to race down the runway.

"Are you going to take her place?"

Julia leaned back against the headrest as the seat tilted and the plane began to lift, trying to suppress another sigh. She did not intend to explain her appointment to this impetuous stranger. "Would you mind if I just closed my eyes and rested for a minute? My day has been impossibly rushed and I have a headache."

"I have something for that in my bag," he told her, and became wildly animated all at once.

"No!" Julia cried, grabbing his arm as he reached for the catch on his seatbelt. He stopped with raised eyebrows, taking a slow look around the cabin as if he was unsure of what he had missed. With an air of total bewilderment, he turned his attention back to her.

"Surely, you don't think I would give you something to harm you. The bottle is still sealed. I can show you."

Julia did not release the pressure on his arm until he leaned back again in his seat.

"The plane is taking off. You are not supposed to move around. Haven't you flown before?"

"Actually I haven't, but how did you know?"

Julia was amused at his naivete. "I'm good at guessing things. They won't even let me buy lottery tickets."

"It doesn't seem fair," he said.

"Life has a tendency to be unfair. Would you mind if I closed my eyes and tried to rest them for a minute?"

"Would you like for me to hold them while you sleep?"

Julia aimed a frown in his direction. "Pardon me?"

"Your valuables."

When Julia continued to frown at him, he said, "In case someone should try to rob you while you're asleep."

She was fully awake now, any possibility of sleep having vanished. "Perhaps you're right," she told him. "I think I'll just sit here and gather my thoughts."

She turned her head toward the window but was uncomfortably aware of his concerned expression reflected in the darkened glass. He was darting glances in her direction like an overly concerned parent on a crowded playground. It was early morning now in Israel. Why had Christopher failed to return her telephone calls?

Had he forgotten or had he decided not to talk with her?

She hesitated, trying to decide what she should do.

I will not call him again, she decided after a moment of thinking about the implications. *I will just show up as if nothing has happened.* She turned her face toward the darkened window, determined to find something soothing and pleasant to occupy her time.

Nevertheless, her mind betrayed her, and she realized she *was* thinking about it and all of the unpleasantness she would have to face tomorrow. Sanura Hamada would be waiting for her in Israel, coming into their home on a daily basis to work with her grandmother. How could Erlich have had the indecency to hire this woman, considering her long involvement with radical causes? During the years she had worked for Al Jazeera, she had joined with every American-hater around the world, making no secret of her loyalties and aims. Despite the impropriety of her actions, Erlich had allowed her to direct the television special based on her grandparent's work. He had even allowed her to twist their findings to advance the Arab cause. This was unthinkable when you considered the fact that Erlich was a German Jew.

Julia tried to force her thoughts away from this unpleasantness, but her weariness allowed her mind to veer again and she found herself thinking of Sanura and of Christopher's involvement with her. At the time of their breakup, she had been focusing on her inward pain, and it was only later she had remembered his stricken expression as she had turned away from him.

Could the expression she remembered have been nothing more than regret?

She turned her head toward the window, but not before the tears forming in her lashes had trickled down the sides of her cheeks.

"Is there some way I can help you?" The young man beside her seemed to be waiting anxiously for her answer.

When she saw the look of concern on his face, she managed a smile. "So this is your first trip to Israel."

"It is, as a matter of fact. I have always dreamed of returning to our homeland. In America, everything is too secular. I want to worship as my ancestors did. Are you Jewish?"

Julia thought about his question for a few seconds then realized it was far too complicated to explain to this stranger. "I have some reading I must do," she said, removing a manuscript from her bag and flicking on the small reading light.

"Is it something for the morning news?" he asked.

"It's a manuscript. My grandmother is an archeologist. It's part of a historical novel."

"Hey, cool! I'm going to Israel for the summer to work at an archeological site."

"Where in Israel?"

"Ashkelon. Are you familiar with it?"

"Yes," she said as she removed the manuscript from the envelope. For some unknown reason, this impetuous young man no longer seemed so strange. He was either mentally deficient, or exceptionally brilliant, and she could not decide which it was. Sometimes these two extremes were the same.

She removed the metal fastener binding the pages together, looking at the bold type of the heading for a moment before she ran her eyes down the length of the first page. The story, she realized, was set in the fifteenth century B.C., though she was surprised the location was Egypt rather than Israel. Well, it really didn't matter. Her grandmother was familiar with the history of the entire region. She glanced again at the title, feeling a mixture of anticipation and happiness as she began to read.

While the old priest was threading his way slowly toward the corner table where he was waiting, Maitland took a careful look around the interior of the restaurant and congratulated himself on

Abraham's Bones

choosing this particular establishment for their meeting place. He had arrived a half-hour early, and after a few euros had exchanged hands, the waiter had escorted him to a table where he had an unobstructed view of the entrance, and also of the street through a wide expanse of leaded glass. He was reasonably sure no one was following Sangallo, but he knew you could never be too careful. Sangallo slowed as he approached the table as if he was uncertain of the welcome he might receive. He was wrath thin, obviously in his early 80's, with the ravenous appearance of a wolf. Maitland climbed quickly to his feet and extended his hand. Sangallo's palm was cold to the touch, the bones of his hand as fragile feeling as the skeleton of a bird. He indicated an empty chair with a wave of his hand and dropped back into his own seat.

"Will you allow me to buy your dinner?" Maitland asked, watching the dour expression alter at the mention of food. It had taken almost a full day to locate the seedy hotel where Sangallo was staying, but it had taken no more than a few minutes to determine the extent of his financial distress. He knew all priests took a vow of poverty, but as he thought about this, he knew that on some level the poverty had to be symbolic. Priests could not travel as extensively as many of them did without currency. This was something he had never really thought about, but this new realization offered a possible solution to his problem. If he offered a monetary gift, would he deposit it in the nearest offering box for the poor, or would he keep it for himself?

"I would be delighted to dine with you," Sangallo said with Old World courtliness. Maitland felt some of his tension ebb, although it did not dissipate completely.

While this restaurant was not on the itinerary of most tour groups, it had some of the best food in the Trastevere. If he was going to loosen Sangallo's tongue, what better way than to ply him with wine and expensive food. As he was modifying his plan, a waiter appeared as if by magic, presenting oversized menus that looked as if Michelangelo had designed them. Sangallo flipped his open and pointed at an item with the practiced familiarity of one who had dined here for years.

"You want to know about the artifacts," Sangallo said as soon as the waiter had taken their orders and departed in the direction of the kitchen.

"How did you know?" he asked, feeling ridiculous because he had underestimated Sangallo.

"To a man of your abilities, it should be obvious."

"Obvious?" Maitland said, not sure he liked Sangallo's assessment of his character.

"I did not mean for that to be synonymous with foolish, Mr. Maitland. You are far from being untutored, but you probably aren't aware of the scope of this. Since last week, someone has followed me almost everywhere I have gone. I turned the artifacts over to the Vatican after I become so desperate I could do nothing else."

"What can you tell me about them?"

"Very little that would be newsworthy, unless your readers were interested in archeology or history. Their importance lies in the effect they are likely to have on the upcoming peace talks."

"And why do you think these artifacts are important to the peace talks?"

"I have absolutely no idea," Sangallo said, making one of those gestures only a Roman seemed capable of making. "The artifacts were among a number of art objects taken from the Jews during World War II. When I realized someone was following me, I had them photographed and sent them to the Vatican for safekeeping. The next day someone brutally murdered the photographer in an alleyway near his shop."

"That could have been a random occurrence," Maitland suggested, examining Sangallo's grave expression.

"During the war I was with the partisans, Mr. Maitland. I have seen every type of savagery the human race is capable of committing. I can assure you this was not a random act. Someone wanted information, and I would suspect these people were successful in obtaining it. I happened upon the body by accident and immediately went to his shop. There were men there from the Ministry of the Interior. One of them was a man I recognized from a time when I was active in politics. His name is Sabatini. There was also an American Colonel. I believe his name is Pierce. These are very dangerous men, Mr. Maitland. If your intentions are to follow Dr. Christopher to Israel, I would definitely reconsider."

"I have faced some dangerous situations before. It is a natural part of my job."

"Are you a spiritual man, Mr. Maitland."

Abraham's Bones

Maitland felt his body stiffen in irritation. He wasn't in the mood to hear any religions nonsense. "No, I am not," he said with a little more heat than he intended.

The small, dark eyes darted toward his, as sharp and intense as the eyes of a crow.

"Before this is over, you may have a need to call on God," Sangallo said softly.

Maitland leaned back in his chair, examining the other man's expression. From the corner of his eye he saw movement and turned his head toward the window. On the opposite side of the street a man was leaned against a lamppost, his attention focused on the door of the restaurant. As he studied the man's lean profile, he realized he had seen him before. He felt a little tremor of uneasiness as the man's head turned slowly in his direction and he found himself gazing directly into his eyes.

Joe Prentis

Chapter 8

"I know this is an imposition, Dr. Christopher, but I wonder if I might speak with you for a few minutes."

Members of the press had been calling the hotel all morning and he had used the side entrance to attend an early morning conference at the Vatican. The name this stranger had given did not ring a bell, nor did the organization he claimed to represent. He wondered if the Gnome Project was the name of a military organization. If it was, it was not one he recognized.

"I'm sorry, Mr. Werner, but I have other commitments."

"And I am sorry for the intrusion, Dr. Christopher. I promise I will take only a few minutes of your time."

Hearing the urgency in Werner's voice, he gave him his room number, wondering if this would turn out to be a needless interruption of an already hectic schedule. In less than a minute, he heard a knock at his door and crossed quickly to the entrance.

"Adam Rosing," Werner said, making the introduction. "I know you time is valuable, so we will be as brief as possible."

Christopher shook hands with both of them, then stepped back from the entrance, motioning toward a couch facing the windows. Werner did not waste any time in getting down to business.

"Our concerns involve several issues which aren't on your agenda, but nevertheless we expect them to surface during the upcoming negotiations. You might not be aware of it, but no one

Abraham's Bones

forced General Zecori to give up his appointment as envoy, as was reported in the press. He tendered his resignation of his own free will when he discovered some rather disturbing facts."

"I only know what I read in the press," Christopher answered, and saw the corners of Werner's mouth lift in a humorless smile.

"Then you are probably aware the press can sometimes be careless with their facts. Many of our leaders are afraid the negotiations might be turned into a public forum against the interest of the Israelis."

"I'm sure both sides have similar concerns," Christopher said.

Rosing looked as if he was prepared to say more, but Werner interrupted. "Some of our contacts have reason to believe certain individuals in the military are formulating plans to drive the Palestinians from the Temple area sometime in the next few weeks."

"I am aware of the rumors, but the Vatican has been in close contact with the Prime Minister's office and the government hasn't attached any importance to these reports," Christopher said.

"We have reason to believe these reports are more than rumors. Some of these radical groups have been in contact with certain officials in the SISMI."

Christopher tried to hide his surprise at Werner's unexpected revelation. The organization to which he was referring was the *Servizio per le Informazioni e la sicurezza Militare*, Italy's military intelligence organization. Liberal reporters had accused them of having a role in passing forged documents to the CIA in the run-up to the invasion of Iraq. These documents, known as the Niger Papers, had come from the Nigerian embassy in Rome. They contained detailed documentation of the purchase of 500 tons of uranium ore by agents of Saddam Hussein. After receiving a vigorous denial of any improper conduct by Roman officials, the same reporters had pointed a finger at a shadowy organization known as Propaganda Due, supposedly disbanded by the Italian Parliament in the early 1980s. While the reporters had never been able to prove their allegations, they had hinted at a close connection between Propaganda Due's former operatives and officials in American intelligence, the Masons, the Trilateral Commission, and a host of other ultra-conservative groups. This story had generated enough interest to make the Grassy-knoll conspirators hide in shame.

"It is hard to believe they would do anything so provocative," Christopher said. "What could anyone hope to gain?"

"They hope to accomplish what Moshe Dyane did not have the courage to do during the War for Independence. He could easily have taken the Temple Mount, but his nerves failed him at the wrong moment."

Christopher examined Werner's angry grimace and tried to maintain a neutral expression. "I don't think it was a lack of courage. He was presented with a number of options and made a decisions based on what he thought would be best for the future."

"With your contacts in the area, I am sure you are aware Israel has already acquired most of the materials necessary for the reconstruction of the temple. They have also made appointments to fill all of the priestly positions from Biblical times, including the 71 members of the Sanhedrin. They have the money, gold, silver, and precious jewels. They have even put pressure on the Pope to return the temple vessels seized by Roman troops 2000 years ago."

Christopher could not see where Werner was going with these arguments, so he replied carefully. "Roman history seems to suggest Emperor Vespasian melted them down to pay for the construct of the coliseum in Rome."

"There is sworn testimony from several reputable sources that the menorah has been in the possession of the Vatican for over fifteen hundred years. If the Vatican wants to improve relations with Israel, returning this relic to its rightful place would be a good place to start."

"I think the cause for peace will be better served if we stick to our agenda and stay away from controversial issues," Christopher said.

Werner's eyes were large and unblinking behind the rimless lenses. "Yesterday, I learned of some heavy construction equipment concealed in a warehouse near the western wall of the temple. They could demolish the existing buildings and have the corner stones moved the short distance to the pavement in a matter of hours."

Variations of Werner's story had risen numerous times since the War for Independence had ended in 1948, always packaged in the fears of the current generation.

"Agreements between the Palestinian Authority and the Israeli government have kept the situation under control for a great number of years," Christopher pointed out. "I expect it will continue in the foreseeable future."

"We are aware of the political situation, Dr. Christopher, but the circumstances have changed dramatically. Someone submitted a sample of DNA to Professor Rosing's laboratory. You might not be aware, but he is one of the leading geneticists in the world. The sample he received came from an excavation site at Machpelah."

To those who were familiar with the Middle East, the cave at Machpelah meant only one thing. Abraham had purchased the cave after the death of his beloved Sarah, and they had both rested there for almost four thousand years. King Herod had constructed a fortress-like building to provide protection for the shrine at the same time he had built the temple in Jerusalem. In 1981, the Director of the Israel Antiquities Authority obtained permission to pass through the bolted doors in Yitzhak Hall, where he discovered the secret entrance to the real burial site, three floors below the north grave chamber. In this small room, he discovered artifacts dating from the time of Abraham. No one had publicized the incident due to the detrimental effect it might have on an already unstable political situation.

"Surely, you aren't suggesting someone has dug up Abraham's bones?" Christopher said.

"You are aware there are some other excavations underway in the immediate area," Rosen said. "There have been some interesting discoveries."

"I have read the reports, but I'm not aware of anything significant."

"One item was a stone knife with a fragment of animal bone attached to the shaft," Werner said.

"I understand one of the tour guides at the excavation site suggested it might have been the knife Abraham used when he attempted to sacrifice Isaac. The statement was picked up by some of the news services."

"How familiar are you with DNA techniques?"

"As an archeologist, I have a working knowledge of genetics, but I wouldn't call myself an expert."

Rosing gave him a thin smile that came and went in a single heartbeat. "I am considered to be one of the leading geneticists in the world, but I wouldn't call myself an expert either. This is oversimplifying, but we have traced the human race back to one Y-chromosome ancestor who lived 60,000 years ago in Africa. Every person who ever lived is a descendent of this man. For obvious reasons, we have called him Adam. Male descendants inherit ancient patterns of mutations repeated indefinitely. Certain short sections of junk DNA, called microsatellites, mutate at a constant rate providing a clock and allowing geneticists to attach a date to a particular form of chromosome. For example, most males of Middle Eastern descent can trace their lineage to an Y-chromosome type called M89 and others to M172. While there is a great deal we do not know about genetics, computer models have allowed us to project backward into time. While our computers can't give us an exact map of Abraham's genetic makeup, they can tell us with a great deal of accuracy what he was like."

"And the significance of this would be what?" Christopher asked.

"We have determined that those people buried in the caves at Machpelah were Amorites," Rosen said.

For a few seconds, Christopher did not see the point Rosing was trying to make, and then, suddenly, he did. Abraham, the first Jew, was an Amorite, having come from the city of Ur in the southern area of present day Iraq. In the centuries following Abraham's journey into Israel, a mass migration of Amorites settled the area east of the Dead Sea and a few centuries later, they inhabited the area along the seacoast. These were the Hibri, the wandering tribesmen who were among the ancestors of the present day inhabitants of the Middle East. Any mention of this by the news media could inflame the masses and derail the peace process before it even got started.

"So you are suggesting the remains taken from these caves were members of Abraham's immediate family," Christopher said.

"I am doing more than suggesting, Dr. Christopher. Samples taken from the caves at Machpelah contain the genetic material that could only have come from the area around Ur during the third millennium B.C. These people were not indigenous to this area. They were the Amorite ancestors of the present day Jews."

"And you think this can be proven from the samples you have taken?" Christopher asked cautiously.

"I believe it can. As you probably recall, Sarah, the mother of the Jews, was an Amorite, while Hagar, the mother of the Arabs, was an Egyptian."

Christopher immediately climbed to his feet and walked to the window, standing with his back to the room. What Werner was suggesting was not unlike the battle fought quietly, but fiercely, in American courts over the past decade. It had started when evidence had surfaced at archeological sites in the Pacific Northwest suggesting Europeans had crossed the Atlantic many thousands of years before the ancestors of the Indians had passed across the land bridge from Asia. Their fears had some justification and he could see the concern of everyone involved if DNA testing provided evidence to support a superior claim by either group.

Werner laced his fingers together and looked down at the carpet. "While I cannot support the militant position of the right-wing elements in my government, I am first and foremost a Jew. Integrity can be a terrible burden, Dr. Christopher. I find myself torn between what I feel is right on one side, and what I am being pressured to do on the other."

"I'm not sure I understand what you're suggesting."

"I would very much like your involvement, Dr. Christopher. There are few men in the Middle East who would doubt your integrity."

"My position is to remain impartial, Mr. Werner."

Werner's eyebrows lifted like twin question marks. "What could be more impartial than the truth?"

"There are many who might not see this as the truth," Christopher said.

"On page fifty-four of you latest book you said an archeologist must always remain impartial, never be guilty of slanting their evidence to support any popular belief, and to report any discovery, even if it runs contrary to the prevailing theories."

"I believe I did say something similar."

"Then I am asking you to do nothing more than what you have already stated in your book. I would like you to select some young person to represent the land of Israel, and I will select someone to represent the Muslim world. We will compare their DNA with the samples taken from the cave at Machpelah."

"To what end? If I were to give support to anything so controversial, the press would make every effort to link me with the agenda of these radical groups."

"Our positions might not be as far apart as you seem to think, Dr. Christopher. While the vast majority of Jews want to see the temple rebuilt, many of them do not think the Zionists are going about it in the right way. It is a shameful, blasphemous thing to bring about such an action when it is not the will of God. You must help us, Dr. Christopher."

"I don't understand why you couldn't carry out your experiments without my involvement."

"Actually, this suggestion came from the Vatican. They see no problem in this at all."

As Christopher studied the troubled expressions of the two men, he could not help wondering what other surprises were in store for him when he returned to Israel.

Chapter 9

"Miss Julia! Oh, Miss Julia! Welcome home," Miriam called from the terrace overlooking the parking area in front of Dr. Siedman's house. After standing for a moment with her hand shading her eyes, she came rushing down the long flight of steps where Julia was removing her luggage from the trunk of the car. From the end of the drive, Julia heard the familiar clamor as the groundskeeper swung the wrought iron gate.

Miriam ran down the last few steps and enfolded Julia in her arms. Miriam and her family were Arab Christians and they had worked for Julia's grandmother for as long as she could remember. When she had entered this house for the first time, Miriam had made her feel welcome, first with soft words, and then by placing her in the midst of her lively brood of children.

"These girls will be your sisters from this time onward," Miriam had told her sons with a sense of repressed excitement.

Eyeing her foreign clothes and the small child clutching her hand, they had inched forward, their warm brown eyes staring into hers. In the following years, they had divided their time between Israel and boarding schools abroad, always returning for extended holidays and for the summer. She had grown to love her grandparents, this large house, and the people who lived here.

"I have missed you so!" Miriam cried, holding her in a fierce embrace, and then backing up a step, she ran her eyes down the length of her slender figure.

"But you are so skinny!" Miriam cried, patting her own ample hips. "You look like those women in the fashion magazines with their bones sticking out ever which way. Come! Come with me and I will get you settled. Sharif, Jamaal! Don't stand there gawking like camels. Carry Miss Julia's bags upstairs," she commanded as her two youngest sons edged shyly around the rear bumper of the automobile.

The two boys smiled indulgently at their mother as they came to greet her. Julia ignored Jamaal's outstretched hand and kissed his cheek. "If you were only older, Jamaal," she teased, and saw the flash of a smile as the blush deepened.

"You do not want that one," Miriam scoffed, wagging a finger at him. "He was a very responsible son until that sister of yours got him started on the Internet. All he wants to do now is sit in front of that ridiculous machine when he could be learning something useful. It is the work of the devil and this one is caught up in its mischief."

"What has she done now?" Julia said. "I'm almost afraid to ask."

"Done?" Miriam cried in a petulant tone. "She had no more than arrived when she went to Rabbi Ghosh's yeshiva. They called the police and had her put out. I hate to think of what she might do next. You must help me before she brings disgrace upon everyone in this household!"

"I will talk to her as soon as I get settled," Julia promised, deciding that Daniella was only seeking attention, while testing the boundaries of her newly discovered adulthood. Daniella had an exceptionally high IQ and had advanced past her peers at school. Now, at 14, she was the youngest member of the freshman class at Harvard.

"Sharif, do you have a kiss for me?" she asked the younger boy who was inching shyly toward her.

"I have missed you terribly," Sharif whispered against her ear as she bent and hugged him.

Abraham's Bones

"And I have missed all of you," Julia told him, then noting the eager expectancy on the younger boy's face, she added, "Especially you! Of all of Miriam's sons, you are definitely my favorite."

"Ah! Did I not tell you, brother? You have heard it from Miss Julia, and she would not lie about something so important."

Miriam encircled the two boys with her arms and pulled them affectionately against her side. "You two thick-headed louts are lucky I don't turn you loose in the streets. Don't let polite words go to your foolish heads. Now get those bags upstairs immediately and let me talk to Miss Julia."

The boys hurried along the sidewalk with her luggage while Julia trailed along behind Miriam's stout figure. Inside the foyer, she stopped and inhaled deeply, smelling the familiar odors of furniture polish and freshly cut flowers. When her grandparents had emigrated from Switzerland after the war, they had built a replica of the Mediterranean villa her grandmother had grown up in on Lake Geneva. It was a large house, built almost entirely of masonry, with dark beams of fire-blackened oak, graceful stucco arches, and floors of highly polished terra-cotta tiles. Miriam motioned her to follow and they passed down the length of the foyer and through a wide archway into the kitchen. The smell of food and pastries was heavy in the air.

Looking through the archway toward the foyer, Julia could see her sister rushing down the long flight of stairs. As she passed Jamaal and Sharif, she drew back her fist, causing both of them to shy away, overcome with fits of laughter.

"Roller-babies!" she called after them as she clattered the rest of the way down.

"What is that all about?" Julia asked.

Miriam clicked her tongue. "She brought some of those awful things home with all of those little wheels in a row. This morning I caught her racing down the driveway backwards, like one of those ice skaters in the Olympics. The moment my back is turned, those two are going to try it too. She will be the death of all my sons."

Julia laughed at Miriam's exaggerations as Daniella ran through the doorway and grabbed her in a tight hug.

"Aren't you a little old for inline skates?" Julia asked, examining the yellow spandex top and purple Lycra shorts her sister was wearing.

Daniella lifted her arms and did a perfect pirouette. "Everyone at Harvard has a pair. Things have changed since you were there back in the Stone Age."

Daniella suddenly stopped, leaning her head sideways as she examined what Julia was wearing. "They look nice on you, but you remind me of Ingrid Bergman in Casablanca."

"At least you didn't compare me to Mary Poppins."

"I was thinking of her, too. Something smells wonderful. What do we have to eat?"

Miriam made a trilling sound with her tongue. "I've been feeding this one a dozen times a day, but she burns it all up running on the beach. Young ladies should be more sensitive and . . ."

"They should be more like Julia!" Daniella suggested impertinently as she reached for a bagel. Miriam was quicker and moved the platter out of her reach.

"You will spoil your dinner."

"Dinner is hours away," Daniella complained. "I'm starving." She turned to Julia for support, but Miriam stopped suddenly and looked embarrassed.

"How terribly rude of me. I had forgotten you have come such a long way. When have you eaten?"

"I can't remember. With the changes in the time zones, I only know I am hungry and sleepy and I want a shower." She looked toward the ceiling. "How is grandmother?"

Miriam sighed. "Not much change since I talked with you on the telephone. She has been working some and I think it is good for her. When John is gone, it occupies her mind."

Julia swung away before either of them could see her reaction. What had seemed workable while she was on the other side of the Atlantic was becoming more disturbing by the hour.

"I think I will take a shower," she said, passing through the archway without looking back.

"I will fix something for you to eat," Miriam called after her as she mounted the stairs.

Julia stopped just inside the doorway of her bedroom and looked slowly around. *John will be here soon and I will have to face the issues I have avoided for such a long time. How will I react when we meet again after not seeing him for almost a year?*

Abraham's Bones

As she turned vaguely away from the window, her eyes fell on a picture made at the President's Christmas Party the previous year. After looking at it for a few seconds, she suddenly turned and went across the hall and through the open doorway of his bedroom. His pictures of her were still on the wall, and on his desk was a large one made in front of the Fountain of the Moor in Rome. She was standing behind him with her arms around his shoulders, her cheek pressed against his in a possessive manner. She did not know if finding these pictures in their proper place was better, or if it made her feel worse. She crossed the carpet and stood for a moment beside his bed, running the tips of her fingers across the coverlet. Suddenly overcome with weariness, she stretched out full length, staring at the ceiling. Her body was restless, achy, but when she turned on her stomach and gathered his pillow into her arms, she could smell the faint aroma of the after-shave he wore. She was instantly on her feet again, pacing back and forth in front of the windows.

She saw the blinking icon on the screen of his computer indicating he had unread e-mail. She bent toward the computer expecting to see the message she had sent the day before from Washington. Instead, she saw the name, Sanura, and a short message dated almost a week before. Why had he not read his e-mail for the past week?

Dr. John Christopher:
I appreciate any help you can give me while I am working with Dr. Siedman on her novel. Living at her residence will certainly solve many problems I might encounter.
Sanura Hamada

Julia frowned at the salutation above the signature, but was unable to determine what it meant. While she could speak and understand Arabic without any difficulty, she had never learned to read it properly. After studying the text for a moment, she decided it probably meant something impersonal, like 'thanks for your help', but she was not completely sure.

What if it was something more intimate?

The message had arrived in the middle of the previous week. Was Sanura here already? She hit the delete button as she turned away. Going directly toward the guestrooms at the far end of the hallway, she started opening doors. Inside the third one, she found two suitcases standing at the end of the bed. She turned on her heel and went down the hallway to her sister's room. Daniella was sprawled face down on the bed reading a magazine, bare legs swinging in rhythm with a CD cranked all the way up. She clicked the off switch on the player and Daniella looked around, surprised at the abrupt cessation of the music.

"Where is Sanura?" she demanded. "You evidently forgot to tell me she was here."

Daniella lifted a hand and waved it vaguely around. "She isn't. Her bags arrived this morning. I think she had something to do in Tel Aviv."

"And where is John? Don't tell me he is in Tel Aviv, too."

Daniella's head swung in her direction. "He's in Rome attending a conference. He's due back sometime tonight."

Julia turned away and then stopped. "Have Sanura's bags moved down to the utility room. Tell Miriam to have her stopped at the gate if she should arrive while I am away. I will not have her staying in this house."

Daniella rolled across the bed with the athletic grace of a gymnast and came effortlessly to her feet. "I don't blame you for dumping him. He's been hitting on her for years, even when you were still in the picture."

Daniella had always known how to push all of her buttons. Julia could feel her blood pressure rising despite her intentions to remain calm. "This has nothing to do with John," she said.

"Like, whatever," Daniella said, turning on her toes like a dancer as she went toward the door. "So many men, so little time."

"Daniella, wait!" Julia called after her, but her sister continued as if she had not heard. She had promised Miriam she would help her with Daniella's behavior, but she had let the opportunity slip away. Perhaps she would speak with John when he returned from Rome and try to elicit his support, but as she thought about this, she realized it would never work. Daniella had almost worshipped John since she had been an infant, and he seemed never to tire of her, regardless of her moods or the extent of her provocation. There would be very little emotional support from him. The problems with their relationship had created a difficult situation. It was far too complicated for someone with Daniella's limited experience to understand. Then she realized something she should have been aware of a long time ago. *She didn't understand it herself.*

Joe Prentis

Chapter 10

Christopher turned away from the telephone and walked to a window of his hotel room overlooking the Via Veneto. As he pulled the curtains back, he could see the Stars and Stripes, snapping sharply in the cold breeze like the jib on a 10-meter yacht. A long line of tourists reaching almost to the intersection at the Via Boncompagni, was already queued up in front of the entrance of the American Consulate General, where complaints of lost passports and stolen luggage were handled on a daily basis. The ones among them who were low on funds would be lining up also, unaware that it was routine practice for embassy personnel to turn them politely, but firmly away, after giving them the suggestion to call home collect, or contact American Express.

Isn't this what we pay you for, the harried embassy personnel were frequently asked, accompanied by irate demands to produce their ambassador. Most of them seemed to believe the role of the State Department involved nothing more than serving their every whim. After another hour of standing in the cold wind, their tempers would be short, and the answers they received would be even shorter.

It was almost three weeks before the start of negotiations, and he had intended to use this time to clear his schedule. He wanted to be able to concentrate on the details of international politics without hundreds of distracting issues clamoring for his attention. As he

Abraham's Bones

focused his attention on the large, fortress-like building housing the diplomatic offices of the embassy, he wondered what impact this unexpected meeting with Ambassador Stoltz would have.

He had met Stoltz almost four years before when he and Julia had taken part in a conference between representatives of the Balkan countries and their NATO counterparts. He had found Stoltz surprisingly well informed with the problems of the Muslim minority in Eastern Europe and with the dangers poised by militant extremist. In the following three years, they had returned on five occasions, spending a total of three months at the embassy, becoming familiar with the general proceedings and the personnel who worked there. When Stoltz had asked him if he could come across for a strategy meeting, he had responded willingly. He had been surprised when the ambassador had insisted on sending someone to escort him. Over the last few days, he had experienced some minor difficulty in evading the more enterprising reporters, but the idea of him needing an escort was ludicrous when the hotel entrance was no more than 50 yards from the embassy gate. As he watched, two Marine guards marched through the gates, the gold buttons on their dark blue jackets flashing in the sunlight, moving all the while toward the entrance of the hotel as of they had just stepped from a recruiting poster. When they disappeared from view below his window, he buttoned the collar of his shirt and reached for his jacket. In less than a minute he heard someone knocking at his door. When he opened it, one of the soldiers responded with a polite 'sir' while the other did an about-face, his attention fastened on a man and woman at the opposite end of the corridor.

Christopher could not help being amused. "Have I missed something?" he asked.

Underneath the perfectly squared bill of a military cap, a pair of steel-blue eyes focused on his. "I hope not, Ambassador Christopher, but you can never be too careful."

When Christopher saw the earnest expression on the young man's face, he nodded and fell in step with them as they went toward the elevator.

Ambassador Stoltz's office was near the center of the building overlooking a narrow strip of lawn. Christopher was surprised when one of his escorts gestured toward a corridor leading to the right, where one of the conference rooms was located. He had been in this windowless room on a couple of occasions, and he knew the embassy personnel restricted its use to matters requiring maximum security. This fortress-like building had been the palace of Queen Margaret of Savoy. Thick masonry walls intended to deflect the charge from a short-range cannon had been the ideal place to house the embassy. It had been over a year since Christopher had been here, and he could see several changes in the never-ending effort to bolster security. The door to the conference room was ajar, and as he entered, he was surprised to see the room almost filled, with most of the ones in attendance being military personnel. Stoltz turned away from a lanky soldier with a major's insignia on his uniform and came toward the door with his hand outstretched. Christopher was not surprised when he realized the man following closely on his heels, was Andre Havran.

"You know Andre. I believe his insight into business affairs will be invaluable," Stoltz said with a wink. "I will allow the others to introduce themselves as we move along. I think you will understand the sense of urgency when you see what Major Pierce has to show us. We are going to have to rush through this. We are setting up a video conference with some of our friends in Washington."

As Christopher made his way to a seat near the head of the table, he realized why Pierce seemed familiar. Almost two years before in Washington, he had attended a strategy meeting at the Pentagon in which Pierce had been present. He had paced energetically back and forth in front of a world map, answering each question without making any conscious effort to come up with the answer. There had been three men in the meeting with stars on their shoulders, but they had seemed to hang on every word Pierce had uttered. The War of Terror had given rise to men like Pierce, special operations officers who commanded combat groups comprised of soldiers and CIA operatives. They were at every trouble spot in the world, acting on their own initiative with few questions asked. He wondered what had happened to bring Pierce here, but before he could speculate any further, Pierce clicked a controller in his hand and a picture appeared on a wide-screen monitor attached to the wall.

"In the immediate future we are going to be dealing with an organization that calls itself Shiva. At this point, we don't know very much about them, but the drawing you see on the screen is their emblem."

Christopher knew that a major part of the defense of the western world depended on advanced planning, and it was especially important to identify groups with the potential of causing trouble before they had all of their strategy in place. He leaned forward and was surprised to see an almost exact reproduction of the drawing in the photographs he had received from Sangallo. In the center was a detailed illustration of the cartouch with two bird-like figures, but it was the other drawing that caught his attention. Two figures, a male and a female, were standing in front of what appeared to be a throne. On the right shoulder of the male figure was the tattoo showing the two winged figures, and on the left, was a shield. The breasts of the female figure exhibited two identical tattoos.

"I wonder if you could hazard a guess to the significance of the emblem?" Pierce asked, looking in Christopher's direction.

"I'm not sure there is one. I have some photographs of something almost identical. It is supposed to be several thousands of years old."

"To my untrained eye, this design appears to be Egyptian."

"This is only speculation, but I'm not sure I would agree with the suggestion of it being Egyptian. There were emerging nations all over the Middle East during this period, but the cultures were very similar. The bird figures are made up of seven straight lines, which might have some significance beyond it being the perfect number."

"The perfect number," someone said in a questioning tone from the end of the table.

"Our mathematical system is based on ten," Christopher said, "reflecting the number of fingers we have. In ancient times, counting usually involved small marketable objects like vegetables. The human brain is programmed in a way that allows us to count up to seven items at a glance. The prevalent theory among mathematicians suggests our counting systems developed in the market place. The merchant could grab seven objects and push them across without having to count. Think about it in terms of a speedy checkout at the supermarket. They have been trying to improve on the system for centuries. I'm not sure there has been much progress."

Everyone around the table laughed, while Pierce continued to focus his attention on the drawing. "I'm wondering if it could it have any other significance?"

"The number seven was also used to represent the deity. The idea being completeness."

"Do you think this could be a religious organization," Pierce said.

"Our experts seem to believe there is definitely a religious connection," a nattily dressed man directly across the table said as Pierce flashed another picture on the screen.

"Our people are making a similar assumption, and if it is true, you are looking at the most dangerous man in the world," Pierce said. "We believe he has it within his power to touch off Armageddon."

Christopher leaned forward where he could focus his attention on the photograph. There was none of the weather-beaten features usually associated with al-Qaeda's operatives, although it was obvious the man in the picture was of Middle Eastern extraction. Examining the crest of the mountain behind him, he realized this was not the barren terrain of Afghanistan, but was probably a location somewhere in Europe. The man was tall, dressed in the thermal lined clothing of a professional mountaineer. A full beard hid his features with nothing visible except for the lower part of his forehead and a pair of piercing eyes. He was holding an AK47 with the careless ease of someone who knew how to use it. According to the caption superimposed at the edge of the photograph, he was an inch over six feet, weighing approximately 190 pounds. The heavily insulated clothing hid any distinguishing features he might have possessed. In the harsh sunlight, he could have been of any one of a dozen nationalities, or a mixture of each. There was something about the picture that bothered him, but he could not decide what it was. While Christopher was trying to puzzle it out, another picture appeared on the screen, and he immediately recognized Congressman Danville trussed up like a farm animal ready for the slaughter.

"We do not think Danville's kidnapping was for the purpose of ransom," Pierce said, "although none of our people are willing to hazard a guess as to what it is all about."

Pierce pressed the controller and another picture followed the others on the screen, This one was of a young man who was obvi-

Abraham's Bones

ously of Arabic stock. Christopher immediately climbed to his feet and moved closer to the screen. The young man was dressed somewhat in the fashion of the person in the first picture, although there was no identifying features in the background.

"Do you recognize someone?" Pierce asked as Christopher continued to study the picture.

"Yes," he said after a moment of hesitation. "This young man worked at the excavation site at Ashkelon for a few months early last year. He was a hard worker but he kept to himself. In retrospect, he seemed to be harmless enough."

"I would have to disagree with your assessment," someone said from the far end of the table.

Christopher turned and saw an impeccably dressed man who had gone unnoticed until he spoke. When he gave him a questioning look, the man said, "I am Dominick Sabatini, Dr. Christopher. I am with the L'Arma dei carabinieri. According to the information we have received, he has been given the assignment of killing you."

The Carabinieri was one of three national police forces in Italy and considered a part of the army, despite the fact that many of their duties involved civilian affairs. Their normal area of responsibility involved guarding military installations and providing the normal police duties for the armed forces, although their duties sometimes overlapped those of the *Guardie di Pubblica Sicurezza*. Before he could ask him to clarify the matter, Sabatini answered in an apologetic voice.

"Someone at the Quirinale asked us to look into the matter, Dr. Christopher. I wouldn't want you to think we were taking unnecessary liberties with international affairs."

Normally, the Carabinieri and the Guardie answered to their respective departments in Defense and the Home Secretary's office. For the Minister of the Interior to have taken such an interest, it suggested something of grave international importance had taken place.

"Am I to assume these men might pose an immanent threat?"

"We are doing more than assuming, Dr. Christopher. We have a very large dossier on the leader of this group. His followers call him the Sheikh, although our investigation seems to indicate that he is actually Jewish. We have reached the surprising conclusion that

Shiva is comprised of Messianic Jews, Arab extremist, with a number of radical Christians thrown in."

Christopher's knowledge of Shiva had come from a brief memo he had read a few months before leaving his position in Washington. He remembered the name was on the State Department's watch list, but he could not remember many of the details. "If what you are assuming is true, we probably need to discount the theory of it being a religious organization," he said.

"Quite the contrary," Pierce said. "It is our understanding that the Sheikh is searching for the roots of Abraham's faith."

Christopher felt a moment of confusion, and then he realized what Pierce was suggesting. Most of the radical groups in Israel seemed to be focused on bringing about a rebuilding of the Temple complex, thinking they could restore the greatness of Solomon's era. Evidently, this man was intending to use a new approach that would bind Jews, Arabs, and radical Christians into one entity and give purpose and intent to all. It was a bold move, but he doubted it would appeal to very many potential followers. When he looked away from the screen at Pierce's expectant gaze, he saw he was already shaking his head.

"This is more than a pipe dream," Dr. Christopher. "He has already attracted many thousands to his cause. We expect them to make some dramatic move in the next few weeks."

During the sixty years of Israel's existence, the government had been ever mindful of the disparate groups within the nation, and had quietly, but forcefully, taken precautions. Christopher knew all of them were waiting for his reaction, but he was reluctant to comment until he had a chance to communicate with his superiors at the Vatican.

"I'm wondering if you have thought out a plan of action?" he asked.

"We have," Pierce said. "I have recommended to the Pentagon that we eliminate this man with any means at our disposal."

The abrupt boldness of Pierce's statement lay in the closed atmosphere of the room like an unexploded artillery round.

A young woman stuck her head through the opening door and gave a signal to Pierce. He clicked the controller and the screen was filled with a live picture of what could only be the cabinet room at the White House. President Rosenfield was setting at the side of the table, his tie loosened, his face drawn and unsmiling. In the background were several military officers gathered in a tight little group. The camera panned toward the president's face, and it took several seconds for Christopher to realize the president was addressing him.

"I understand Colonel Pierce has briefed you," Rosenfield said.

"Yes, Mr. President."

"Then I am going to brief and to the point because we have another crisis brewing here. The situation over there could get out of control in a heartbeat. That is the reason I sent Pierce to assist you. I'm not going to mince words with you. We have suddenly and unexpectedly been caught up in a major crisis with worldwide implications. If the unexpected happens, we might not have time to gather around this table, or to summon the Pentagon brass from their golf game. I have given Pierce the authorization to act in any way necessary to protect the interest of the United States and our allies. We will have the meetings and sign the papers after the buttons have been pushed. Do you understand your role in this?"

Christopher felt as if his body had received a numbing blow. "Sir, I don't think . . ."

"That you are qualified?" Rosenfield waved his hand and looked toward the corner of the room. "Back that camera up," he commanded. The camera immediately panned backward, showing the entire room and the group gathered just beyond the table.

"This is not my cabinet," Rosenfield said, moving his hands outward to include the men seated around him at the long table. "This is our morning prayer session. Pierce has a battle group under his command, but there might not to be time for consultation if something goes wrong. Only the good Lord can help you with this."

Christopher opened his mouth to reply as he saw Rosenfield's finger stab downward toward the device setting in front of him. The screen immediately went dark.

Joe Prentis

Chapter 11

Dr. Siedman unfolded the letter, carefully smoothing the pages as she began to read.

Dear Dr. Sideman:

I was pleased yesterday to receive the first chapter of your novel. I cannot think of anyone more knowledgeable about the ancient past, or who is more capable of making this era understandable to the average reader. I am honored you have selected me to help you with this task . . .

She ran her eye down the length of the page to Christopher's signature, and then refolded the letter and placed it on the corner of her desk. She felt a great rush of happiness he had taken time away from his busy schedule to write to her.

She loved him. Oh, she loved him so much!

John Christopher had walked into her life one magical morning when a group of student workers had arrived from stateside to work at the excavation site. He had been a tall, gangling high school student with a boundless supply of energy. In those early years, he had seldom been more than a pace or two away from her granddaughter. On one occasion he had fallen headlong into a pit when he could not take his eyes from Julia long enough to see where to place his feet.

During the summers when they were here, the sound of their laughter had made this vast mausoleum of a house come alive again.

Abraham's Bones

As she thought about this now, she remembered something she had forgotten. Julia had presented her with a legal document, but for some reason, the details of this memory eluded her. She seemed to recall tearing the document in half and throwing it in her wastebasket. Julia had been furious with her.

"You care more about John than you do about me!" Julia had cried in frustration and anger.

"You are wrong, my dear," she had argued. "I do not care more about him, for that would be impossible. He is like a son to me. I don't understand why you have never married him."

She had stopped there and questioned her no more, for her emotional turmoil had been too painful to watch. The next day Julia had flown back to America without another word on the subject and she had not seen her since.

She touched her temple, rubbing gently along the edge of her hairline. The area above her ear felt sensitive, and she decided it was probably the onset of a headache. *Or was it? Could she have fallen again?* It had been over a year since the accident. She had avoided the narrow staircase at the rear of the house since this unfortunate event—*or had she?* The rear stairs was involved with something more recent, and then she remembered what it was.

Her publisher, Dr. Erlich, had arrived with his lawyer and they had discussed the possibility of a pending lawsuit. With a sudden, jarring sense of clarity, this disagreeable episode came flooding back. She gripped the arms of her chair as her mind veered quickly away. Taking a calming breath, she forced her mind back to a more pleasant time when John had been such an eager student and he and Julia had been so happy together. This had been a magical time in her life. Without knowing exactly how it had happened, she had become his teacher, his mentor, and his friend. She had felt an uncommon amount of pride in everything he did, even flying to America to attend his graduation from the university, and again when he had received his doctorate.

National Geographic had published an article about her once, and the strongly opinionated young woman had described her as 'one of the world's greatest archeologist, brilliant, knowledgeable, but as plain as a pikestaff.'

She had decided this last observation was probably true. There had never been sufficient time to worry about her appearance. Of all her achievements, her relationship with Christopher stood above the other milestones in her life. Her only child had been a daughter who had spent most of her life in Washington with nothing to show for it except an obscene amount of money and a divorce. The only bright spot in this troubled affair had been the birth of the children she had eventually claimed as her own. Julia had been born first and then much later, Daniella. This latter incident had occurred almost on the eve of her daughter's pending divorce. Her career-driven daughter had not even had the decency to name her youngest child!

So she had named her Daniella, which was Hebrew for 'God is my judge.'

And God had judged her in those years for her thick anger against her only daughter. Julia had grown like a flower, while Daniella had developed into a brilliant but headstrong child, secretive and given to strange silences.

She sighed, knowing it was useless to dwell on the past, and forced her mind back to the present. Scattered among the framed awards on the walls of her office were pictures showing the four of them posed with various leaders in the Middle East. In one of them, she was squinting in the harsh sunlight holding some worthless piece of rubble the photographer's assistant had plucked from the pottery table.

"This is about life," she had protested after he had snapped the shutter, gesturing at the mound behind her where a million people had lived and died during countless millennia. The news team had not understood what she was trying to explain. Suddenly tired of the whole thing, she had dropped the object and walked away.

After John and Julia had received their doctorates in archeology and returned to Ashkelon to work full time, she had refused to pose for any photographer unless John, Julia, and Daniella were there to share the honor. *This young man is like a son to me*, she had wanted to say to the world, but this was something she had not dared to utter. *Would he have considered her a foolish old woman if he knew how much she loved him and how much she wanted them to be married?*

I am a foolish old woman, she decided. *Oh, why did I start this impossible task? Everything I have written is non-fiction. What do I know about writing a novel?*

The shelf above her computer contained a row of thick editions she had written over the last forty years. All of them were

Abraham's Bones

books on archeology. She had arranged them in order, starting with the first one she had written when she was working at Bethlehem. *The Stones Speak: What Capernaum Means to the Modern World.* She had dedicated one of these books to John, even daring to address him as her son in the dedication. At the last minute, she had lost her nerve and had called the publisher. They had finally settled on, 'John Christopher, friend and colleague.'

But this was years ago! Now she was old and afflicted with Alzheimer's disease. How could she hope to complete a novel when there were so many days when she could not remember where she was?

She sat looking at her computer and frowned to herself. Julia had presented her with a videocassette and had insisted she watch it in its entirety. It had something to do with Dr. Erlich and a documentary he had filmed for television.

I never watch documentaries on television. Why would Julia want me to watch a documentary?

Julia had also mentioned the lovely young woman she had seen so often on Al Jazeera giving the news about the Middle East. She seemed to recall her name was Sanura. As she thought about this now, she seemed to recall she had talked to Sanura recently, and she had seen her here in this house. How could this be possible? Then she remembered something else she had learned about Sanura, and felt a sudden, breathless fluttering in her chest. An old friend had given her a document many years ago, and she had locked it in the wall safe in her bedroom. Was this document something she had intended to give to Julia and Daniella, or was it something she was trying to conceal from them? It was all so utterly confusing.

She jumped slightly when she felt a hand touch her shoulder and looked up to find Julia standing at her side. She covered Julia's hand with her own as she saw the concerned expression on her granddaughter's face.

Julia had returned from Washington to visit with her, although she had forgotten this. Where was Daniella, she wondered, and then she remembered. Daniella was on her way from America to work at the excavation site. Or was she already here? She could not remember.

Does John know both of them will be here when he gets back? For a moment, this troubled her, but she could not remember why.

"It's time for your medication," Julia said and presented a small paper cup with a capsule resting in the bottom.

"Oh, I don't want to take my medication. It makes me sleepy, and I want to spend all of my time with you. Just think, dear. The four of us will have the entire summer together."

Julia's hand immediately fell away from her shoulder. "It means John and I will be working together and nothing more. He will be staying at the hotel when he returns. It is really out of the question for him to be staying here."

"But this is his home, dear! Surely, you don't think I could turn him away. I know something has happened between the two of you, but you must not let your anger come between you and what you know is the right thing to do."

Julia turned her head away, but not quick enough to keep her from seeing her expression.

Oh, Julia, please! You love him. I know you do.

"You need your rest now," Julia said, avoiding her eyes. "There will be plenty of time to work on your novel."

"I just can't seem to get started," she said. "Oh, I know it's foolish for an old woman to think she can be productive forever, but this is one last project I want to complete. You can't imagine how important this is to me."

"You know how important your nap and medications are. Besides, you have written twenty pages today, and I think it is a respectable amount of work for just one morning."

Julia was not the kind of person to resort to sarcasm just to make a point, but she did not understand what she had meant. As she tried to puzzle it out, Julia leaned past her and hit the Page-Up key several times in rapid succession. She saw pages full of text scroll past. Julia leaned toward the computer screen, studying it intently.

"Would you mind if I read a few paragraphs of this chapter?"

She shook her head, not trusting herself to speak. She looked at the first line of text as it came swimming into view.

I don't remember writing any of this, she thought, feeling a moment of confusion and alarm. Julia read on for a moment and then murmured a compliment she scarcely heard.

There was a faint sound near her ear and she realized it was the voices speaking to her again. At first, it had frightened her, but now she felt a great comfort when they spoke to her, telling her things too wonderful to imagine. Ignoring Julia, she placed her wrist on the edge of the keyboard. She tried to focus her eyes on the monitor, but was only aware of the voices whispering in her ear.

Yes, yes! Egypt, the 15th century BC.

Now she recalled what she had written and remembered she was at the beginning of another chapter. She hit Enter, and then after studying the text where she had left off, her fingers started to dance rapidly on the keyboard.

Christopher came out of a gift shop and stood for a moment on the top step, looking down the length of the Quattro Fontane where honking automobiles had backed up all the way to the Piazza Barberini. He glanced in both directions, then went quickly down the steps and turned toward the plaza. Pedestrians crowded the sidewalk, making it difficult to make any headway through the milling throng. Everyone seemed to be going in opposite directions. They were mostly young, high spirited, and caught up in a festive mood. He continued to push through the crowd until he had reached a group of students standing dangerously close to the curb. The passing automobiles were almost brushing against them as they rolled past. This group of young people was looking up at the ornamental stonework on top of the monastery of San Cario, while one of them adjusted his camera. As he inched slowly past them, a young couple broke away from the group and rushed toward the busy intersection.

"*A domani!*" the girl called over her shoulder as they dashed between the honking automobiles to the far side of the street. The others in the group waved and shouted after them as Christopher continued to force his way through the slowly moving crowd.

It had rained earlier and the dampness was still lingering in the air. Normally, the unseasonable coolness would not have bothered him, but this evening he found himself shivering and turned up the collar on his raincoat. It would not only protect him from the raw breeze but would prevent him from being recognized. During the last two days he had been followed almost everywhere by the paparazzi, and it was becoming increasingly difficult to avoid them. He had ducked through the side entrance of the ABC Grill earlier in the day to attend a meeting at the Vatican.

Pushing his hands into the pockets, he avoided a tour group just inside the porta as he headed in the direction of Rosati's Bar. He shook his head in dismay, regretting that he had agreed to this meeting. He could not imagine how Keith Maitland had been able to obtain the number of his cell phone when so many others had failed. Maitland had suggested a 10 o'clock meeting at the well-known bar within easy walking distance of his hotel.

He crossed the plaza toward the entrance, pushing his way past a group of tourist huddled together while they consulted their guidebooks. Behind him, the sudden snarl of a Vespa drowned out a question one of the tourists had asked. As he paused, looking at the man's guidebook, there was a loud report he thought was the backfiring of an engine. The man in front of him gave a sharp cry and fell to the pavement in a boneless heap.

Christopher bent toward the fallen man and turned him gently on his back. His face was ashen and he was gasping for breath. A small hole in the center of his chest was bleeding profusely. Christopher grabbed his cell phone and had started to punch in the numbers when someone grasped his elbow and turned him about.

"Please come with us, Dr. Christopher," the man said in a low voice that was lost in the shouting from the crowd. Christopher found himself looking into the face of a police officer. Two other men dressed in dark suits crowded between him and the crowd. He opened his mouth to protest, but the police officers were already leading him away.

Chapter 12

Julia clicked the TV remote, rapidly advancing through the channels until she had reached the last one and started around again. She had seen the announcement on CNN but had only heard the last part of TV anchorman Bill Bridell's comment about Christopher's appearance on television. He had not mentioned the network. She would have guessed it to be European News International, but she had clicked past it twice, finding the continuing coverage of an airline crash in Romania.

After another minute of searching, she found the right channel and was relieved to see Christopher had not started his speech. She had always liked public television and the similar unaffiliated stations around the world. There was something magical in the impromptu nature of those broadcasts missing from programs carried by the major networks. The camera was panning randomly around the auditorium and she could see only a few empty seats with a large crowd milling about at the rear of the auditorium. Technicians were still in the process of shifting their equipment around, giving the upcoming program the appearance of an opening night at an off-Broadway production. A woman with a clipboard in the crook of her arm was checking the microphone at the podium. After a few seconds, she gave a signal to someone behind one of the cameras and walked off stage.

Then she saw him crossing the floor from the left side of the auditorium, his long legs moving slowly, but carrying him along at a rapid pace, making it difficult for the short, plumpish man at his side to keep up. There were two men following closely behind them, dressed in dark suits, and she guessed them to be policemen. They took up positions directly in front of the stage, while Christopher's escort walked with him to the podium. Almost as soon as he came to a stop behind the microphone, the plump man started to speak, giving an elaborate description of his own title and position, and then turned the microphone over to Christopher with only a brief, perfunctory introduction. An enthusiastic patter of applause continued to build as he lifted both of his hands and gave a relaxed smile to the audience.

He really loves this, Julia thought as the crowd continued to applaud. He waited patiently, lifting a hand to acknowledge someone in the balcony, and then gave a thumbs-up to another person seated in the front row. Julia marveled at how relaxed he appeared, knowing this came from long experience from having done this many times on lecture tours around the world.

Then she wondered who these people were. The reporter on CNN had not said, but as the camera panned across the crowd again, she saw most of them were young adults—students perhaps—with a few individuals scattered among them the right age to be their teachers. When the camera panned slowly around the auditorium, she realized it did not have the appearance of a civic center or theater. It was a university, no doubt, but not one she recognized.

"Thanks for inviting me here," Christopher said as the camera moved in close for a headshot. It seemed as if his eyes were gazing directly into hers.

She took the towel from around her shoulders and patted along the edge of her hairline, and then as she leaned back to listen, she folded it into a neat turban around her damp hair.

"I hope all of you in this detention hall have learned your lesson so we won't have to do this again."

Jade Larkin, in My Miserable Summer, Julia remembered, but she found herself laughing along with the students. They had seen the movie together almost two years before in Washington. It was not a particularly clever line, but he had the deft touch and timing of a professional comedian. This particular talent had advanced him in his former position as one of Washington's most skilled negotiators. Two years before, they had taken part in a series of meetings in Ramallah concerning issues in the West Bank. During one of the most difficult session when it seemed all of the progress they had made was suddenly coming apart, Christopher had made a joke at his own expense. The members of the delegation had joined in the laughter and the tension had dissolved in the midst of the unexpected merriment. Both of them had dined at the home of the Palestinian Prime Minister that night, finding him and his wife to be charming host. Julia closed her eyes, remembering . . . then realized he was speaking again and she had missed the first minute or so of what he was saying. It had been thirty-six hours since she had slept and her attention was wandering. She wanted to hear this speech before she went to sleep, for she knew he would refer to the upcoming negotiations. Leaning her head against the back of the chair, she tried to focus her attention on the television screen. His expression had become serious, and as the camera cut to the crowd, she saw they were listening intently.

"During the last few weeks we have experienced growing unrest in Israel. There have been terrorist bombings with many incidents aimed at religious sites, although we have been fortunate to experience nothing of a serious nature at Ashkelon. Nevertheless, the news media has focused a great deal of attention on some minor occurrences, while important events have passed them by.

"My appointment as Ambassador came about because I know many of the leaders in the Middle East and feel honored I can call them my friends. Negotiations sometimes lead to bitterness. Desperate people cannot live with the outcome of treaties dealing with the problems of government, but offer nothing to the people they represent. We live in a crucial time when it would be easy for events to spin out of control. I covet the prayers and support of each of you and from people of good will around the world. Those of us in the western world must not arrogantly assume God is concerned only with people who are Christians. If His word is to teach us anything, we must understand it contains a message of love and concern for every person on the face of this earth. God loves those who are faithful to him, but He also loves the ones who have strayed from His loving care. He loves the rich and poor alike. He loves those who struggle and those who are sheltered from the troubles of life. We must not forget that God also loves those who bring trouble into the world and those who are unlovely. He loves the prostitute, the murderer, and the thief, the man or woman setting on death row in prison, and those without hope. A love of this nature is not easy for us to understand, but as we meet with others in negotiation—or in the classroom, in cafe's, or within the privacy of our homes—we must remember God loves them just as much as he loves you and me."

Julia closed her eyes, feeling an unmistakable tingling of anxiety and alarm.

The world was not ready for this message two thousand years ago and it is not prepared to receive it now. There are men in high places who profited from danger and fear. Words of love were dangerous words, and there were many prepared to kill those who proclaimed them.

Julia awoke with a start, lifting her head to peer at the television screen. She had not meant to let her attention wander, and she had certainly not intended to go to sleep. When she focused on the television again, she realized the atmosphere had changed dramatically. This was evidently a question and answer period. Someone, she guessed to be a reporter, was standing with a microphone at the rear of the hall, and from his posture, it was obvious he was not in agreement with anything he had heard. She grabbed the remote and turned the sound up where she could hear it better.

The reporter was delivering an angry diatribe, speaking so rapidly she could not understand everything he was saying.

"I am sorry if you have misunderstood," Christopher said after a moment. "I have never taken this position nor do I know anyone who has."

"But it is right here in the newspaper! Can you deny the accuracy of this?" he asked, waving the paper wildly around until it lay in shreds at his feet.

Then he was off again in a rant, leaning close to the microphone. Julia heard the name Angus McLeish, rebuilding the temple, and DNA, all in one rambling sentence.

Suddenly, there were two security guards at the reporter's side leading him away. When the camera switched back to the stage, the small, round man who had introduced Christopher was at his side, shaking his hand. The camera moved across the crowd and she saw all of them were on their feet, applauding, their faces lifted in rapt attention.

What have I missed? Julia wondered. The camera panned forward as the two guards hustled the reporter through the doorway. There was something in his expression she could not define—something that chilled her to the marrow of her bones.

The crowd was thicker here, but he knew it would be foolish to try to close the distance separating them. Judging from the clothing most of the pedestrians were wearing, they were tourists, wandering aimlessly with their guidebooks as they scanned the storefronts. He lost sight of her briefly as she circled a small group of women wearing long black dresses and head coverings. He guessed them to be nuns. She was walking fast and he knew this was dangerous, for the ones who had trained him had said it was easy to spot someone tailing you if you walked faster than the other pedestrians. A quick glance into a storefront window was all that was required to detect someone matching your rapid pace.

Glancing toward the intersection, he saw two young men standing under a streetlight and decided they were Americans. His brother had come back from America dressed as they were, and his father had put him out of the house.

The clothes of a girl, he had said, contemptuously.

These two young men were holding what appeared to be a street map, and were rotating it as they examined the signs at the street crossing. *Trouble*, he thought, knowing they would notice her confidant pace and attractive features, and use it for an excuse to ask for directions. Just as he had feared, one of them saw Daniella approaching and elbowed his companion. Both of them turned with expectant grins already in place.

He had slowed his pace not wanting to catch her, but knowing it was unwise to stop completely. If he stopped, she would be certain to notice him. After a moment of hesitancy, he moved to the edge of the sidewalk and pretended to be tying his shoelace.

"*Ata meayim anglit?*" the young man said hopefully, pointing at an entry in his phrase book as Daniella drew abreast of them. She stopped, giving them a startled look, then threw back her head and laughed. She tried unsuccessfully to smother it with her hand, and then turned in a complete circle, dancing from one foot to the other.

"I don't think you pronounced that correctly," one of he young men said to his companion.

He had tied his shoelace, but hesitated now as a pedestrian brushed against him, mumbling an apology. He couldn't stay here all night bent over on the sidewalk. She was certain to notice. He turned his back to them and moved to the edge of the street. He could hear her smothered laughter and the apologetic sound of the young man's voice.

"I think you are right," the other agreed, but he was laughing too. "What did he say?" he asked her after a moment. Her laughter came floating back.

"You don't want to know," she told him. "Now put that book away before both of you get arrested."

"Was it that bad?"

"Are you kidding? You could cause someone to walk into traffic and be killed. Where are you trying to go?"

"It is a restaurant someone told us about," the one with the map said. "I think it is called the *kivkul keva* or something or the other.

"*Shut up!*" she said, darting a quick glance at the pedestrians who were passing them. "Are you two for real? Where did you learn this stuff?"

"Well . . . from one of our fraternity brothers at college. He said just a few phrases would really help us out when we got here."

"Both of you are pledges, right?"

He could hear the amusement in her voice, and the brief interval of silence before either of them answered.

"We are, as a matter of fact, but how did you know?"

He could not hear her reply, for she had linked her arms with theirs and was leading them toward the intersection. *These two are harmless,* he decided as he quickened his pace to stay in sight of them, but continuing to scan the faces all around him on the sidewalk. He did not see anyone who appeared threatening, he decided as he approached the crossing.

Chapter 13

Why on earth did I leave this place? Julia asked herself as she made her way down the path to the wide expanse of beach below her grandmother's sprawling villa. Stopping at the edge of the hard packed sand, she faced into the freshening wind, while it danced the hem of her short skirt against the top of her legs. Coming off the surface of the wide expanse of water, it was sharp and brisk, and it smelled . . . Oh, it smelled heavenly! In the last four years, she had traveled the shores of the Atlantic from Maine to the tip of Florida, but here were the sights and smells of the three continents surrounding this deep and mysterious sea. She turned in a complete circle with her arms raised, while the wind whirled her hair around the tops of her shoulders. She had always liked the feel of the wind in her hair, and who could resist this. In the last week, she had rushed from one impossible task to another, but here there was none of the mind-numbing routine of a vast and mundane bureaucracy. This was vibrant and alive. This was intoxicating!

She stood for another moment savoring the fresh salt air, then turned down the beach toward the excavation site, stopping only long enough to slip her sandals from her feet and dig her toes into the cool, damp sand. In the distance, she could see the tumble of stones marking the location of the sea gates, and the vast mound of reddish earth containing the ruins of one of the oldest cities on earth.

She quickened her pace, anxious to examine the progress at the excavation site. After reading the weekly bulletins from the project's staff, she had tried to picture each discovery, but was anxious now to see it firsthand. A fence ran along the edge of the ridge preventing access from below, but it was only a short distance along the beach to the front of the King David Hotel. A paved walk provided a smooth pathway from the seashore to the large glass doors opening into the lobby. It was early, but as she continued to walk, she could see there was already a respectable number of tourists sprawled on the sand along the edge of the waterline. In the distance, she could see a long line of yachts tied up at the docks, and the larger sailing craft anchored inside the breakwater. She stopped at the bottom of the walk and slipped her sandals on, then went briskly up the steps.

For several years, the excavation staff had maintained a suite of offices in the hotel. The entrance to the excavation site was nearby, and it was much easier to take advantage of the close proximity of the hotel, rather than having to drive back and forth to some less costly accommodations across town.

The door sighed open as she approached. Inside the entrance she turned toward the desk, where Kevin Krishnan was sorting through some newly arrived messages. Kevin had been working at the hotel for the last four years, having accompanied his sister to Israel while she was a student at Hebrew University. She had graduated recently, but he had stayed on. He had worked at the excavation site in the mornings for the last three years and had corresponded with Daniella on her website almost on a daily basis. As Julia approached the desk, she saw him look up with his eyes widening in surprise. He came around the end of the desk and threw his arms around her in a quick, enthusiastic embrace, then backed up, smiling down at her face.

"You look . . . different," he said, and she realized he was looking at her hair. In the last year, she had let it grow to shoulder length, but now it was a tangled mess. She reached up and ran her fingers through it, then laughed self-consciously.

"I know I'm a mess, but I just came from the beach. Does this look better?" She was aware of his eyes darting around her face, and then his mouth widened in a pleased grin.

"It looks even lovelier," he said. "You look like . . ."

Abraham's Bones

"Yes?" Julia said, wishing she had stopped at the bathroom before she had approached the desk. Her hair was a mess. It had to be.

"You look like . . . your sister," he said, but even as he said this, she knew it was not what he had originally intended to say.

"Has she been hanging around the desk?" she asked. When she was 12 years old, Daniella had developed an adolescent crush on Kevin, while he reacted to her infatuation with a great deal of amusement. He had visited Washington in December and the roles had undergone an astonishing reversal. She had gone from smitten to smug, and Julia had a feeling smug would trump smitten every time.

"Regretfully, no," he said looking wistful. "She has been giving me a patronizing wave whenever she rushes through the lobby."

"Should I tell her you are dying of unrequited love?" Julia teased.

"She already knows, but it doesn't matter. She comes through here with some big *motzetz*, and he waves too. I think his name is Gideon."

Julia laughed while Kevin grinned self-consciously. He had made a serious effort to extend his knowledge of Hebrew beyond what he had learned at yeshiva. *Motzetz*, which referred to a store mannequin, was not the word he was seeking, but it was close enough. Suddenly he leaned toward her and lowered his voice. "I think Gideon might be a problem."

Seeing his serious expression, Julia's smile faded. "For you or for her?" she asked.

"I'm interfering in your private affairs," he said, his hands suddenly becoming busy. "There was someone asking for you about an hour ago. His name is Angus McLeish. He looked vaguely familiar, but I couldn't place him."

Angus McLeish was a living legend among history buffs, although his name did not arouse the same kind of admiration among the ranks of professional archeologists. He had appeared on countless television specials over the last few years, all of them dealing with fanciful theories about archeology and human history. He had covered Noah's flood, the disappearance of the Ark of the Covenant, Sodom and Gomorrah, and the true nature of the plagues in Egypt. Most of it was harmless showmanship in the tradition of

P.T. Barnum, but occasionally he made some startling announcement that was later proven to be true. Many professionals were unhappy with his brazen notoriety. She could not imagine what McLeish could want with her.

She decided the best thing would be for her to slip down the corridor to Dr. De Silva's office, but when she looked up McLeish was crossing the lobby. Kevin waved and pointed at her. He immediately changed directions. She realized he was looking at her hair in the same manner as Kevin, but when she tried to smooth it down it stubbornly refused to obey. He stopped directly in front of her, his eyes darting around her face.

"I'm Angus McLeish," he said, almost shyly, and extended his hand. McLeish was an Irishman of medium height with a head of dark, straight hair, combed back from his forehead. He was sunburned, muscular, and she could feel the full force of his magnetic personality.

"Julia Siedman," she said, letting her fingers brush against his.

"I wonder, Miss Siedman, if I could speak with you for a minute?"

Julia had started to make an excuse, but after studying the frown line between his eyebrows, she decided to relent. "Only for a few minutes," she said. "I have just returned home and I would like to renew some old acquaintances. Negotiations will be starting in a matter of days, and there isn't sufficient time to devote to matters not pertaining to our mission."

"Well, actually, this has something to do with your mission in an indirect way. I wonder if I could buy you a cup of coffee."

Julia had started to refuse, but she had skipped breakfast and a cup of coffee would be nice. She followed him across the lobby and into the brightly lit restaurant. A waiter led the way to a table near the windows. McLeish ordered coffee for them in passable Hebrew, and then turned his worried expression in her direction.

"I wonder if you have spoken with Dr. Christopher recently?"

"This is in relation to what?" she asked, not wanting to explain their strained relationship or the fact she had not spoken to him in almost a year.

"Have you heard of the Moroccan Stelae?"

Abraham's Bones

Julia gave a negative shake of her head, wondered if this was something he would be using in another overblown television documentary.

"Then let me explain. The Moroccan Stelae was unearthed almost ten years ago. It has gone almost unnoticed by the archeological community, although I have sent a report detailing its importance to a number of authorities on ancient languages. The fragment was broken and only the upper half of the text was visible. Subsequent tests on the patina have proven the artifact was originally from Palestine, and probably from this immediate area. While I am not an expert linguist, I believe the text is some form of Proto-Greek language, preceding Linear B by a great number of years."

Linear B was the oldest example of the Greek language anyone had been able to decipher, dating from around 1250 B.C. While historically important, she could not see how McLeish could make any of this into a documentary. The audience would be likely to yawn themselves to death. "This is very interesting, but what connection does that have with the upcoming negotiations?"

"Dr. Christopher has received some photographs of a number of artifacts, clay tablets, to be precise. I understand they have an inscription in the same language as the Moroccan Stelae. These photographs are supposedly very legible. I understand there are seven of them."

"I haven't discussed this with Dr. Christopher," Julia said, still wondering where he was going with this.

McLeish leaned toward her. "This is of extreme importance, Miss Siedman. I have reasons to believe the Moroccan Stelae is much older than anyone has suspected and could very easily be the primordial language."

Linguistic experts had tried for years to trace languages back to their roots, working on the theory that all languages had evolved from one common source. Trying to recover the language of Adam and Eve was a hopeless dream, in her opinion, but it was the thing that made overblown television documentaries possible.

"I'm afraid you would have an uphill battle trying to prove it to the scientific community," she said.

"Once I place the proof in their hands, there will be no way they can deny it," he said, somewhat defensively.

"What proof are you referring to, Mr. McLeish?"

"I believe the text on these artifacts will lead us to a great storehouse of historical treasures. Father Ricci, who is one of the Vatican's most accomplished theologians, was in the process of making a translation when he had a stroke. I have a summation of his translation in my possession, but it did not include a copy of the text. I have several friends who are expert linguist. I would like them to complete what Father Ricci was attempting to do. In the meantime, I intend to follow the information I already have, incomplete as it is. I might get lucky again." McLeish reached into his pocket and removed a small tissue wrapped package. "There is also this," he said, as he unfolded the paper and placed it carefully in front of her.

The object was a small pendant suspended from a gold chain. It was probably made of alabaster, very similar to the cartouches found in the tombs of the Egyptian Pharaohs, although this one was much smaller. She could see two birdlike figures composed of seven straight lines, with a row of text underneath the drawings. There was nothing remarkable about it, for untold numbers of similar objects had been found in recent years. "Is this the text on the other artifacts?" she asked.

"It is, but I wonder if you have seen something similar?"

"Similar, but nothing identical that I can recall. You might want to consult with Dr. De Silva. He might be able to refer you to a catalogue for comparison."

"Actually, this is of recent manufacture, although a number of them have been found in the past. This is what makes it so interesting. I am told this is the emblem of a terrorists organization called Shiva."

Julia wondered where McLeish had obtained his information, but did not intend to confirm anything he suspected. "I'm afraid I won't be able to be of any help you," she said.

"I would have waited until Dr. Christopher arrived, but I thought an indirect approach might be more effective than simply leaving a note."

"I will pass on your message, Mr. McLeish, but I can't guarantee Dr. Christopher will be interested."

"I couldn't ask for more, Miss Siedman."

Looking past McLeish's shoulder, Julia could see Daniella approaching with an envelope clutched in her hand. She stopped on

Abraham's Bones

the far side of the table with the message hovering just out of her reach. She was aware of Daniella's startled expression, and the careful way she was looking at her hair. She resisted the urge to reach up and run her hands through it again. *What was wrong with her hair?* McLeish shifted in his chair, looking at Daniella for a few seconds, and then his eyes darted away. Daniella dropped the envelope on the table, then turned in a teenage huff and retraced her steps toward the lobby.

"You really must excuse me," Julia said, fighting to maintain her composure while barely able to restrain herself from squirming in her chair.

"Certainly," McLeish said, climbing to his feet as she scooted her chair back. Julia shook hands with him again, and then made a detour toward the restroom. As she rounded the corner of the partition and approached the mirror, she stopped and drew in her breath. Her hair had always been thick and full, and on several occasions, she had let her hairdresser thin it along the sides. As she stared back at her reflection in the mirror, she could hardly believe what she was seeing. Sanura Hamada had made her windblown coiffure famous on the last occasion when she had played at Wimbledon. This picture had subsequently appeared on the cover of *Vanity Fair*. When she came face to face with her, would she think she was some kind of pathetic groupie? This was awful! *Tomorrow I will have it cut,* she promised herself.

Chapter 14

Rachel Richardson was not what Julia had expected. Richardson was to be their advance representative, responsible for setting up her office and putting the necessary security and communications equipment in place. She had agreed to meet her in the restaurant of the King David Hotel at noon. She had been expecting someone who looked like Hollywood's version of an FBI agent, and was surprised to see Richardson did not look much different from the many thousands of tourists you could see on any street in Israel. She was dressed casually in a pair of jeans with a sleeveless blouse faded around the collar. Richardson smiled in a distracted way as she scooted a chair out on the opposite side of the table and immediately got down to business.

"I don't like this location. I think there might be a security problem if we try to set up your office here."

"Have you been to Israel before?" Julia asked. "If you haven't, you might not be aware there is a security problem everywhere. We aren't likely to change anything if we hide behind the walls of a fortress."

"I'm sure there are a number of details to work out, but Senator Cauldfield has asked for our help in securing Congressman Danville's release."

"I don't understand why any of this would require elaborate security measures."

"I assumed you had already discussed this with Gary Maser before you left Washington," Richardson said, aiming a frown in her direction.

Julia leaned forward. "Look, Ms. Richardson . . ."

"Rachel."

"Rachel, I have no intention of working with Gary Maser."

"I'm afraid there's little choice in the matter. Congressman Danville's staff has already discussed this with Senator Cauldfield and he has requested the cooperation of everyone involved."

"Maybe you didn't hear me. There is no way I will work with him."

Rachel gave her an amused smile and wiped an imaginary crumb from the gleaming surface of the table. "We had intended to go through the embassy to secure his release, but this will be better for everyone concerned. If everything doesn't work out as we have planned, the political fallout will not be as damaging."

In the last four years, Julia had taken part in all of the negotiations between the Palestine Authority and Israel. She had naturally assumed Cauldfield had chosen her because of her qualifications and the success of the previous missions. Instead of being flattered, she felt insulted and used.

"Political fallout is not my number one priority. I intend to keep my focus on the prospects of world peace," she said stubbornly. Before Rachel had time to reply, she saw the shifting of her eyes and turned to look toward the entrance of the restaurant. At first, she could not believe the message her eyes were sending, and then she realized the man approaching their table, was indeed, Gary Maser.

Mario Falconi had a commanding presence for a man of such short stature, but Christopher could not decide if it was his family connections with the House of Savoy, or if it had something to do with the way his father and grandfather had deftly sidestepped the zealots who had prosecuted the fallen at Nuremberg. Not only had they survived, they had flourished, and it was this remarkable success that had brought Christopher, Pierce, and Ambassador Stoltz to his office for a late afternoon meeting. Serious financial matters in Italy required the involvement of Falconi, or at least his knowledge and support. His bank was an imposing structure with a neo-classical façade, as solid appearing as the European fortunes that backed it financially.

"I am afraid this photograph means nothing to me," Falconi said from behind a teakwood desk as wide as the transom of a sailing yacht. He had started to return the photo to Pierce when he stopped and angled it toward the light.

"If I was hazarding a guess, I would say that this photo was made at *Mürren*, in south central Switzerland. It is an alpine village situated high above the *Lauterbrunnen* Valley. My father was one of the founders of the *Kanhahar* Ski Club. I go there often for skiing and also some ballooning during the summer months."

Christopher thought it strange that Falconi had not asked for the man's identity but had only given the photo a cursory glance before passing it back. When he became aware of the careful way in which Christopher was watching him, he said, "The world of international finance is a very small club. If this man had made any serious financial transactions in the last quarter-century, I would have been one of the first to know. I'm naturally curious as to why you think I might be able to recognize him."

"Some of our people believe he has been financing some terrorists groups in the Middle East over the last decade."

"Are you talking about serious money?" Falconi said rather doubtfully.

"We are sure that it runs into the millions," Pierce said.

Falconi made an elegant gesture with his hand, and then paused as he chose his words carefully. "Financing a terrorist organization on the level of al-Qaeda would require several billion each year. There is always some loose money floating around any trouble spot in the world, but nothing significant is likely to happen unless you have serious money. I'm sure you are aware that most of the financing of these groups comes from government and religious organizations around the world." He darted a quick glance in Christopher's direction as if he was suddenly remembering his connections with the Vatican.

"Is there any way large amounts of money could be moved around the world without you being aware?" Pierce asked.

Falconi paused. "There is a system called hawala. Some people believe it dates from Abraham's day. It was actually the model for

Abraham's Bones

today's international banking system. Money brokers charge a fee for guaranteeing payment. It was very useful centuries ago when caravans transported most of the merchandise. It was not necessary to send gold along on a perilous journey. Someone at each end took care of receiving or paying out the necessary amounts. They used little clay jars with marble sized pellets inside to represent the amount involved. The jar was sealed and had the guarantor's seal affixed. It was a simple, but ingeniously secure system."

"Like today's wire transfers between banks," Pierce suggested.

"Exactly. It is still used extensively in third-world countries, as I am sure Dr. Christopher is aware."

"It is still in use all over the Middle East," Christopher agreed. "Conformation is made over the Internet or by phone. They don't need the little jars with the pellets inside."

Pierce looked thoughtful. "I think I have heard of this, but I seem to remember it involved only small amounts."

"Most of the transfers are small, but it also involves large amounts as well. Al-Qaeda uses hawala quite extensively, as well as making use of larger banking organizations. It has occurred to me while we have been speaking, that this might be a way to track down this man, if indeed that is what you are intending to do."

"That is why we have come to you," Pierce said. "How should we go about doing this?"

"Terrorists organizations collect money from many millions of persons from around the world. Find the hawala brokers who are moving these funds. You might get lucky. It might take time, but I think it might be the best way to guarantee success."

"Time is the one thing we don't have," Pierce said. "We have to find some other way."

Falconi looked thoughtful for a moment, his eyes directed at the surface of his desk. "It is my understanding that you already have someone who is an expert in these matters. It was my intentions to hire her away from CITI a few years ago, but one of your intelligence services managed to do so before I could make my move. Her name is Rachel Richardson."

"I believe Ms. Richardson is in charge of setting up security measures for the American delegation," Pierce said.

Falconi's mouth moved in what might have been a smile. "If Ms. Richardson is in Israel, I can assure you there is more involved than setting up a security system. You might want to explore this problem with her."

"It might not be that simple," Pierce said.

"Then I wish you luck," Falconi said. Christopher realized this was Falconi's way of dismissing them.

Julia hit the redial button on her phone, then quickly made a note as she heard it ringing on the other end. She had been able to contact the Palestinian Authority in Ramallah without difficulty, but had been unable to get past the receptionist in Jerusalem. She looked with dismay at the pile of papers she had accumulated since her arrival. She had hoped to have a little free time before she became involved in the millions of details surrounding this negotiation session, but evidently, this was not to be the case.

"Naava Ludvic," the receptionist said.

"This is Julia Siedman in Ashkelon," she said. "You were supposed to have someone in the Prime Minister's office return my call."

There was a brief pause, and then the woman said, "Who is this again, please?"

"Julia Siedman, from the American Department of State," she added for emphasis, somewhat exasperated that this young woman could not remember the three calls she had made in the last hour.

"Ah, yes, I do remember. I did make a note to have Yosef Arav telephone you when he returns," she said in a lilting voice. "Is there anything else?"

Julia had started to reply when she heard a male voice, somewhat indistinct, and then much louder, as if the person had stopped somewhere near the telephone.

"No, not today, I have other things to do!"

Then the voice stopped abruptly as if the receptionist had placed her hand over the receiver.

Julia waited, frowning down at the open folder on her desk until the young woman came back on the line.

"General Arav left the office before your first call. I understand he will not return before the end of the day. Would you like to leave a message?"

Abraham's Bones

Julia had heard the man's voice for only a second, but she had known Yosef Arav for all of her life. She was certain the voice was his.

"Yes," she had started to say, and then realized the connection had already been broken.

Chapter 15

If you were required to describe Israel in one sentence, you could use the words 'stinking hot,' Maitland decided as he wiped his neck and threw the damp towel toward the bathroom. He had spent weeks in third world countries where there was no hot water, but in this abominable place, nothing was cold. He would have liked to spend another five minutes standing in the shower, but the water from the showerhead was as tepid as freshly brewed tea. The weak blast of air coming from the vents was cool, but in another hour, the inside of the room would be as hot as a sauna. Tourists came to Israel from every part of the world to get closer to their God, but he strongly suspected Hades was only a few feet underneath the hot, flinty soil.

In the early years of his career, he had received an assignment to write an article about the Jewish community in Jerusalem, and he had reported they had mistakenly believed God loved them, while there was a preponderance of evidence that suggested the opposite. *If God did not hate them as much as the rest of the world did, then why did he give this accursed wilderness to them as their homeland?* When he had written this article, he had not known his editor was Jewish and discovered, belatedly, that he did not have a sense of humor.

Before leaving Rome, he had arranged a flight scheduled to arrive in Tel Aviv in the early hours of the morning. He had then secured transportation to this seedy hotel near the business district of Ashkelon. He wanted to spend his first few days going quietly about his business where he could conduct his investigation without any interference from the authorities. During the early years of his career, a reporter could depend upon the cooperation of government agencies, but now, he frequently found himself under surveillance, his proper role in society having undergone an unfortunate reversal.

He glanced at his watch and realized he had almost a half-hour before he was to meet his contact. There were also a couple of telephone calls, but he knew it would be foolhardy to conduct his business over his cell phone. Electronic surveillance was rampant throughout the world and you could never be too careful. He would use one of the pay phones along one of the side streets or in a shop.

Before leaving the airport, he had picked up a copy of Independent America where his latest article was due to appear. He had done one rewrite when the editor had disagreed on several essential points, but had refused to change some others. Examining the cover of the magazine, he did not see his article mentioned as he had expected, and when he flipped to the inside, he could not find it on the title page. The two longest articles were by Bryan Fredrick, and two of the staff writers had written the others. Then on page four he saw his article and was enraged to see a complete rewrite by one of the editor's toadies. The essence of the story was still there, but it had been twisted 180 degrees, making it say exactly the opposite of what he had intended. He had done some extensive research on unwarranted surveillance in the private sector, and had been alarmed at what he had discovered. Few people were aware of the electronic devices which made this possible, and almost no one knew of the intrusion by the government into their private lives. The affordable prices of electronic surveillance equipment made it possible for private industry to launch their own assault on the rights of their employees. In the near future, Radio Frequency ID's attached to every article sold in stores, would allow anyone with the proper equipment to track a package from manufacturer to consumer. A small airplane could carry the necessary equipment to scan an entire city with one pass and produce a printout of the recently purchased merchandise in any home or apartment. Companies were insisting this would lower cost by allowing retailers to have rapid checkout at their stores and would aid in inventory control. None of them, however, could explain why retailers needed the ability to continue monitoring merchandise long after it had left their stores. Cell phones carried similar devices, allowing government agencies to pinpoint the location of a caller anywhere in the world. Equipment available on the Internet allowed stalkers to keep track of their prey without the victim's knowledge. New automobiles were already equipped with GPS capability and a 'black box' producing a recording of every mile the automobile traveled. Hidden surveillance cameras now monitored 95 percent of American employees while they were on the job. Many employees had identification cards allowing their supervisors to track them 24/7. Some of them had tracking devices the size of a grain of rice implanted underneath their skin. These devices were coated with a kind of surgical superglue that made it impossible to remove them unless you wanted to remove a thumb-sized lump of flesh. Information databases recorded pertinent details of the lives of each citizen from birth to death, while government officials were assuring a gullible public this was in accordance with their best interest. *Trust us,* they had said. It made him want to laugh. The bootlicker who had appropriated his article had twisted it into a flaming mess and would probably get him elevated to a better job on the same floor with the CEO. He had hoped this article would be a wake-up call to the public, but the evil ones had thwarted him again.

Maitland threw the magazine into the wastebasket and rubbed the palm of his hand along the back of his neck. In Rome, he had been a 'person of interest' to the Carabinieri. Once the authorities knew he was here, he had no doubt Shin Bit, or one of the other covert organizations within the Israeli intelligence community, would have him under surveillance. Only a few things in his investigation remained, and he hoped he would have time to complete the remaining details before he confronted Christopher with his shocking evidence.

He opened the envelope and began thumbing through its contents until he found the pictures he had made of Daniella. The camera had caught her in mid-stride coming down the steps of a restaurant, long legs flashing underneath the hem of an abbreviated skirt. In another, he had snapped the shutter just as she had licked at a cone of ice cream, leaving a pink smear on the edge of her lip. At the curb, he had focused on her feet and could see the stitching along the soles of a pair of beaded sandals, and the small pink toes curled slightly as she lifted her foot from the pavement. He had seen something similar on a movie actress in Rome, and realized they were Manolo Blahnik sandals and had probably cost close to a thousand dollars. Was she trying to impress the brainless looking kid following along behind her? He looked as humorless as a donkey and as dumb as an ox. He would not have noticed if she had worn a pair of pink flip-flops. Glancing at the back of the photograph, he saw that his name was Gideon. He looked vaguely familiar, but he could not identify him.

In the next shot, the sunlight was striking the soft skin on the side of Daniella's throat. He could not believe she was only fourteen. Eve had probably looked something like this when she had lured Adam into an act of sin.

Thumbing slowly through the file, he began to examine the other documents. There were airline tickets, a large assortment of letters printed from the Internet, her school reports, phone numbers . . . It was all here, but as yet, there were large portions of it he did not understand. Daniella was the weak link in his investigation, and with a little more research, he would be able to exploit this weakness.

He had saved the other picture for last. Someone had made it from a great distance through a telephoto lens. The background was compressed and without any detail. The bikini she was wearing was make of some kind of shiny, elasticized material that appeared wet, although there was no evidence of moisture on her skin. The wind had caught her hair, whipping it around the back of her neck and leaving the sides of her face exposed. Her mouth was open, and it was obvious she was calling to someone across the pool. Was it a boyfriend? There had been nothing in the file to indicate any serious relationships, although there were a large number of male friends. Did she like older men, or was the age difference a result of being in a prestigious college at such an early age? As he continued to study the photograph, he suddenly noticed something he had not noticed before. He flipped his equipment case open and found his magnifying glass. There was nothing in the background to identify the location, but he could see someone standing just beyond the fence looking in Daniella's direction. The young man's forehead was indistinct, shadowed by the bill of a baseball cap, but he could see the rest of his face. There could be no doubt that this was Gideon. A date printed on the lower right-handed corner of the picture indicated that someone had made it the previous summer in Boston. The list of workers he had obtained at the hotel listed Gideon as a student at a small university in Hungary. Was he actually a policeman, CIA, FBI or just some nut who was following a pretty girl around the world? He closed his eyes and felt a little tremor of uneasiness travel up his spine.

Chapter 16

Having been a world traveler for most of his life, Christopher was accustomed to the inconveniences airline passengers encountered at airports around the world. In his years at the State Department, he had traveled extensively in the Middle East and had occasionally accompanied others with diplomatic passports. Seeing these officials ushered past customs, while he had to endure a thorough search of his luggage, had always made him envious. Heads turned as an impeccably dressed customs administrator escorted him past the checkpoints.

During the last two days, he had sat in conference after conference with officials from a dozen Vatican offices. There had been elaborate praise for his abilities and cautious optimism concerning the future. They had reminded him, with a great deal of delicacy, that the aspirations of the church were sometimes contrary to the procedures to which he had grown accustomed.

He had intended to call Havran as soon as he arrived, but decided to wait until later. A last minute change in plans had delayed his departure, and he had booked a later flight.

When they reached the gate, the customs official handed him off to a sturdy looking young man who had been holding a sign aloft in the center of the concourse.

"I'm Benji, Dr. Christopher. Leora is waiting beside her car."

Benji inquired politely about his flight as they made their way to the curb where Leora was standing beside the door of a silver-gray Honda. She was a third generation Sabra, as the native born Israelis were known, with healthy good looks and an alluring smile. The young man quickly stowed the bags in the rear floorboard and swung effortlessly into the back. Christopher took the passenger seat as Leora ran around to the driver's door and hopped behind the wheel.

"We barely made it in time," she said as they fastened their seatbelts. She took a quick look at the slowly moving traffic, then stabbed the accelerator with her sandal, darting the little car in front of a honking automobile.

Christopher glanced in the mirror and saw a van with official markings force its way into the space behind them, but did not see the blue lights come to life as he had expected. Leora swerved again and headed toward the street.

"Did you have problems with the traffic?" he said, grabbing the armrest and pulling himself upright again in the seat.

"A truck blew up," she said, making a gesture toward her left. "They have some of the roads blocked."

Leora had grown up in a nation where armed conflict was a frequent occurrence. Like most of the young adults of her generation, she had served in the military and now held the rank of lieutenant in the reserve. She was currently the pottery expert at the excavation site and took the responsibilities of her work seriously. He was touched she had taken time from her busy schedule to pick him up at the airport. She had not explained who Benji was, but judging from the number of times she had taken her hand from the wheel to touch the oversized boot jammed between their seats, their involvement went beyond a casual relationship.

Leora did a racing change with the shift and then continued to alternate her foot between the brake and the accelerator as she whipped in and out of traffic. In less than a minute, he was thoroughly lost, occasionally seeing a sign with the name of some unfamiliar landmark. After passing a sign pointing toward *Rishon Le Zion*, he realized they had skirted the southern part of Tel Aviv and were now racing toward Ashkelon. It was past midnight and the traffic was thinning considerably. Leora increased her speed and

Abraham's Bones

took her eyes off the road long enough to give him a searching look.

"I checked your e-mail before I left the office," she said, passing a sheaf of papers to him. He tucked them inside the pocket of his jacket without looking.

"Was there anything interesting?"

"There doesn't seem to be anything of earthshattering importance. Dr. De Silva had already gone for the day so I just printed them out and brought them along."

Gilbert De Silva was the head of the excavation project at Ashkelon, having received this position when Dr. Siedman's health had forced her into retirement. He was an able administrator and one of his dearest friends. It was their arrangement for De Silva to handle any important items of business when he was away. The way Leora had answered his question made him aware something was troubling her. Her profile was visible in the faint light from the dash and he could see her worrying her bottom lip between her teeth.

"It couldn't be as bad as all that," he said. "Why don't you tell me?"

She shifted the position of her hands on the wheel and took a deep breath. "There was a message from Julia. She came home yesterday."

He leaned back in the seat and took a deep breath of his own. He had not seen Julia since he resigned his position in Washington almost a year before, although he had called her office on numerous occasions. The young woman who answered her telephone had informed him with a crisp voice that Miss Siedman was not available. Messages he left at her apartment had gone unanswered as well.

He suddenly realized Leora was waiting for him to comment, but this was so unexpected he did not know how to form an answer. Julia's previous visit had coincided with a trip he had scheduled to Egypt. Returning to the house tonight would create the same uncomfortable situation he had managed to avoid the previous year. He was exhausted from a full day of almost frantic activity, plus the flight home. The best solution would be to check into the hotel for the night and deal with this awkward situation when he had all of his wits about him.

"Are you working at the excavation site," he asked, glancing over the seat at Benji. Instead of an answer, he saw him exchange glances with Leora in the rearview mirror.

"Do you think we should tell him," Leora asked. Benji seemed to be considering it for a moment before giving a quick nod of his head.

Leora tilted her head and changed the position of her hands on the wheel. "Benji is Palestinian," she said.

Leora had lived for a short time at a kibbutz in the West Bank, and he wondered if she had met Benji while she was there. There was little social contact between Palestinians and Jews in Israel, and marriage between them was a rare event. When he turned his head slightly where he could study her profile, she moved her mouth nervously and continued.

"When I first met Benji, he told me he had gone to college in America, but he did not tell me he was an Arab, or that he had changed his name so no one would know he was originally from the West Bank. He waited until I was hopelessly involved with him and then he told me. When he invited me to attend an interfaith worship service, I accepted. We have been meeting in some of the member's homes each week, and it is something I can't really explain. I am a Jew and I will always be a Jew, but when I see what is happening all over the world because everyone is having problems with the way other people worship, I can't help wondering if everything isn't mixed up somehow."

She suddenly stopped speaking and they rode along for a moment until Benji broke the silence.

"I was having the same problems, Dr. Christopher. I am a Muslim and my family has faithfully followed the teaching of the Qur'an for centuries, but like Leora, I have come to realize there is more to religion than condemnation. At first, we went to the services out of curiosity. Our curiosity turned to interest when we heard the simple message the leaders proclaimed. Muslims and Jews claim to be descendants of Abraham with their own distinct and separate truths, yet the simple message we heard that night was about the same things Abraham believed. There was nothing about how far a man could travel on the Sabbath or about the punishment of an unfaithful wife. Jews, Muslims, and Christians worship the

Abraham's Bones

same God. We want to worship without the thousands of rules forcing men away from God. Faith should be simple."

Suddenly he stopped and looked embarrassed. "I'm sorry, Dr. Christopher. I didn't mean to sound disrespectful of religion, but . . ."

"Sounds like good Catholic doctrine to me."

Benji laughed. "Most of my American friends tell me I sound like a Presbyterian."

Christopher had not noticed the army fatigues Benji was wearing until that moment.

"Are you with the military?" he said, but almost immediately regretted having asked the question when he saw Benji's eyes dart toward the mirror again.

"Yes, I'm on active duty. While Palestinians are not subject to the draft, we are allowed to serve voluntarily."

"He's with Special Forces," Leora said with a little note of pride in her voice.

Like America's counterpart, Israel's Special Forces worked hand-in-hand with their intelligence services, frequently carrying out missions for Mossad, Israel's equivalent of the CIA. It was an elite group made up of the military's finest soldiers.

"I know what you are probably thinking, Dr. Christopher. My superiors are aware of my personal history, while the men I serve with are not. It's rather complicated and it isn't easy to explain to someone who isn't familiar with the situation."

"Dr. Christopher is an expert on Israel's political situation," Leora said rather quickly. "Why do you think he is involved in the upcoming negotiations?"

"Oh, no, I am talking about my personal life. I grew up in a camp in the West Bank. My parents were dead by the time I was twelve, killed by artillery rounds fired into our apartment. I was full of anger and hostility because of my misfortune. I hated everything Jewish—their religion, their customs, and their funny clothes—until I met a Rabbi from Milwaukee. He came to Israel to organize a protest movement against the Zionist and he never left. I used to treat his injuries when no one could force him to go to a doctor. I did not understand why anyone could take so much punishment and go back for more. I thought at first it was his liberal views, so I asked him to teach me about his religion. He told me he did not want to convert me to Judaism. He wanted to transform me into an Israeli. He said Israel would never know peace until it opened its doors to people of every religion and creed and allowed them to be equal citizens under the law. He believed it passionately and it got him killed. I am an Israeli, Dr. Christopher, but at the same time, I am one of the new breed. Our numbers are growing daily, and it is frightening to some of our citizens. It even frightens me sometimes."

There was a sudden flash of headlights behind them as a small delivery truck swung out and went racing past. Another vehicle moved up to take the position the truck had just vacated, then dropped back a respectable distance where the low beams were no longer shining through the glass. Benji had fallen silent and was studying the vehicle directly in front of them.

Christopher glanced at his watch and saw it was almost one o'clock. He had spoken to Dr. De Silva only once during his absence, and as he thought about this now, he felt a rekindling of his anxiety. De Silva's call had been short and cryptic, urging him to return to Israel at the first possible moment. Even when pressed, he had refused to explain the reason for his concern. It would be late when they arrived in Ashkelon and he would have to postpone any discussion with him until morning. He was still thinking of his own problems when he realized Benji had spoken to him from the rear seat. He swung his head around and saw Benji had a cell phone pressed to his ear and was looking through the rear glass at the car following them. It had started to creep up again with the lights on high beam, causing a blinding glare in the mirror. Another set of lights above the roof snapped on and Leora made a sound of frustration and let off on the gas. Directly in front of them, someone had lifted the rear door of the truck and he could see a figure outlined in the bright light. The man seemed to be tilting something upward at a sharp angle. Before he could shout a warning, there was a loud thump from underneath their tires and the car went careening toward the shoulder. Leora fought the steering wheel trying to keep the car under control. She rode hard on the brakes and came to a stop with the front end pointed toward the ditch. The automobile behind them had swung out to avoid a collision and went skidding past their rear bumper with the tires crying in protest. There was the strong smell of hot metal and burned rubber in the air. The

Abraham's Bones

automobile had almost collided with them was a white van with government markings. This was the same vehicle Leora had cut in front of as they were leaving the terminal.

Christopher ducked as someone in the van fired a short burst with an automatic weapon. The door on the passenger side slid open and two men jumped out and continued to shoot at the escaping truck. It was several hundred yards away, the sound of the rapidly accelerating motor beating loudly against the damp night air. Suddenly, a blinding flash filled the inside of the car with a brilliant light. The car shook as the pressure wave rolled over them.

"Plastic explosives," Benji said in a calm voice from the rear seat. "There must have been one hundred kilos or more."

Christopher tried to focus his eyes but could see nothing except the yellow impression of the explosion on his retina. Two men from the van had approached and were leaning through the window. As his vision cleared, he saw both of them were wearing military uniforms. One of them shined his flashlight along the ground.

"All of your tires seem to have gone flat," he said, giving a low whistle as he examined the gouges where the wheel rims had cut into the pavement.

"There's a guru bed lying back there in the ditch," another soldier said, moving his light to illuminate an object some distance away on the shoulder of the road.

A guru bed was the slang term for the deadly device terrorists sometimes used to stop unsuspecting motorists. They were miracles of improvisation, easily constructed by driving rows of nails through a sheet of plywood. Thrown into the path of an automobile, there was little time to swerve and the result was sometimes deadly. They had avoided an accident because of their good fortune, but mostly because Leora was an excellent driver.

Benji had joined the group of soldiers near the van. Blue lights were flashing in the distance as a car came rapidly toward them. Swinging wide around the burning vehicle, it came to a halt in front of the government car. The passenger door opened and a man dressed in a dark suit came across to where they were standing.

"My name is Cohen, Ambassador Christopher. I am with the police. I would suggest all of you come with us and we will see you safely home."

Leora was assessing the damage to her car with a stricken expression.

"Please," Cohen said as he gestured toward the government vehicle. "This is dangerous. We must be on our way. Our friends here will arrange to have your car transported into town. A set of tires will make it as good as new."

When they were all jammed together in the back seat of the police car, the driver made a tight turn and they went racing toward the city. Cohen spoke into a microphone for a few seconds, talking rapidly and pausing to listen to the brusque replies from the other end. The driver kept his foot to the floor and the heavy car seemed to be floating just above the pavement. He did not attempt to slow until they reached the edge of Ashkelon, and then went racing through the streets at a slower but still reckless speed. At the center of town, the driver turned away from the police station toward Dr. Siedman's residence. Christopher opened his mouth to protest and then closed it again, knowing it would serve no useful purpose to delay the inevitable.

Julia was here and he must face her, if not tonight, then certainly when tomorrow came.

Julia flipped through the stack of messages, and made another quick note in the margin of her notepad. She had talked briefly to her staff in Washington and had left a message at Senator Cauldfield's office when she had not been able to speak with anyone in authority. Glancing at her watch, she was surprised to see it was after midnight.

She was getting ready to shut her computer down when she saw a blinking icon indicating she had received another e-mail. Clicking the 'mail' button, she bent toward the bottom drawer of her desk, shoved the folder inside, and had just straightened in her seat when she saw the message consisted of a single word. She experienced a feeling of annoyance when she saw URGENT printed in capitol letters, and a telephone number centered underneath it on the second line. The person who had sent this message had probably not known how to make the letters blink, or they would have arranged this as well.

Abraham's Bones

Midnight was not the best time for melodrama, and it was a relief to see there was not any cute faces following the message. Some adolescent game-master had probably sent this same e-mail simultaneously to ten thousand addresses, and was breathlessly waiting to count the number of telephone messages it would generate.

She glanced at the area code and realized this message had originated from the Washington area, although it was not a number she recognized. Suppressing a sigh, she picked up the telephone and punched in the numbers as she searched for her pen. There was a brief pause before she heard someone answer with a cryptic word that sounded like *dater*. Her first impulse was to hang up, but before she could shift the phone to her other hand, she heard her name in a questioning tone, then someone with a Back Bay accent reminiscent of John Kennedy, began speaking in a rapid-fire manner.

"This is George Cardigan at the National Data Center."

"I just received your message, Mr. Cardigan. How may I help you?"

"I wouldn't bother you after hours, Miss Siedman, but your submission was marked priority, so I thought I should notify you we couldn't process your request."

"My request?"

"Yes, you see, we aren't authorized to access data banks containing confidential government information."

"Was this request submitted by my office in Washington?" she asked, wondering if her secretary or someone on the team had requested the search and left instructions to forward it to her. Before she could ask him to clarify the matter, he spoke up again.

"We work in the private sector and do research almost exclusively for industry."

Julia hesitated. "Can you tell me the name of the person who submitted the request?"

"I have your name, Miss Siedman, and your e-mail address."

"And can you tell me the subject you were asked to research?"

"Actually, there were two requests. The first was for information about an organization called Shiva."

Julia wondered if her grandmother had submitted a request for information and gave the wrong e-mail address. She knew she had used an agency in California for many years to do the detailed research for her books, but she could not imagine why she would want information on a terrorists group. This was very puzzling.

"And what was the second request?"

"We were given the name, Angus McLeish. I believe he is a rather well known archeologist. This request is completely beyond the depth of what we normally do. One of our experts said this was the type of information someone could use to obtain the GPS coordinates of his cell phone."

"Thank you for your trouble, Mr. Cardigan," Julia said, after a moment of considering what he had said.

"No problem, Miss Siedman. I'm sorry we couldn't be of help."

Julia replaced the receiver and sat for a moment, turning this incident over carefully in her mind. After considering each aspect of the matter, she realized she could not think of any explanation for this particular mix-up. She made a note to call her office in the morning and see if she could find out who had made the request.

Then she realized something she should have thought of a moment before. The e-mail address Cardigan had accessed was her old account. She had not used it for over a year.

The person initiating this request had evidently done so from this computer.

Her hands hovered over the keyboard for a moment, and then she decided tomorrow would be soon enough to contact Geoffrey Benner in Washington.

She tore the sheet from her notepad, and as she started to discard it in her wastebasket, she saw a small scrap of paper lying on the carpet underneath the edge of her desk. Smoothing the creases, she turned the note toward the light and saw the words, National Data Center, inscribed in a small neat script. She realized it was Daniella's handwriting.

Chapter 17

Standing on the upper floor balcony overlooking a darkened expanse of beach, Christopher could easily imagine how this place had appeared as the first travelers had wandered along these shores from the far reaches of Africa. This was an enchanting place, and it was stranger still when he remembered how his relationship with it had first begun.

Both of his parents had been tenured professors at the University of Chicago and had spent all of their summers doing fieldwork in the southwestern United States. His earliest memories were of sitting alone in the corner of a tent while they hunched over a table examining some newly discovered artifact. Usually they spent the entire summer in dreary wilderness areas in what was probably Arizona or New Mexico. It really did not matter where they were, for it was all the same.

When he was thirteen, his grandparents deposited a generous sum in a trust fund to pay for his college education. They had also advanced some badly needed funds for a family trip abroad. He had been thrilled when his parents had decided to go to Israel. Anything would be an improvement over the mind-numbing summers he had learned to dread. Three weeks later, they had flown to Israel and passed down the coast to Ashkelon with a tour group.

On his first visit to the excavation site, he had hung around the workers making a general nuisance of himself until his parents had dragged him away. He was surprised to discover archeology students did most of the manual labor at the excavation site. Each year they arrived from schools around the world, usually at their own expense. The intermixture of languages they spoke blended like a lively symphony. *This is where I belong,* he had immediately decided. *This was the reason for which I was born!*

When he was sixteen, he had pestered his parents until they had allowed him to return to Ashkelon for the summer as a volunteer worker. He had arrived back in Israel in late April, seeing the area through older, more adult eyes. He could not wait to get his hands on a shovel and start digging in the hard, red earth.

As the child of two of the world's leading archeologists, he was soon to learn he was unbelievably naive. It was hard, grueling work, but he had loved every minute he spent at the excavation site. He was the first one out of the bed each morning and the others would find him sitting in the darkness gazing expectantly toward the ruins. Somewhere beneath those layers of earth was the house where Herod had been born. There were markets where Samson and Delilah had strolled hand in hand, and wandering through it all were the cobbled streets where the astonished citizenry had witnessed the arrival of Alexander the Great. They were digging through rubble left by Arabs, Romans, Greeks, Phoenicians, Philistines, and Canaanites.

All of the doubts he had experienced in recent days were swept aside as he continued to stand quietly by the railing looking out on his adopted homeland. Julia would probably be sleeping late this morning and his early departure would allow him to escape before she was awake.

He checked the e-mail Leora had given to him the night before. The first message was from Andre Havran informing him he would be arriving in Tel Aviv the following day and would be in Ashkelon as soon as his schedule permitted. There were also a number of e-mails from unknown individuals accusing him of having links with al-Qaeda. Judging from the irate tone of these messages, all of them had been reading Maitland's newspaper articles. He separated these messages from the others and discarded them in the wastebasket without reading any further.

He glanced at his watch again, feeling an overpowering sense of urgency to hurry to his office after an absence of almost two

Abraham's Bones

weeks. He decided he would skip breakfast. This would give him time to consult with De Silva at the excavation site before he started his own workday.

He dressed quickly then clicked the television on, but kept the sound low so he would not disturb anyone. He flipped past several stations but stopped when a picture of Julia filled the screen. He moved closer to the set as they switched to a spokesperson at the Senate Office Building in Washington. As the man started to read from his prepared text, the television suddenly clicked off. He stood for a few seconds wondering what had happened, then realized someone was standing in the doorway behind him. When he turned, Julia dropped the remote on the table and crossed her arms, drawing the neckline of her robe together. Seeing the direction of his gaze, she combed her fingers self-consciously through her hair. After a moment of standing uncertainly in the doorway, she seated herself on his couch, tucking her bare feet underneath the hem of her robe.

"I think you should hear it from me first," she said.

"I did hear just a bit before you clicked off the set. I'm delighted to be working with you again."

She regarded him for a few seconds before speaking, and then looked away, her face filled with indecision and pain. "Senator Cauldfield asked me to represent Washington's interest in the upcoming negotiations. I understand he had a hand in bringing about your own appointment."

"In a manner of speaking. How did he drag you into this?"

"My appointment was a spur of the moment thing. I had gone to see Senator Cauldfield on another matter. He mentioned the peace proposal and asked if I would mind working with you. I guess I didn't stop to think how awkward it would be."

"It doesn't have to be awkward," he said. In Washington, almost a year ago, he had offered his apologies but had failed miserably.

"This is *so* awkward for me, John. In the last year, I have tried to determine what went wrong between us, and I have decided some of the fault was probably mine. The thing I cannot forget is the painful way in which you broke off our engagement. I don't think I will ever be able to forgive you."

He was speechless for a moment before he managed to find his voice. "I was not the one who broke off our engagement."

Her eyes came up to meet his, widening slightly, and then wavered away. Her lips parted and he could see the quick denial trembling on the tip of her tongue.

"You told Jeannie . . ." she began and suddenly stopped.

Jeannie Carson was one of Julia's most loyal friends, but she was also fiercely protective. He felt a sudden rush of anger and betrayal.

"I called you office on numerous occasions, and left dozens of messages on the answering machine at your apartment. It was never my intention to break off our engagement."

Her eyes wavered slightly and then settled on his. "I saw those awful pictures. You betrayed me," she said with a note of finality in her voice.

He did not have a clue as to what she meant or how she had reached this startling conclusion. He had tried repeatedly to contact her. After two weeks of fruitless endeavor, he had backed off to give her some breathing room. This lonely interval had quickly stretched into a year. As he tried to puzzle everything out, Julia suddenly started speaking again without looking in his direction. He tried to focus on what she was saying, but realized he had missed something.

"Grandmother has always entertained this ridiculous notion we would marry one day," she said, giving him a quick, sharp look as if she was daring him to disagree. Before he could answer, she was on her feet again, clutching at the collar of her robe.

"Please let me explain," he began, but she continued to speak as if she was not aware of his interruption.

"Having you here in grandmother's house is awkward. I cannot imagine why you have continued to live here."

In all the years he had worked in Ashkelon, he had always considered this imposing villa to be his home, even from the first moment when Dr. Siedman had invited him for dinner and had insisted he move his things from the hotel. The previous summer she had revised her will, granting both of them joint ownership of the house after her death.

"You are family," she had insisted as if the matter required no further discussion.

"Your grandmother is one of my dearest friends," he pointed out, but even as he said this, he knew she was right and he was in denial, caught up in an impossible situation. Her eyes wavered and then settled on his again, this time a little more firmly.

"While I was away there was no problem, you must realize it is no longer appropriate for you to continue to live here. Your room is directly across the hallway from mine."

He started to speak and then stopped, stung by the implication of what she had just said. "I've been across the hallway from you for half of our lives."

"But it's never been like this!" she cried.

He had intended to finish what he had started a moment before, and then relented, knowing any further discussion would be fruitless. As he moved past her, he placed his hand gently on her shoulder. She turned her head, looking down at it without speaking.

"I'll send for my things," he told her, letting his hand fall away.

"No!" she cried, coming alive all at once to grasp the cuff of his sleeve. Suddenly she was on her feet with her arms wrapped around his neck, her mouth pressed firmly against his. Before he could return her embrace, she had spun away, her face full of indecision and pain.

"If you leave it will only make things worse! I am terribly sorry. I should not have said what I did. I just wanted you to realize things have changed between us. There should be a word besides awkward to describe how I feel about this, but I cannot think of one. I have tried to determine what went wrong between us, but it is so utterly confusing. I do love you, John. I don't think I could bear it if we were no longer friends."

When he gave her a brief nod of acceptance, she turned her face away and spoke, almost as if it were an afterthought. "I have to go into Ramallah today. I probably won't be back until the day after tomorrow. I have a long list of things I have to do in the meantime. My hair is too long, and I *hate* it like this. I am thinking of having it cut short again."

She had gathered her hair in her hands as if she was trying to hide it from him. He hesitated before he answered, not sure what she had intended with this surprising remark. "Not if you are going to be facing an Arab delegation and a roomful of Orthodox Jews."

Her eyes slid away and she made a face. "You're right," she said, "but I can't go around like this. It's shaggy and it needs to be trimmed. It looks awful."

"It didn't look awful just a moment ago on television. I thought it looked lovely."

During the summers when they were teenagers, she had usually worn her hair in a ponytail. Her hair was one of her most attractive features, and as she combed it away from the upturned collar of her robe, he could see the long sweep of her neck and the delicate structure of her throat. Standing there now in a shapeless terrycloth robe, she looked as if she was sixteen again. She looked up and caught him staring. Her eyes wavered away and she turned her back to him, staring through the darkened windows as if it took all of her concentration.

"We need to get together sometime today and work out our separate itineraries," he suggested as the silence stretched on between them. "We won't be meeting with anyone until the end of the month, but there are some social arrangements we have to make rather quickly. I had intended to have a reception here toward the middle of next week to get everyone acquainted."

She didn't say anything for a minute, staring off into the distance, and then she gave him a tentative smile. "A reception sounds like a wonderful idea. What I had scheduled for tomorrow has nothing to do with the meetings. I have spoken with the senator's office and they have received some information which might have some bearing on Congressman Danville's abduction."

"There are already some things in progress," he said, wondered where Cauldfield had obtained his information and the reliability of the source.

She looked as if she was considering a number of options but made no effort to tell him what they were.

"Very well," she said after a moment. "I will give you until after the weekend, but you must realize I will be answering directly to Senator Cauldfield."

He turned away and almost collided with a young woman who had suddenly appeared in the doorway. As he looked around, her mouth widened, transforming her whole face. Daniella had always been a thin child, but in the last year, her face and figure had taken on the fullness of maturity. She was poised and mature in appearance, radiating athleticism like an aerobic instructor at a fitness center. He could not help wondering how far this new maturity extended below the surface.

"Excuse us, Daniella," Julia said. "We were having a private discussion."

"If I didn't know you better, I would think you were having an argument. I could hear you from the far end of the hallway."

Daniella threw her arms around him and gave him a kiss on the cheek. "This is for both of us," she said. "We've missed you terribly and don't let her tell you otherwise."

"Daniella," Julia warned, but Daniella swept past her as if she had not heard, making a circle of the sitting room, and then took a quick peek through the archway, examining the unmade bed with a pillow propped against the headboard. Daniella spun around with the fluid grace of a model while removing the rubber band holding her glossy hair in place. It fell just above her shoulders, framing a face with large brown eyes, high cheekbones, and soft red lips. Julia had crossed her arms again, her face red with embarrassment. She turned suddenly, with a swirl of nightclothes, and almost ran from the room.

"What did I do?" Daniella asked, her expression a study in innocence.

"Nothing," Christopher said, amazed at the indelicate manner in which she had thrust herself into their private affairs.

"I'll talk to her," she said in a fierce whisper. "Sometimes Julia can be such an idiot."

"Just give it a little time," he said, looking at his watch, but she ignored the gesture, moving in close and fastening her hand on his sleeve.

"But you aren't moving out, are you?" she asked, studying him intently like a harried parent with an obstinate child.

For a brief moment, he considered trying to explain the problem to her but decided against it. "No," he said. "I think we worked it out."

Her eyebrows arched. "She's only trying to get you to chase her, you know. Why don't you send her some flowers?"

He tried to suppress a smile. "You've been reading too many romance novels."

Her mouth opened and her face took on a slack, disbelieving expression. "I know how women think."

"How, you're barely fourteen?"

"Barely fourteen!" she said, her expression alternating between exasperation and amusement, but it was amusement that won out in the end. "I bet I could tell you a few things," she said, tilting her head in a flirtatious manner.

"I probably wouldn't want to hear this. Behave yourself and let Julia sort it out in her own way. I'll talk to her later in the day," he said, pulling her close and kissing the part in her hair.

Daniella jerked her head back, giving him a look that was impudent and strangely challenging. "I'm not a kid anymore, okay?"

"I can see that, but my problem with Julia is rather complicated—and private. Don't make it more difficult than it already is," he explained, but she no longer seemed to be listening. Her face had suddenly grown serious, her eyes watchful.

"I want you to tell me about Sanura."

"I'm not sure of what you're asking."

"Neither am I, but she is here and Julia is livid."

"Here? Why?"

"The publisher hired her to edit grandmother's book, and Julia has been having a hissy fit. Julia was going to prohibit her from coming into the house but this is in the contract as well. She thinks you had something to do with the arrangements."

"I offered to be first reader, but I don't know anything about the business arrangements. I thought all of it was in Julia's hands. Who is the publisher?"

"Richard Erlich."

Christopher closed his eyes and ran a weary hand across his forehead. Erlich Publications was one of New York's leading publishers, and they had handled all of Dr. Siedman's previous books. It was surprising to learn they were planning to branch out into the literary world after more than a half century of exclusively publishing nonfiction.

"Where is Sanura now?" he asked, unable to suppress a weary sigh.

"Somewhere in town. She wanted to stay here but Julia threw her bags out and refused to let her move in.

This large sprawling villa had a full time staff, more than capable of handling a large number of guests without any difficulty. Working with Dr. Siedman through the coming months would be a difficult and challenging task. Sanura was an excellent writer and had published three books about the political climate in the Middle East. All of them were from an Arab's viewpoint and had stirred up controversy in Israel and many other places around the world. While there was little doubt she would be equal to the task, he could not help wondering why Erlich had made such a controversial choice. Then he decided Erlich had made the decision with full knowledge of the implications, but simply didn't care.

"I'll talk to Julia later in the day," he said, giving Daniella a reassuring pat on her shoulder.

"You still haven't answered my question," she said.

His eyes came up to meet hers. "What question?"

She frowned as if she suspected him of being deliberately deceitful. "I've never understood this thing with Sanura. What is she to you?"

"I thought I answered your question."

"I want to know about your *personal* relationship with her," Daniella said, moving in close while she straightened the collar on his shirt.

"What makes you think there is a personal relationship?"

She did a slow eye-roll, tracing a path across the darkened ceiling. "I saw you on *Good Morning America* when you were promoting grandmother's book on Gaza. Your whole face lit up when the newswoman asked you about her."

"A perceptive observation, I'm sure, but it is early in the morning and I am in somewhat of a hurry. We can talk about this later," he said but she did not seem to be listening.

"And there was a picture of you and her in *Paris Match* last fall at some kind of social event. It showed the inside of her apartment. You were leaning against the mantle as if you belonged there."

Paris Match was one of the leading magazines in France, covering the social scene as well as the news. This was hardly the type of thing he would have expected Daniella to be reading. "You've been snooping," he said.

She tried to hide her smirk behind a bland, innocent expression. He placed his finger under her chin and tilted her face up at his. Her eyes darted away and the blush deepened.

"I just happened to run across it on the Internet," she argued, and then her voice changed, becoming low and intimate, her mouth forming a soft pout. "Something is going on and I want to know what it is."

"Go play with your dolls, Daniella."

"She's in love with you!" she cried, appalled at his ignorance.

He frowned at her, but her expression did not change.

"Who?" he asked.

"Both of them, you idiot. A woman has a way of sensing things."

"And you probably would if you were a woman, but you are a fourteen year old . . ."

"Sophomore at Harvard!" she finished for him, exasperated because he kept bringing up her age as if there was any possible significance in that. "I'm the youngest student in my class and I've been at the top academically since the entrance exams—and I've had a few flings of my own."

"For the last time, Daniella, behave yourself. Do I have your promise?" he asked, his hand tightening on her shoulder.

"No!" she said, jerking her arm loose as she marched through the doorway, only to spin on her bare feet and confront him again.

"This isn't a sorority house at Harvard," he warned before she had a chance to continue her argument.

"Well, I think it is, and we've handled more than a few like Sanura Hamada, with her cute little face, and her cute little hair, and her *so* cute little uniform."

He gave a weary sigh. "She may have to stay here, Daniella. If she does, you'll have to learn to deal with it."

"Stay here?" she said, her voice rising. "The only kind of *stay* she is going to know about is the kind that goes with *heel!* I have a whole bunch of little doggy tricks I'm going to teach her, starting with a short leash."

"Daniella, wait."

Before he could stop her, she was walking rapidly in the direction in which Julia had taken.

Chapter 18

Christopher could hear the ringing of the telephone as he pushed his way through the doorway into the small room he used for an office at the King David Hotel. He placed his attache case on the floor beside his desk and propped the telephone under his chin, wondering what someone could be wanting at this early hour.

"Christopher," he said, reaching for the stack of mail that had accumulated over the last two weeks.

"Dr. Christopher, this is Axel Tobin in Washington. I am Senator Cauldfield's executive assistant. He has been trying to reach you for quite some time."

There was a short pause at the end of Tobin's statement as if he was waiting for him to explain why he had not been available. "I just arrived at the office. Please put him on."

"He has stepped out for a moment. When you didn't reply to any of his messages, he naturally wondered if there was some kind of difficulty."

"It's five o'clock in the morning, Mr. Tobin."

"I didn't mean to suggest you had done anything improper."

"Can you give me some idea of the nature of Senator Cauldfield's problem?"

"I wouldn't classify any of it as a problem, but he's concerned over some of the unfavorable publicity in the newspapers."

"*Inaccurate* publicity would be a better way to describe the situation," Christopher said.

"Inaccuracy is not as much an issue as you might imagine. A careful explanation has to be crafted to answer each allegation."

Christopher could not help being amused. "So you're saying if I really am Osama bin Laden's brother, there won't be any problem as long as we have a politically correct explanation."

"Oh, dear me, nothing is ever so simple."

"Could you be more specific?"

"I don't think it would be advisable under the circumstances. Are you speaking over a secure phone?"

"This is the regular office telephone. It will probably be tomorrow before the equipment is installed."

"Then you need to contact General Zecori immediately so you can communicate with us through his office."

"I understood General Zecori's appointment had been withdrawn," Christopher said, wondering if anyone in Washington was aware of Zecori's political ambitions.

"Oh, I think I see what you're saying. In a situation like this, you have to understand withdrawn does not necessarily mean he no longer has any connection with the peace process. He will remain there in an unofficial capacity to give you any assistance you may require."

Christopher could not help wondering how long it had been since Tobin had been absorbed in video games to the exclusion of everything else. Washington had always had the ability to generate an endless supply of legal-speak, but these comments seemed to come from some mystical realm where you had Borks, Orks, and incantations with magical powers. Tobin sounded awfully young and inexperienced to be the executive assistant to anyone.

"I don't mean to be rude Mr. Tobin, but I have other commitments. Could you give me a hint, in general terms, of what Senator Cauldfield thinks I can do for him?"

Tobin's voice became brisk and businesslike.

"Senator Cauldfield naturally assumed you would give him your full cooperation. After all, you did work for the government for a number of years. If we are to accomplish anything during these negotiations, it will require careful preparations. Even the slightest suggestion at a conference table can be misconstrued and

Abraham's Bones

have a great deal of significance when it is least expected. I'm Senator Cauldfield's executive assistant so you might want to clear everything with me."

"I was appointed by the Vatican as their envoy, Mr. Tobin. You might want to direct your inquiries through the attache to the Holy See."

"Dr. Christopher, you couldn't possibly be so unenlightened you have forgotten this is an election year."

"Whose election? I was appointed to my current position."

Tobin sniffed his nose delicately. "I think you are putting me on, Dr. Christopher. Senator Cauldfield expects your full cooperation and I would suggest you speak with him as soon as you can do so. While we are on the subject, I would like for you to give me your itinerary so I can reach you whenever it becomes necessary."

"Goodbye Mr. Tobin," he said, and hung up.

In less than a minute, the telephone rang again. He picked it up, but before he could speak, Tobin said, "I'm certainly sorry if I sounded hasty, Dr. Christopher. Do you think it's possible for us to back up and start again?"

"I see no problem, Mr. Tobin. How may I help you?"

"General Zecori has secure communications in his van. He is now in Tel Aviv. That is how many minutes away from where you are?"

"There have been some problems during the night. It will probably take an hour for him to get here."

"I was thinking in terms of you driving to Tel Aviv."

"General Zecori can find me at my office or perhaps at the excavation site. Is there anything else I can do for you?"

After a short pause Tobin said, "I will inform General Zecori."

When Julia entered the breakfast room, Daniella was standing beside the table, smearing a thick layer of some gelatinous substance on the top of a bagel. She came to a halt just inside the doorway, examining the clothes she was wearing—a lace trim cami skimming the bottom of her ribcage, and a pleated prairie skirt hanging dangerously low from one hip. The only thing she was wearing that passed inspection was a pair of double-strap sandals with two-inch heels.

Julia could not suppress a grimace when she saw the bowl of rice sprinkled with coconut, and a tall glass of lemon drink. She snatched the bowl and glass from the table as she passed and dumped the contents into the garbage disposal in the kitchen. When she returned, Daniella was staring back at her, her mouth filled with something looking suspiciously like potato chips.

"That was my breakfast," Daniella complained, digging around in the bottom of a cellophane bag.

"The cook is fixing our breakfast," Julia said as Miriam came through the archway from the kitchen carrying two plates. She placed both of them on the table, and then without a pause, picked up the platter containing the bagel. Julia winced as she sailed regally past, seeing the thick layer of lox on the hard, brown crust.

"No more sickening things at the breakfast table," Julia said as she slid a chair out on the opposite side and seated herself. "And sit down while you eat."

Daniella stopped chewing for a few seconds, then dropped into the other chair and rotated her plate ninety degrees before she started to eat again, chewing with her mouth open. When she became aware of Julia's disapproving look, she straightened in her chair, dropping one hand in her lap.

Julia had not slept well since her arrival and she was feeling grumpy, resentful even, at the way Daniella was dressed. *Surely, she wasn't intending to go to the office dressed in that fashion.*

I need to shut up, Julia cautioned herself, but when she examined the hair pulled up on top of her head like a teenage strumpet in a French movie, she had an almost uncontrollable desire to scream. She closed her mouth, but somehow the words came slithering between her clinched teeth.

"You graduated last year from one of the most prestigious schools in Europe and now you are at Harvard. Why do you eat like a pig? Surely you didn't do that in Switzerland with the headmistress breathing down your neck."

Daniella's startled expression changed into a grin. "She wasn't always around. This was when we had our food fights. My table usually won."

It took Julia a few seconds to realize she wasn't joking. "You were eating in a dinning hall with a royal princess. The one from Denmark or wherever. What was her name? I can't remember."

"Gibralta. She was at our table. She was one of our best team members."

Despite Julia's intentions to remain calm, her voice went up an octave. "And you had food fights?"

Daniella's smile spread. It reminded her of the time when she was a child and she had . . .

Her mind veered quickly away, not wanting to think about this while she was eating.

"Anything else you want to complain about?" Daniella asked. The smile had changed into a self-satisfied smirk.

"The way you are dressed."

"Right."

"And your hair."

"Got that," Daniella said, licking the back of her spoon.

Suddenly, Julia was seething. How could someone so lovable and attractive, be so irritating at inappropriate times? The only person in the world she couldn't drive up the wall was John. He always seemed amused whenever she slipped into her bratty mode. Julia ran her hand into the pocket of her robe. Her fingers closed around the note she had found underneath her desk the night before. She slapped it on the table beside Daniella's plate. Daniella stopped chewing and looked down at the paper.

"What?" she said after a moment.

"I found this under the corner of my desk. I spoke to someone at the National Data Center and he said you made a request for some information about a terrorists organization."

"Right, and you thought . . . what?"

"I wondered if you were playing a dangerous game," she said, watching Daniella's fork as she cut a ridiculously small bite and placed it in her mouth, then chased it with a delicate sip of milk. She chewed for an impossible length of time before she swallowed. Julia could feel her blood pressure rising as the second hand on the clock raced around the dial.

"I was doing some research for mother," Daniella said in a prim little voice. "You can ask her."

Julia felt some of the tension going out of her body like the unwinding of a spring. "I'm sorry," she said after a moment. "I guess I'm letting the pressure get to me. It is always like this before a negotiation session starts, and this time it isn't going to be business as usual. Congressman Danville's disappearance is creating a major crisis, and the reporters are going to be hounding us continually. It simply isn't appropriate for you to go around . . ."

"Looking like this at the office," Daniella finished for her.

Julia started to nod in agreement, and then a thought occurred to her. *If she knows it is inappropriate, then why is she dressed in this fashion?* She hesitated for a slow count of ten, trying to modify the tone of her voice. "You look lovely, and what you are wearing would be appropriate at a party with your friends, but you simply can't go to the office like that. Why don't you dress like the other students. You are going to be making countless trips to the tel to deliver messages, and what you are wearing wouldn't be practical."

"Right," Daniella said in an agreeable tone as she popped up from her chair. "I'll go change."

Julia had started to relax when Daniella reached across the table and grabbed the French Toast from her plate. She crammed the whole slice of bread in her mouth, grinning at her as she whirled away, chewing with her mouth open. Julia sat looking at the empty doorway for a few seconds, and then clamped her hand over her mouth. She could not suppress the laughter as it came bubbling up out of control. Hearing footsteps, she realized Miriam had stopped in the doorway and was looking at her in a questioning way. She sat for another moment with her shoulders shaking, then threw back her head and laughed.

Christopher was searching through his appointment book when he became aware that someone had stopped in the doorway behind him. He turned in his chair and was relieved to see Gilbert De Silva, the head of the excavation project. De Silva was carrying a thick bundle of office files with one hand, while balancing a box with the other. Christopher had left the house early, hoping he would have time to speak with him before he left for the excavation site. When De Silva had called him in Rome, he had caught the next flight home. De Silva had chosen not to make an explanation over an open telephone line, but Christopher knew the matter was serious or he would not have urged him to return before the end of the week.

"I can't tell you how glad I am to see you, my friend," De Silva said.

"If you've been carrying those papers around since I left, I can see why."

"Nothing quite that dramatic," De Silva said, "but you will be flattered to know that nothing has gone right since you left."

"Maybe you should put me back on the payroll."

"As long as I can depend on your advice and support, I can spread the largess around where it will be appreciated." De Silva was now pawing thorough a thick bundle of papers threatening to spill from their folders.

"I'm in a pickle, or I should say, both of us are. When I received this message from the IAA, I immediately called you in Rome." He found the folder he was searching for and threw it open on the desk, extracting three sheets of paper. He examined them briefly and handed one of them to Christopher.

Scanning through the first two paragraphs, he realized it was a request from the Israeli Antiques Authority for information. He ran his eyes down the length of the page with a growing sense of uneasiness until he reached the last paragraph.

We request a through accounting of all artifacts having left the work site, copies of shipping authorization, and the names of the laboratories to which they were sent.

Universities around the world received artifacts from excavation sites on a regular basis to confirm the findings of the project specialists. This was routine procedure and he could not understand why someone at the IAA would suddenly want a written report. There could be little doubt Maitland had already been at work, hoping to produce some catastrophic reaction, and then he had another thought occurred to him, more disturbing than all the rest. Maitland was one of the most skilled investigative reporters in the business. There was no doubt he was investigating each aspect of the upcoming negotiations.

"Have you discussed this with anyone?" Christopher asked, desperately hoping there was a simple explanation. They had always kept meticulous records and had exercised every precaution to stay within the law.

"I spoke with Reuven Goldman as soon as I received this request," De Silva said. "He seemed to think it came from some low-level administrator in Tel Aviv. I have gone about as high as I can go without ruffling some feathers. I thought you might be able to contact someone in the government and find out what is going on before some over-zealous bureaucrat shuts us down."

In all of the years they had worked at Ashkelon, there had never been a request of this nature. Visits from officials within the IAA were a frequent occurrence. On most occasions, these visits were nothing more than a social call from someone with a personal interest in archeology and a desire to examine some of the work in progress.

As Christopher turned this problem over slowly in his mind, he realized there was another possibility. While the IAA was primarily involved in supervising Israel's antiquities, it was also involved in trying to prohibit the illegal trading of artifacts. This was a lucrative enterprise in a nation where unemployment was rampant, despite violators being prosecuted to the fullest extent of the law. Any archeological site might produce many thousands of identical objects with no archeological significance. Many of them passed legally into the hands of licensed artifact dealers. Countless individuals would pay large sums of money for an artifact from some Biblical site. Careful documentation helped to prevent theft, fraud, and other types of illegal activity.

"I'll call Goldman and see if he has anything to report. If he hasn't, I'll contact someone in Jerusalem," Christopher said.

"The rest of this can wait until later," De Silva said, as he waved the papers around and then crammed them back in the folder. "I passed your photographs along to Levenston but haven't heard anything yet. He's been too busy butting heads with Jacob Davidi."

Davidi was the director of a large excavation project in Jerusalem, and one of Levenston's strongest critics. Levenston was the project's epigrapher and a member of the excavation staff. They had almost come to blows at an archeological symposium the previous year. De Silva had found himself caught in the middle of their never-ending rivalry on a number of occasions.

"It's almost 5 o'clock," De Silva said. "I have some things to check at the work site. Most of our summer students will be arriving next week and I don't have to tell you what this means."

"I have one phone call to make and then I'll join you at the tent."

De Silva was an able administrator and was not inclined to worry unnecessarily, nor was he likely to exaggerate some trivial difficulty. He wondered if Levenston had been talking to the press again. It seemed unlikely, considering the difficulty he had encountered the previous year. As Christopher reached for the telephone, he felt a strange stirring of uneasiness and a vague sense of urgency.

The breeze was cool now, but with the rising of the sun the temperature would start to climb, making it almost unbearable inside the small camouflaged tent. He shifted his body into a more comfortable position as he lifted the glasses to his eyes. In the distance, more than a kilometer away, was a row of lights. As he focused the glasses on the dim florescence, he could see the outline of a freighter making its way up the coast toward Tel Aviv. To his right, the lights along the stretch of public beach seemed to be growing dimmer as the sky lost some of its inkiness. Only a handful of stars were visible in the sky, twinkling like bright shards of glass. Swinging the glasses in the opposite direction, he pointed them toward the dark bulk of the house. He could see a dim radiance coming from some of the windows along the upper floor and a bright glow from the kitchen. The car had left almost thirty minutes before, but he knew she would not be leaving for another few minutes. Reaching out with his booted foot, he kicked the sole of Chanda's tennis shoe and heard her grunt in reply. Leaning back against the bole of the tree, he settled down to wait.

Chapter 19

As Christopher approached the fence leading into the excavation site, he could see an armed guard standing at the entrance of a small kiosk. In the last year, there had been heavy damage at several archeological sites and threats of violence against the ones who worked there. Had something occurred that De Silva had not told him about?

Hearing the sound of his footsteps on the walkway, the guard turned casually around with an assault rifle pointed in his direction. There was nothing menacing in the gesture, but it was obvious the young man was ready for any difficulty. As he drew nearer, he realized the small shelter beside the gate was one of the portable units recently acquired by the military. They were made of ceramics and bullet resistant Kevlar and could be set up at any trouble spot with only a moment's notice. A shadow moved inside the enclosure and a second figure materialized in the darkness. As Christopher clambered to the top of the steep incline, the soldier's hand moved where it was hovering over the handle of his pistol.

Christopher called out a greeting and received a quick *shalom* in response. He answered in Hebrew and the younger of the two men smiled while asking for his papers. Stepping inside the enclosure, the soldier shined a light and then squeezed through the opening again and extended the documents.

Abraham's Bones

"Your group is waiting at the upper gate, Dr. Christopher. If you should need us, there will be someone here around the clock."

"Has there been another incident?"

"We arrested a group of terrorists a few days ago. They had been involved in some minor acts of vandalism. This time they were getting ready for something a lot more serious. We found some explosives and a large cache of automatic weapons. Our commanding officer was quite concerned when we found a detailed map of the excavation site."

Christopher looked toward the dark bulk of the tel, barely discernable against the faint glow of the eastern sky. There were dozens of trenches and exploratory shafts scattered over the area. A few well-placed explosives could wreck havoc with the remaining work. The most serious incident had occurred when a group of protesters had tried to block access to the site. There had been some pushing and shoving but fortunately, no serious injuries. He had not expected an occurrence leading to violence. Ashkelon had produced few shrines of interest to Palestinians or Israelis. At some of the other sites in Israel, death threats against the workers had caused some of them to quit. They had evidently found a reason to target this one.

"I don't suppose you've learned the identity of the group they represent?"

"We were rather lucky in that regard. The police received a tip of something illegal going on at a local Internet site," the younger of the two soldiers explained. "When they examined some of their files, they thought they had found a computer virus. A software-consulting firm examined the programming code and discovered some hidden messages addressed to a terrorists group. They turned the problem over to military intelligence."

"In this case it looks like they were caught by their own cleverness," Christopher said.

The soldier was quick to disagree. "There are some in military intelligence who think catching them was too easy. They believe this whole operation was some kind of clever ruse, but no one is willing to hazard a guess. It makes you wonder if we were intended to catch them."

"Maybe their leaders wanted them eliminated."

"In that case, they would have used a bomb. It would have silenced them effectively and provided an excellent propaganda opportunity. They could have claimed Mossad was responsible."

During World War II, the American military had used Native American soldiers to transmit secret information in obscure tribal dialects, but even with 6,800 languages in the world today, obscurity no longer offered the security it once had. The large computer systems operated by the NSA monitored telephone calls and Internet messages around the world. Computers recorded any suspicious messages they encountered and could instantly translate them into English.

Christopher looked up to find the young soldier watching him intently. He could not have been much more than seventeen, but he had a wiseacre grin plastered across his face. It was the same expression you might see on the face of a kid in a video parlor who knew he was good and was prepared to demonstrate his prowess. Christopher lifted his eyebrows in question and the grin widened.

"What they're doing is the twenty-first century version of a procedure called steganography, which is the technique of hiding something in plain sight. Herodotus coined the phrase in his account of a secret message sent to the Greeks. Passing through the enemy lines required a thorough search, so they shaved the soldier's head and tattooed the message on his scalp. They waited until his hair had grown back before they sent him on his journey. No one thought about looking under his hair. When he reached his destination, the Greeks shaved his head to reveal the message. On the Internet they use a similar technique to hide secret messages in unused bits of programming code, and not in the body of the message where you would expect it to be."

"But it can be ferreted out with modern techniques," Christopher suggested.

"It can be found but not traced to its source."

Christopher blinked as he realized what the soldier was suggesting. Everyone on the Internet received dozens of unsolicited e-mails every week, with some of them containing viruses. Once the virus was inside your system, it could send a copy to each person in your address book. One message could multiply itself into millions of copies in a single day. There was no way any government agency would be able to trace the message back to its source, regardless of the size or complexity of their system. It seemed as if the evil ones were always one step ahead of the good guys. Across the darkened Mediterranean, he could hear the incessant rumbling of thunder. It sounded like a bad omen.

"Have they found a connection between this group and any other terrorists organizations?" Christopher asked.

The soldier hesitated for a second as if he was reluctant to make the admission. "This time they weren't Palestinians. They were ultra-Orthodox Jews. At first, they suspected some of the messages might have been from al-Qaeda because of some references to the Sheikh. Military intelligence is still working on the problem."

Christopher felt a stirring of uneasiness. "Is this the group monitoring our radio transmissions?"

"It's not the same bunch, sir."

This had been a problem in recent years. Groups of ultra conservative Jews had objected to disturbing graves found at excavation sites. He wondered if the group arrested by military intelligence had a connection with Shiva, or if this was a coincidence.

He thanked the soldiers and tucked his papers away. Archeology had never been an easy task, but in recent years, it had become increasingly expensive, with most of the funds coming from private sources. Something with the far-reaching implications of human history deserved the coordinated efforts of the respective governments. The laws of most of the Middle Eastern nations served more as an impediment to their work than to any other useful purpose, and now there was terrorism to deal with as well. He thanked the soldiers and turned up the path toward the upper gate.

There was a bright flash of light as the front door flew open and he could see her outlined dimly against the dark row of hedge. Jafar gave a low whistle and heard an answering call from Chanda on the path below. He swung the glasses a few inches to the left and saw the wrought iron gate rolling back inside the stone wall as she drew near, and the slender outline of Jamaal standing in the center of the drive. As she approached, Jamaal lifted his arm. She did not pause as she slapped her palm against his hand, and then she was running hard. Her stride lengthened as she went into the curve at the end of the drive, the whiteness of her legs flashing as she passed the illuminated sign marking the entrance. Swinging the glasses in the opposite direction, he saw Chanda moving with the speed of an Olympic runner as she continued along the path toward the roadway. He placed the glasses back into their fitted case and crawled on his hands and knees toward the opening of the tent. Today was his chance to sleep. Tomorrow perhaps . . .

He yawned heavily as he stretched out on the pallet and was instantly asleep.

Abraham's Bones

Chapter 20

Julia had not unpacked her suitcases when she arrived, and as she examined the contents of them now, she saw a hopeless tangle of clothes like something you might find on a bargain table at a suburban yard sale. The previous weekend she had spent an entire Saturday shopping and had donated most of her old things to charity. She examined the linen duster that had caught her eye the moment she had entered the boutique. It had a shirt collar and a front placket of pretty buttons, shaped in the front and back with darts. Without any insistence from the salesclerk, she had purchased all of the accessories in the display including a Peking jade necklace and a pair of brown mules. Hooking the ribbon-trim straps of a Voile sundress over her finger, she shook her head in dismay. She suddenly realized someone had stopped just inside the doorway.

"You have two visitors, Miss Julia! One of them said his name is Havran and the other . . ."

Before Jamaal could finish what he had started to say, Julia went rushing past him and ran quickly downstairs where she could hear the murmur of voices coming from the direction of the foyer.

"Oh, Andre!" she cried, seeing the quick flash of his smile as he turned away from Miriam, who was in the process of fastening the front door.

"Every time I see you, I think you have grown lovelier," he said as she rushed into his arms.

Seeing the pleased smile, she placed her fingers gently against the side of his cheek. "And you, my friend, are the most handsome man on earth."

Havran threw back his head and laughed. "You have discovered if you flatter me I will do anything you ask."

Julia's expression suddenly became serious. "I can never repay you for the trip you made to Switzerland. Daniella was there on a two-week exchange program and I was afraid it would reflect unfavorably if the headmistress sent a report back to the dean. I was at my wits end when I called you."

"It was no trouble at all. Daniella never knew I was there and the problem was not as serious as the headmistress made it out to be."

Julia breathed a sigh of relief. She had worried about this for endless days, but apparently, there had been little reason for concern. She placed her head against his chest and hugged him again, drawing strength from the strong muscles she could feel underneath the palms of her hands. When she lifted her head and looked up at him again, his face had grown serious.

"Will you be here through the weekend?" she asked hopefully, and felt her heart sink when he gave her a reproving look.

"I am sorry, my dear, but that unfinished business in Egypt is going to require several more days to complete. When I return, I will spoil you shamelessly."

"You are far too good to me," she said and felt her smile spread until her features felt tight, her eyes swimming with tears. Before she was able to say anything else, he cupped her face between his hands and kissed her forehead softly.

"Nonsense, my dear, it is no more than you deserve."

Since breaking off her relationship with John the previous year, she had begun to depend upon Andre, confiding in him in the same manner she had once confided in John. She had never thought of herself as clingy, but she had grown to depend on his help, missing him terribly when he was not around. He had flown into Washington frequently to visit the American branch of his investment firm, and they had spent their evenings together, going to fashionable restaurants and to social events. He had never asked anything of her, and this had given her an undefined feeling of guilt. She had known from the beginning their relationship could never ripen into romance, for he was old enough to be her father.

The father I never had.

During the last few months there were many times when contact with him had been impossible while he was traveling into areas of the world where the possession of a cell phone could attract some unwelcome attention. This had caused her to worry for days on end when she was unable to reach him. As he stood smiling into her face, she knew he was safe again, and she was reluctant to remove her hands from his shoulders.

Suddenly remembered there was someone with him, she lowered her arms and turned toward the man standing just inside the front door. For a brief instant, she could not comprehend what she was seeing, and then her joy at seeing Andre faded. Before she could speak, Andre's hands tightened on her shoulders, forcing her to look up at him again.

"I'm terribly sorry, my dear. I should have called ahead, but there's some urgency involved and I thought it would be best if I explained in person."

"If you're thinking of making an introduction, it's hardly necessary," she said, meeting Gary Maser's unblinking gaze and having the satisfaction of seeing him color slightly.

"I'm sorry to have intruded," Maser began, but before he could finish, Havran placed his arm around her shoulders again and turned her around to face him.

"This whole thing is my fault," Havran explained, "but when you hear what he has to say, I don't think you will judge him too harshly."

"I have heard what he has to say on two occasions."

"Miss Siedman, please. I know this is an imposition, but it is terribly important I speak with you. I have received a videotape from the kidnappers and I would like you to see it before you make any decision. It will only take a few minutes. If you still choose not to help me, I will be on my way without any further argument."

Julia's first reaction was to refuse, but instead of opening the door and shoving him outside, as she would have liked to do, she took the tape from his outstretched hand and turned toward the den. She wished Christopher had been here, but as she thought about this, she decided he would probably have sided with the other two men.

She swung the doors open on the entertainment center and inserted the tape into the VCR. The screen showed blue for a moment and then a voice started to speak, low and indistinct, and then much louder, echoing hollowly in the close confines of the room. She walked quickly to the table, found the remote, and turned the volume down.

Since the beginning of the war in Iraq, she had viewed countless tapes of kidnapped victims on the evening news, their faces filled with pain and suffering, but this scene was different, almost as if this tape had been left over from the Abu Ghraib prisoner abuse scandal. There was a growing sense of revulsion as she stared at the flickering images. A man with his face concealed behind a ski mask was battering Congressman Danville with what appeared to be a police officer's nightstick, stopping occasionally to inflict some unspeakable act of torment on his defenseless body. The cries coming from Danville's throat did not sound human. They were high and thin like the gibbering of a wounded animal. She endured it for another few seconds, then closed her eyes and whirled away, placing her hands tightly over her ears.

"I should have warned you," Havran said softly, gathering her into his arms. "I wasn't thinking. Actually, it's the last part of the tape I wanted you to see."

Julia would have dashed from the room, but she heard someone speaking her name and realized the voice was coming from the television. She swung abruptly around and saw Danville, lying in a fetal position on the floor, and crying softly. The camera shifted, focused now on the hooded man's face. She tried to look away, but his eyes held hers almost hypnotically.

"There is some purpose in this madness, Miss Siedman. From what you have seen, I am sure you understand the seriousness of our demands. We want one million dollars for the continued safety of Congressman Danville. We will inform you through our intermediary of what you need to do in the immediate future. Please do not disappoint me. There is a lot more at stake than you might imagine."

The screen immediately turned red as if someone had dashed a container of blood into the lens of the camera. Julia drew in her breath sharply and tried to stifle the cry building in the back of her throat.

There was a group waiting in front of the upper gate, and although Christopher could not make out their identity from a distance, he could recognize De Silva's rich baritone above the loud clamor of voices. Someone with a Brooklyn accent was trying by sheer volume to override whatever he was saying. De Silva did not seem to be aware of this and his quiet rumble continued to cut through whatever point the man was trying to make. Another voice had stridently joined in and Christopher realized this one was familiar. As he skirted a pile of rubble at the bottom of the wall and came up to where the group was waiting, he could see De Silva's thick mane of hair blowing in the breeze. Although it was not yet daylight, he could see the man confronting De Silva was dressed inappropriately in a business suit, while the woman was wearing army fatigues with her hair caught up underneath a beret. Having planned to contact Sanura later in the morning, he was surprised to find her here at this early hour. The man beside her was Keith Maitland. Both of them were standing in almost identical postures reminding him of a pair of enraged jackals confronting an angry lion. Something moved in the shadows behind De Silva and Christopher realized it was five heavily armed soldiers. On the crest of the hill, the members of the excavation staff stood against the golden light of the sky like miniature warriors on a chessboard.

"Maybe you can talk some sense into this idiot!" Sanura called to him as he approached. She seemed determined to draw him into the argument on her side, even thought they had parted company on less than friendly terms. The loud voices from the rest of the group had quieted to a murmur.

"I seem to have missed something," Christopher said, keeping his tone as light as possible.

"You've missed nothing," De Silva announced in the same imperious tone he used in his classroom at the university. Sanura turned toward Christopher, fanning her notepad in agitation.

"I've left some important business this morning to come here, but it was obviously a waste of time."

"Why don't we get together in an hour or so at my office?" Christopher said.

"Our group of summer workers are due to arrive on Monday," De Silva rumbled. "I'll take a few questions but I can't waste a lot of time on this news conference, or whatever it is."

"Must we stand out here on this hideous pile of dirt?" Sanura complained. "Why can't we go inside where we can be seated?"

De Silva had started to refuse when Christopher nodded toward the upper gate. "Okay," De Silva agreed with ill grace. "Let's go up to the tent."

De Silva turned abruptly away and went rapidly up the walk to the top of the tel, while the whole group trooped along behind him in silence.

The tent was located near the center of the massive tel where it would be convenient for each of the separate teams working at the excavation site. Placed near the gnarled trunk of a sycamore tree, it received the benefit of the sparse shade and could catch the intermittent breeze rising up the hillside. De Silva shoved the tent flaps aside and took his place at the head of the table, while the others scrambled for the remaining seats. The group quieted and everyone received his full attention, except for Sanura, who kept darting glances in Christopher's direction. Before anyone else could speak, her hand shot into the air. When De Silva gave her a reluctant nod, she was quick to pounce.

"Getting back to the question you refused to answer earlier."

"I believe I gave you an honest answer and I refuse to discuss this any further. Does anyone else have a question they would like to ask?"

A large man seated on the opposite side of the table lifted his hand. The Egyptian accent seemed familiar, and as Christopher examined the narrow green tie, the memory came flooding back. He had been a member of the Wahhabi sect, one of the most radical branches of Islam, but had broken with the group after the bombing of the World Trade Center. If he remembered correctly, he was now working with a network based in London.

"I spent most of the night speaking with an investigator from Rome," the reporter announced in a slow, ponderous tone. "I've had no sleep since night before last."

Abraham's Bones

"Don't blame me," De Silva growled from the end of the table. The other reporters laughed at his quick wit and Christopher began to relax.

"I'm more worried about what he told me than I am about the loss of sleep."

"Concerning?"

"Your financial arrangements with Marshall Wurman Associates."

De Silva gave him a puzzled frown. "The only financial arrangement I'm aware of is with AccuTel Financial. Who is Marshall Wurman, and what is your concern?"

"He is Jewish."

De Silva did not comment nor did he ask for any further clarification. Christopher had seen this same performance in De Silva's classroom, when some student asked a particularly foolish question and received the same withering silence. After a moment of staring back at him, De Silva pointed at another reporter seated at the foot of the table. "I believe you had your hand raised."

"But you didn't answer my question, Dr. De Silva," the first reporter interrupted rather testily.

"I didn't hear a question, sir, and I'm afraid I don't know your name."

"Rasheed, Dr. De Silva. My information suggests you are to be the recipient of a large financial grant from Marshall Wurman Associates."

"Then you know more than I do, Mr. Rasheed. AccuTel controls all of the financial arrangements for this project. You might want to direct your inquiries to their accounting office for clarification. Next question," he said briskly and was in the act of pointing to a man at the foot of the table when Rasheed came lumbering to his feet.

"Perhaps I should explain."

"Is this a question or did you have a statement to make about Mr. Wurman?"

"I guess it's a little of both. Mr. Wurman is determined to prove the identity of the pharaoh of the Exodus."

"Mr. Rasheed," De Silva began, rubbing the tips of his fingers across his forehead as if he was examining a mortal wound. "Investigations of this nature should be confined to the pages of the tabloids rather than to serious academic discussion."

"There are religious and political implications. This could be of tremendous importance."

"Believe me, Mr. Rasheed. What you are suggesting falls under the classification of *who cares*. If you do not understand what I am saying, you might want to look it up. I really don't have time to go all the way through Archeology 101."

"I'm not arguing the academic merit of such a project, Dr. De Silva. I am simply repeating some information I learned from an associate in Rome. I believe what he told me is accurate."

"As long as we can meet operating expenses, I don't care if the funds come from al-Qaeda. It isn't likely to change the focus of our work."

"This is where we disagree. My friend in Rome seems to think there is a political agenda attached to Mr. Wurman's request. He is also financing Angus McLeish, I understand."

De Silva gave a weary sigh. "I don't know any of these people you have mentioned, nor do I understand why you think any political importance could be attached to what we do here? This is an archeological project."

"But you do know Angus McLeish."

"I met him once at an archeological symposium," De Silva growled. "I can't say that I know him."

"It is my understanding that he is involved with a group of radical Zionist who are intending to take possession of the Arab section of Jerusalem."

"He produces television documentaries on sensational subjects. While I don't approve of his credentials, he seems harmless enough."

"Harmless is hardly the word I would use, Dr. De Silva. His last documentary touched off riots in Jerusalem that lasted a week. The peace we have enjoyed for the past year is fragile at best. Dangerous radicals like McLeish need to be silenced at all cost."

"I'm sure Dr. Christopher already has a plan in motion that will be more than adequate to meet all of the needs, whatever they might be."

"Do I need to remind you that Dr. Christopher has contacts with every evildoer and fanatic in the Middle East. No more than two days ago, my informant saw him dining in a restaurant with Andre Havran."

"Who is Andre Havran?" De Silva asked, looking puzzled.

"He supplies the funds for some Jewish terrorist's organizations, but there are some who suspect he is really an employee of the American CIA."

De Silva's hard stare did not waver. "I think you have spent too much time in the sun and not enough time doing your research. Do you have any proof to back up these allegations?"

"Proof," Rasheed cried out, looking at De Silva in astonishment. "Dr. Christopher has received an ambassadorship from the Vatican? What other proof do you need?"

"Dr. Christopher was selected for this peace mission because he is a man of integrity. Every Arab State in the region has requested his help. You have twisted some commonly known facts and reached a bizarre conclusion," De Silva said.

"The reason for my conclusions should be obvious. Mr. Wurman's real agenda is to prove the Israelis have superior territorial rights to the land areas claimed by the Palestinians. This whole issue in the Middle East is about territory?"

"You have been reading too many conspiracy theories in the tabloids, Mr. Rasheed."

Acting as if De Silva had issued a challenge, Rasheed produced a newspaper from the battered equipment case he had dropped on the floor beside his chair.

"Have you seen this?" he asked, as he held it underneath the flickering lantern suspended from the center pole of the tent. The headlines covered the upper third of the front page.

Jewish underworld figure supplies funds for archeological dig.

Underneath this was the teaser in ominous bold print.

How are Washington playboy John Christopher and missing congressman linked to Marshall Wurman Associates? Our readers would like to know!

"I hope you aren't taking this drivel seriously? You'll be telling me the business arrangements were conducted onboard a UFO."

The corners of Rasheed's mouth had turned downward in an ugly sneer. "I was skeptical until I checked my facts. I strongly suggest you do the same."

De Silva made no attempt to hide his amusement. "We don't do conspiracy theories here, Mr. Rasheed. We only deal with scientific fact."

Maitland slapped the top of the table with both hands, producing a thunderclap of sound startling everyone in the tent. Several of the reporters jumped and aimed anxious looks in his direction. On the far side of the tent, the soldiers had moved forward in perfect unison. Something in their flat expressions suggested they were zeroing in on individual targets if the need should arise. The reporters seemed to be having difficulty in tearing their eyes away from their weapons.

Maitland wagged his finger at De Silva. "I resent the implications of what you have just said. I wrote the article my colleague has just shown to you, and I have no apology for its content. I assure you everything I said can be proven."

"I'm sure it can, Mr. Maitland, but the question concerning me is the rapid shifting of your accusations. A few days ago, you implied Dr. Christopher was strongly in support of radical Muslims, and now you insist he is taking the side of Israel. You even went so far as to insinuate he has some nefarious connection with al-Qaeda. Which is it, Mr. Maitland, or have you decided?"

"I have done no such thing, and I can show you documentation to back up every charge I have made. I will thank you, sir, not to throw suspicion on my character. I have given an honest evaluation of these events and I think all of my readers will agree."

"Everyone who has read one of your columns has acquired a lasting impression of your honesty." De Silva said.

"When this is over we will see who is remembered for their honesty!" Maitland replied hotly.

Sanura had been sitting uncharacteristically still during the entire exchange, but now spoke up, although she had dropped the biting tone she had used to address De Silva a few minutes before. She seemed to be trying to distance herself from Maitland's theatrics.

"Just for the record, you categorically deny you met with Congressman Danville, and you know nothing about a coffin case disappearing from this site?"

"We have never found a coffin case at any time at this site. A number of them have been found in Gaza in recent years, but none here."

Abraham's Bones

"And you refuse to describe the objects found inside the case."

"Same answer." De Silva said, pointing to one of the reporters standing near the rear of the tent. "Did I see someone back there with their hand raised?"

Sanura ejected herself from her chair, causing it to topple with a loud clatter. "You have refused to answer my direct questions!"

"I answered your questions," De Silva insisted, "and I resent the implications of what you have implied."

Sanura pointed at the tabloid Maitland had spread open on the table. "I'm not talking about that fabricated nonsense! Any legitimate reporter resents this kind of sensationalism as much as you do. I demand an explanation and I think everyone seated around this table would like to hear it."

Maitland's face had blanched at Sanura's pointed criticism. He had started to rise when Rasheed placed a restraining hand on his shoulder.

"I did not evade your question," De Silva rumbled. "I simply refused to give you the answer you wanted. You are trying to put words into my mouth to confirm a rumor."

"This is ridiculous!" she cried, and seemed on the verge of beating her fist against the table as she had criticized Maitland for doing only a moment before.

This time Maitland did not attempt to climb to his feet, but leaned away from the table and spoke without looking in her direction. "You need to go back to playing tennis, young lady, and leave the news to trained professionals."

"I *am* a professional," she shot back.

"You're a dilettante working for a dysfunctional network. No one takes them seriously, even in the Middle East."

"How dare you pass judgment on my professionalism or upon my employers! More than eighty million people watch Al Jazeera every day, which is more than there are watching FOX, CNN, or the despicable little network where you are employed."

Maitland waved her words away. "What you do isn't reporting. Anyone can read the news off a Teleprompter in an air-conditioned studio. I liked you better in your tennis outfit than I do in your ridiculous uniform. What army do you claim to represent?"

Christopher moved around the end of the table. When he stopped directly behind her, she looked sharply around and swayed her body away. He stopped her by placing his hands on her shoulders and turned her around where she was facing him. This time she did not move away, but lifted her eyes in injured silence and gazed back into his.

"If you would give us a little time, I'm sure Dr. De Silva would be glad to answer your questions. I am also curious about the source of your information. It might not be as reliable as you think."

"My sources are confidential," Sanura snapped. "You know I can't comment."

"What you are saying may be true," De Silva said, "but these press conferences are voluntary, and you seem to be working under the assumption you have the upper hand. If something disappeared from this work site, it would be a matter between my staff and the Israeli Antiquities Authority. As far as I am aware, the government of Qatar does not have any interest here."

Christopher could see her eyes glittering in the light from the camp lantern. "I have been hired by Richard Erlich to work with Dr. Siedman on a new book she is writing. I have an interest here whether you like it or not. And just for the record, I am a representative of Al Jazeera news service and not a government employee as you seem to imply."

De Silva made a sweeping motion toward the open flap of the tent. "Al Jazeera is a government controlled news agency."

In response to De Silva's mulishness, Sanura seemed to have grown an inch or two in stature. "I find your inference insulting! You ought to stop what you're doing and listen to yourself."

Christopher had intended to allow De Silva to handle this, but Sanura had no intentions of remaining silent. He tightened his grip on her shoulder until she broke eye contact with De Silva.

"I will personally see this problem is thoroughly investigated, and I will answer any questions you have before the end of the day. For now, I think we ought to allow Dr. De Silva to continue."

Sanura's wounded expression turned in his direction and her eyes settled on his. "I seem to have no choice in the matter. I accept your offer."

Maitland was immediately on his feet, his hands clenched into fists. Christopher remained motionless as Maitland swung around where he was facing him across the corner of the table. Direct con-

Abraham's Bones

frontation with Maitland was the last thing he wanted. At the far end of the tent, a reporter removed the lens cap from his camera and pointed it in their direction. As the reporter adjusted the lens, the camera slipped from his grasp and landed on the table with a loud clatter. Maitland's face jerked but his attention did not waver.

"I think the information should be shared with all of the news services," Maitland complained. "I don't want to hear something on Al Jazeera you didn't offer to the rest of us."

"This conference is over," De Silva said. He had started to turn away when the man seated at the lower end of the table lifted his hand.

"Dr. De Silva, please! We have come a long way to investigate Congressman Danville's disappearance. I wonder if there is anything you can tell us."

"The only thing I can tell you is I have a pressing appointment and don't have any more time to waste."

Sanura was quick to pounce despite the warning pressure of Christopher's hands on her shoulders.

"While I don't agree with Mr. Rasheed's assessment of the situation, I do have information Danville met with you the morning he disappeared. Do you think he has been kidnapped or did terrorists kill him as was earlier reported?"

De Silva had already turned toward the tent flap. He stopped but did give her the courtesy of turning all of the way around. "I'm sure you have far more knowledge of terrorists than I do," he flung over his shoulder as he disappeared into the darkness.

When Christopher attempted to follow, Sanura whirled around, blocking his path. "John, please," she said rather frantically. "This is as important to you as it is to me. Try to get him to listen to reason. Please, if not for me, then for your own sake."

Almost immediately, one of the soldiers took hold of her arm and pulled her rather forcefully in his direction. She stumbled, almost losing her balance, and then turned her head toward the soldier.

"Take your hands *off* me!" she cried, and then as she attempted to jerk her arm from the soldier's grasp, her beret came off and her dark hair fell around her shoulders.

"I want to speak with her for a moment," Christopher said to the sturdy looking soldier who seemed determined to hustle her off like a barroom drunk. The young man hesitated, and then gave her a little shove in Christopher's direction as if he was relieved to be able to shift the responsibility to someone else. Sanura stumbled, and then rounded on the soldier as if she intended to push the confrontation to the limit. Christopher turned her around like someone handling a child and pointed her toward the flap at the side of the tent. The other reporters were moving unceremoniously in the direction of the gate. Sanura tried to evade his hands in an effort to fight her way back to the soldier, but he lifted her from the ground and swung her around again. She was a small bundle of fury, wrestling frantically as he forced her through the exit.

"Turn me loose, John," she pleaded, leaning away from him. The soldier had stopped indecisively in the opening at the far end of the tent as if he could not decide if he had made a mistake in turning the problem over to someone else.

Not wanting to give the soldier a chance to reconsider, Christopher placed his hands on her shoulders and forced her along the path leading to the deep trench where the ancient sea gates had been uncovered. She attempted to resist, and then allowed him to herd her along like a balky sheep.

Chapter 21

"I'm sorry, Mr. Maser," but all of our rooms are taken at the moment. They have been reserved for a number of weeks now. If you like, I might be able to find you some accommodations at one of the nearby hotels."

Julia had refused to help him, and he could not help feeling an increasing embitterment, like a cold rage settling around his heart. Two crucial years of his life had been invested in the law firm, and now he was going to loose his job. Cassie had wanted a June wedding and had sent out the invitations weeks ago. She had even made reservations at the country club . . . and then he remembered her parents. They had overlooked his lack of social standing because he was working for a prestigious firm. There were the possibilities of quick advancement, and beyond that were the stock options and the possibility of a partnership.

He glanced at his watch, trying to determine the time in Washington, then happened to notice the row of clocks suspended on the wall behind the desk, showing the time in some of the major capitols around the world. The one on his left read Washington. He decided he would call his office as soon as he had moved his luggage to the hotel, and then realized it was the early hours of the morning in Washington, rather than the middle of the afternoon. It would be hours before he would be able to contact anyone. Would it be wise to delay the inevitable in the hope he could work something out? Julia had made it plain that she would not help him, although he had insisted her mission could not move forward unless Congressman Danville's release was successful. A lovely girl, surely, but he could think of only one term that fit her lack of regard for one of her fellow citizens. She was uncaring, and then as he thought about this for a moment, he decided it was more than a lack of caring. She was cold-hearted.

He realized the desk clerk was looking at him rather oddly, so he nodded in agreement. He had no car, but if the hotel was nearby he would be able to secure a taxi, or perhaps walk back and forth once he had moved his luggage.

The clerk immediately picked up the phone as he turned away, leaning his elbow against the edge of the desk. He saw movement from the corner of his eye and turned to face a girl approaching the desk. At first he thought it was Julia, but when he focused on her face he realized she was much younger, but the strong resemblance made him certain this was her younger sister. She was wearing a lace-up capri that stopped at the center of her knee, and a tunic-length tank top. It was the type of outfit Cassie would have selected for herself. Keith Maitland had assured him that she was a member of Shiva, a terrorist organization, but as he studied her face, he decided it was improbable. This was the type of face usually described as wholesome, the kind of teenager you usually saw in a cosmetic ad. He had started to turn away when he realized she had aimed her smile at the desk clerk.

No one has ever smiled at me like that, he thought, with a sudden, stabbing pang of jealously.

"This room is in the Holiday Inn, and they are expecting you," the desk clerk said, writing the number down on a small card and sliding it in his direction. "I can have your bags sent across."

"If Kevin has your bags sent across, you will probably never see them again," the girl said as he slipped the card into the pocket of his shirt.

"She is joking," the young man said quickly, but the smile he aimed in her direction did not diminish.

"I'm not joking," she said in a lovely voice filled with mock indignation. "He is irresponsible, careless, and is probably the reason you don't have reservations here."

Abraham's Bones

Maser could not help being amused at the good natured banter going back and forth between these two. It was obvious they liked each other and he wondered what their relationship might be.

"I don't have any choice, so I will take a chance on him," Maser said. "He has an honest face."

"Honest is hardly the word I would use to describe him. I wanted to go out with him for the last year, but my sister has forbidden it after finding out what he is really like. She has even threatened to have him deported."

"You're Julia's sister," Maser said, and saw the quick movement of her head. She gave him a quick appraisal and then was looking into his eyes.

"Do you know her?"

"I . . . do as a matter of fact. We met in Washington."

"I'm Daniella. If you are going to the hotel, I'll walk across with you. I wouldn't be going in that direction, but Kevin the Inept has misdirected some of our supplies and I have no choice."

Somehow, the despair he had experienced only a few minutes before had vanished in the presence of this self-assured young woman, and then he wondered how old she actually was. She could have been anywhere from seventeen to twenty-three, but something instinctively told him she was younger.

"She's fourteen," Kevin said as if he had read his thoughts. Her smile dimmed slightly as she stared back at the young man in a challenging way. For some unexplainable reason, he felt better than he had felt in days.

"Jobs are scarce in this part of the world, Mr. Maitland, and this has ruined my business."

Maitland resisted the urge to wave the foul smelling smoke away from the table, wishing desperately for a light breeze that would carry the noxious fumes away. He remembered the smell of marijuana from his college days, but this was more foul, rank almost, as if he was burning garbage. It had been his choice to sit here, underneath this outdoor awning rather than going inside this small cafe. *Wasn't smoke supposed to rise rather than wrapping itself around your head in a toxic halo?*

Joe Prentis

The man's name was Muhammad, but he didn't appear to be to be an Arab or a Palestinian. He could have, in fact, been a European Jew, a German, a Pole, Irish, French, or anything beside a Muhammad. He had sauntered past the tables twice before Muhammad had called him over, complaining that he didn't look like an American. He had spent the previous day trying to locate him and he wanted to hear his story. He was surprised when he returned to his hotel and found the message waiting for him. He wondered if it could be a trap of some kind, but he was willing to take a chance.

"So you were doing what?" Maitland asked, eyeing the pastry the man was eating. Smoking and eating at the same time. It the smoke didn't kill him, the cholesterol filled pastry probably would.

"I was doing what I was hired to do!" the man said around a thick mouthful of food. "I am a carpenter, one of the best in the business. Dr. Siedman's housekeeper hired me to renovate her office, which I did in a professional manner. There was no complaint regarding my work. It was the camera."

Maitland already knew this part of the story, but there was no point in letting him know he had paid over a hundred dollars to obtain his information from one of his competitors. He nodded his head and made a sympathetic noise while the little carpenter continued to chew. He was not in the least interested in his tale of woe, or the fact they had caught him prowling through the contents of Dr. Siedman's desk. He did not need to know all of these tiresome details. What he wanted to know was what the manuscript *said*. He leaned forward, supporting himself on his elbows while he continued to commiserate with him, assuring him that what he had done was nothing more than normal curiosity. *What did the manuscript say!* he wanted to shout at him as he heard his voice droning on.

"I worked at the excavation site for a couple of years, but I was discharged when they started using more students. They work them for free, you know. Why pay someone when you can get some kid to do it for nothing?"

"I wasn't aware of that," Maitland said. He had researched this, too—knew about the eight hours of college credit, the letter that would be forwarded to their respective universities—but he tried to keep his expression sympatic, trying to judge the exact moment when he should make his offer. *How much should he pay?* He was so absorbed in his own thoughts that he did not immediately comprehend what Muhammad had said.

I have a copy of the disk!

When he looked up, trying to keep his astonishment from showing at this unbelievable stroke of luck, Muhammad said, "I wonder if you would be interested in buying it from me?"

Maitland could feel his palms tingling and could barely restrain himself from grabbing for his wallet and emptying the contents on the surface of the table.

"Yes," Maitland said cautiously, and was astonished at how calm his voice sounded. "I think I would be interested if the price isn't too high."

"American money?"

"If you prefer."

The man looked thoughtful and then leaned his head at an angel. "Do you think 100 dollars, would be too much?"

One hundred dollars would definitely not be too much, nor would a thousand, or ten thousand. "I am a little short on cash at the moment, but yes, I think I could manage 100 dollars. I am interested in archeology and I am quite a fan of hers." When he felt something touch his knee, he reached under the table and felt the corners of a CD case as it was slipped into his hand.

Chapter 22

When Christopher attempted to place his arm around Sanura's shoulders, she shoved it aside and increased her pace, not even bothering to look in his direction. Reckless confrontations were almost a way of life for her, resulting in her abduction by rebel forces on three separate occasions. It had happened once in Iran and twice in Afghanistan while she was covering news events for Al Jazeera. A picture showing her with her head thrown defiantly back, while a curved sword was pressed against the underside of her throat, had caught the attention of the world.

'Do it!' she had taunted her captors. The look of pride and defiance had been so compelling you could not look upon this picture without experiencing the powerful message it conveyed. The photo had become a poster and her defiant words appeared on T-shirts and bumper stickers around the world. It had also become the title of a book on the bestseller list for twenty weeks and the rallying cry of oppressed women everywhere. It had been only a matter of weeks since she had played an exhibition game at Roland Garros Stadium in Paris. Thousands of adoring fans had delayed the start of the match by standing in the bleachers, cheering and pumping their fist in the air. One magazine had declared her the Muslim's version of Joan of Arc. It was not a role she played by choice. It was simply who she was.

Abraham's Bones

Neither of them spoke until they had reached the trench where the ancient sea gates had been uncovered. She suddenly spun around to face him, her face fierce with anger.

"He's such a liar!" she cried, without making any effort to explain exactly what she meant.

Christopher had not had time to talk to De Silva about the problems that had occurred while he was in Rome. She obviously thought he was involved in whatever De Silva was trying to conceal from her. Despite the direct opposition of their political beliefs, they had always been scrupulously honest with each other. There was something in her manner now as if she suspected him of recklessly breaking that trust. She had not accused him of betrayal, as she once had, but the accusation was there in her face. He resented this more than he should have.

"I didn't get home until late last night," he said. "I haven't had an opportunity to consult with anyone."

"Then maybe you should at your first opportunity. De Silva is trying to cover up for Levenston again. He's going to involve you in this if you aren't careful."

Sanura had uncovered an investigation by the IAA the precious year with political and religious implications. Andrew Levenston, one of De Silva's staff members, had authenticated some important artifacts, subsequently questioned by some other authorities. The attacks in the press had raged on for months until De Silva had come to Levenston's defense. On this previous occasion, Sanura had written a blistering expose accusing Levenston of a lack of scholarship. Thinking of the far-reaching implications of their unending quarrel, he could feel a sudden weariness seep into his bones.

"I think it would be better if you would give this a little rest," he suggested.

For an instant, he thought she was going to strike him as she shrugged his hands aside, her eyes moving over his features as if she had never really seen him before.

"I was only trying to help you and you treat me like this," she said, holding up a sleeve with the seam ripped from the elbow to her shoulder. After a moment of silently inspecting a bruise on the underside of her arm, her anger began to rise again and her voice became so thick with rage she could barely speak.

"You . . . you Americans are so smug, so arrogant. No American should be a Christian, for it mixes two kinds of craziness! You act as if every Muslim is a terrorist, and even the Jews you pretend to like, you secretly despise as if they were inferior beasts. I cannot understand why Allah does not strike you dead!"

He moved his hand from her shoulder to the back of her neck. She resisted, trying to push his hands away, then gave a little wounded cry as he pulled her against his chest where her cheek was resting against his own. He was amazed at how good it felt to have her in his arms again.

"Turn me *loose*, John, I hate you!"

"If you would only allow me to help you," he began softly, but she was infuriated now because he had broached a forbidden subject. He had promised her in Paris he would never bring it up again.

Her head came up and she started to rail at him, cursing him in a dialect as old as the ancient ruins dotting her homeland. Her hands had closed into fist and she began to beat them ineffectually against his chest. He caught her by the arms and pulled her against him again. He held her tightly until she stopped struggling, although he could still feel the tension in her shoulders and the small sobbing sounds escaping her throat. He kissed her eyes, and after a moment, she lifted her softly swollen mouth to his. After a moment of clinging to him in a fierce embrace, she suddenly turned her head aside.

"I tried almost continually to reach you over the weekend. When I attempted to leave a message, Daniella refused to pass it along to you."

"I had no idea," he assured her.

Her eyes moved across his face. "It doesn't matter now. Something serious has come up. I think you ought to look at this before you do something stupid again."

She held his eyes for a moment, and then passed a package to him, aiming her flashlight as he slid a report from a wrinkled manila envelope. He saw Department of Defense printed on the cover sheet and immediately felt a little stirring of uneasiness. He realized this was in reference to a spy satellite, although he did not understand the significance of the information.

"This report contains classified information," he said. "Where did you get this?"

Abraham's Bones

"Look at the last page," she said, making an impatient gesture toward the report.

At first, he could not tell what he was looking at, and then as he rotated it slightly, a picture suddenly took form in front of his eyes. It was a computer-generated drawing of the western wall of the city. Two objects having the shape and appearance of a coffin case were setting in the center of a chamber more than sixty feet below the surface of the earth. Remembering the angry exchange between Sanura and De Silva, he wondered how long this document had been in her possession. De Silva had vehemently denied having any knowledge of a coffin case, while Sanura had insisted he was being deceptive.

"Where did you get this?" he demanded, realizing he was not likely to get an answer. How could he explain this breach of security to his friends in Washington without drawing her more deeply into trouble?

"Someone searched my room last night while I was eating dinner. Fortunately, I had this with me. When I couldn't reach you I decided to make some changes in my plans."

"Where did you spend the night?" he asked, realizing she was in serious danger, more serious perhaps than she realized.

She nodded toward the ridge of hills above the tel. "I spent the night up there. I didn't feel safe in my room, and I was afraid to go anywhere else."

"We have to get you somewhere where you will be safe."

She closed her eyes for a few seconds and then she was looking at him again. "I am going to tell you something important. You cannot tell anyone, for it could have some far-reaching implication. You must promise."

"You know I wouldn't betray you," he began, but she swung her head away, not answering for a moment, then her eyes came up again looking frightened and uncertain.

"Congressman Danville is already dead," she said in a flat voice, but when he started to question her, she held up her hand to stop him. "That isn't the worst of it. No more than an hour ago . . ." she began, and then stopped as if she was weighing the implications of what she had already told him.

"You've come this far. Why don't you tell me the rest of it?"

It was growing lighter now and he could see the dim outline of her face, her bottom lip caught between her teeth. "Forget what you think you know. There is a conspiracy. There are high-ranking officers in the military as well as some officials in government who are a part of this. They are intending to take over the government."

"Are you sure of your source. If anything was underway, someone in Washington would know about it."

"Don't you understand," she said in a fierce whisper. "There are high-ranking officials in Washington who are in on this as well. They have already killed Danville, and if you get in their way, they will kill you too."

He returned the report to the envelope, and after a moment of considering the alternatives, he handed it back to her.

Seeing movement from the corner of his eye, he realized someone was coming up the path from the lower gate. The girl was dressed in a pair of knee-length capri pants and had a quick, athletic stride. At the top of the ramp, she stopped and shaded her eyes, then changed direction and came around the edge of the excavation toward the place where they were standing. He suddenly realized it was Daniella and wondered what she was doing here. She came to a stop a few feet away with one of her sandals propped on a broken piece of stone. He had not seen the list of summer workers and had assumed Daniella was in Israel for a short visit with her grandmother. She was apparently here for the summer and was intending to work for the excavation staff as she had in the past. He wondered if Julia was aware of her intentions. He was trying to think of how he should handle this awkward situation when Daniella broke the silence.

"I'm sorry I am late. I had to run some errands and it delayed me," she said, regarding Sanura with one raised eyebrow. Aware of the careful scrutiny, Sanura shifted her position and returned Daniella's brazen stare with one of her own.

"You'll find the excavation team over by the tent," he told her, wanting her to leave so he could finish what he had started. Their argument had opened some old wounds and he could not walk away from this now.

"Actually, I wanted to talk to you for a minute if it's convenient," Daniella said in a contrite manner. Her confident gaze did not match the submissive tone of her voice.

"Later, would be better for me. We can get together late this afternoon."

Sanura moved back a few inches, but continued to stand with the palms of her hands against his chest. After a moment, she turned reluctantly away, walking along the side of the trench until she was barely visible in the darkness. She seemed to be studying something in the bottom of the excavation as if it required the full focus of her attention.

Daniella dug into her pocket and pulled out a scrap of paper. "Julia wants you to call her. You can reach her at this number. She says it's very important."

Christopher took the offered note and buttoned it in the pocket of his shirt. Daniella took a couple of steps backwards with a show of reluctance.

"Something important has come up," he said before she could turn away. "I want you to help Sanura move her things to Dr. Siedman's house." Daniella's body stiffened and he could hear the sharp intake of her breath.

"Are you crazy?" she hissed at him, speaking in a loud whisper while Sanura was standing no more than a dozen feet away.

"I'm sure Julia won't object," he said, but Daniella's chin had come up and she was staring defiantly back at him, her hair twitching against the top of her shoulders like the mane of a spirited colt.

"*Object?* She's going to blow her cork!"

"I don't have time to explain. I'll talk to you this afternoon," he said, but even as he said this, he realized Daniella was not ready to agree with his suggestion.

"This is a joke, right?"

"I'm completely serious."

Aware of Daniella's careful examination, Sanura came walking back to where they were standing. Christopher remembered the summer when someone had accused a 10-year-old Daniella of putting a frog in the water cooler at grid 50. The father of one of the student workers had threatened to sue when his daughter had become ill and returned home before the end of the season. When he had confronted Daniella, she had protested her innocence and had cried, inconsolably, when Dr. Siedman had confined her to her room for the remainder of the week. Feeling guilty over the harsh punishment her grandmother had imposed, he had apologized for his own involvement and had taken her to her favorite restaurant over the weekend. He had even bought her an expensive present. Several months later, she had admitted her guilt to Julia. Daniella was looking at him now with the same innocent expression.

"I'll get back with you," he told Sanura, but she did not seem to be listening. Sanura's attention had shifted in the same way heat from a furnace will find an open doorway on a cold day.

Daniella had starting a slow creep in Sanura's direction until she had moved invasively into her personal space. Sanura had been a world class tennis player, but she had never been able to match Daniella for aggressiveness on the court. Daniella seemed to have a knack of discovering infuriating things to do to the other players. She had won most of her matches before her opponents had stepped on the court.

"Daniella," he warned under his breath, remembering their conversation no more than an hour before. Before he could say anything else, Sanura placed her notepad under her arm and turned abruptly away.

"I'm going to love this," Daniella mouthed back at him, an impish grin exposing her front teeth. Taking a couple of quick steps to catch up with her, they went rapidly down the path toward the lower gate.

Chapter 23

"I can assure you that we had not intended for this meeting to add to your discomfort," the taller of the two policemen said as he dropped a file on top of his desk and leaned back in his chair.

Maitland could feel his rage building as he examined the bland expression and the immaculately pressed uniform this police officer was wearing. The neatly trimmed mustache and a head of closely cropped hair made him look more like a military officer than a policeman. He had no idea of the man's rank, and after a careful examination of the brass nameplate setting squarely at the front of his desk, he did not learn anything new. In Europe, even if you did not know the language, you could usually get a rudimentary idea of the contents of some unknown message by making a careful examination of the text. The other policeman was standing behind his chair where he could not see him without turning his head. Maitland knew that this was a variation of the good cop, bad cop routine used in almost every police station in the western world. Then he reminded himself, with a little tremor of uneasiness, that this was not the western world. This was Israel, a modern country, but with a way of handling human rights issues, completely at odds with what he had grown to expect in Rome and in Washington.

"No offence taken," Maitland said, trying to force his breath into an even rhythm, despite the rapid hammering of his heart.

"A commendable attitude, I am sure. Just a few questions to complete our report and then we will let you be on your way. Did you get a good look at the driver of the car? It is my understanding that he made no effort to stop and render assistance."

"It was a dark car with a tented windshield. I couldn't see the driver and I have no idea of the license number. It all happened so quickly."

Maitland looked down at his knees. The bandages were showing through the rips in the fabric and he could smell diesel fuel and tar on his clothing, but overpowering everything else, was the unmistakable odor of blood. The fender had struck his hip, throwing him from the pathway of the front wheel. He remembered a feeling—almost of euphoria—that he had not been hurt. And then, as if everything was happening in slow motion, he found his body tumbling along the rough surface of the pavement, catching brief glimpses of the frightened faces of the other drivers and the pedestrian gawking from the sidewalk. After an endless time had passed, he was slammed into the curb and lost consciousness. The next thing he remembered was someone leaning over him shouting in some incomprehensible language. The only thing he could understand was that they had identified him as an American—as if this was the sort of irritating thing Americans did every day.

"Some of the witnesses have told me this seemed to be deliberate. Do you know of anyone who would want to harm you?"

"No," he said quickly, and then paused as he studied the policeman's narrowed eyes and the careful, appraising look. He knew this seemingly innocent question was an attempt to trap him into making some damaging omission.

But what kind of trap was it? He had done nothing since his arrival that could have violated any of their laws, unless his careful movements could have been misconstrued.

Then he remembered the angry exchange at the excavation site. Were they using this incident as a pretext to hound him because he was trying to uncover an important news story? Disagreeing with another reporter was nothing more than could be expected in his line of work, and he knew that none of them would have taken his remarks personally, unless Sanura . . .

This was ridiculous, he decided after a moment of reflection. They were not friends, would never be friends, but she would not have done something like this. This was more than a warning. It was an assassination attempt by someone who knew exactly what he was doing. It was cold and brutal and it was only by a rare stroke of luck that he had managed to twist away just as the car had swerved in his direction. As he looked up and saw the inquisitive expression on the policeman's face, he knew that he had made another serious error, but he had no idea of what this second mistake could have been.

"There is also another matter that we wanted to speak with you about. Certain inquiries have been made in Rome by the father of a young lady in your acquaintance. In the absence of formal charges, this is no more than a formality. Her name is Giulietta Bellarmini."

He had taken pity on Giulietta and allowed her to move into his apartment after finding her wading in the cold waters of a fountain. It was obvious that she had not eaten in days, but when he had offered to buy her dinner, she had refused. "I am not hungry," she had insisted, and told him that she made her living posing as a model for an artist who sometimes taught at a nearby university. She had also told him that she did not have a father. All of this had obviously been a lie.

"She was little more than a street urchin when we met," he said, trying to downplay any negative conclusions these policemen had reached. "I hired her to run errands for me on occasion."

"Ah! Then that explains everything. Has she ever done any house sitting? There was a complaint from the building manager that she is living in your apartment."

Maitland gazed back at the bland expression on the Policeman's face, but he had no idea where he was going with this. Was this a warning that he was under investigation for having a relationship with an underage child? This would not be so surprising, for this was the Middle East. These people had no idea of the social norms of a modern European society. They were stiff and formal, only a generation or two away from archaic customs of a tribal society.

"Has something happened to her?" he asked, trying to keep his voice neutral despite the fact that he could feel his heart galloping away at an alarming rate.

"An accident, more or less, but she was not seriously injured."

"An accident," he echoed dumbly. "What kind of accident?"

The policeman's mouth widened and he could not decide if he was trying to reassure him, or if he was trying to communicate the fact that he had placed his neck into a noose.

"It was an automobile accident, more or less. A car swerved in her direction when she was crossing a street. The police seemed to think that it was nothing more than a trivial occurrence, automobile drivers being as they are in Rome. I'm sure there is nothing to be concerned about."

The policeman was on his feet and Maitland knew that the interview was over. He turned away, trying to force himself to make an unhurried exit, but he had taken no more than two steps when the policeman spoke again.

"Do be careful, Mr. Maitland," he said.

Maitland did not know if this was a word of advice or if it was a warning.

Someone had tried to run Giulietta over in Rome, and someone had tried to kill him in the same manner here. Was this a strange coincidence or was he caught up in some unexplainable conspiracy that was bigger than he could possibly imagine?

As Christopher made his way along the walkway on top of the tel, he saw two visitors coming through the upper gate. One of them was tall with a military posture, while the other was much younger with the broad shoulders of someone who worked out regularly at a fitness center. The guard escorting the two men pointed in Christopher's direction. The younger one immediately increased his pace and arrived at the edge of the trench some distance ahead of the others.

"I'm Larry Walcott, Dr. Christopher. I want to have a word with you before you speak with General Zecori."

Christopher took the offered hand, wondering how long Walcott had been running interference for Zecori, then decided it probably hadn't been very long, judging from the nervous mannerisms and the way he kept looking over his shoulder. Zecori had stopped at the top of the embankment, while the guard pointed into the distance as if he were giving him an abbreviated tour of the excavation site.

"How may I help you, Mr. Walcott?"

Abraham's Bones

Walcott was wearing a pair of tinted aviator glasses. He whipped them off and slid them into the lapel pocket of his suit. "I spoke with Axel Tobin and he is concerned that you might make some imprudent remark and offend General Zecori."

It would have been better if Walcott had not removed his glasses, Christopher decided as Walcott's eyebrow lifted, displaying an eyeball that was bloodshot, embittered, and withdrawn. He could not help wondering what role General Zecori had played in this.

"Did Tobin remind you this is an election year?"

Walcott made a little sound of surprise. "Well . . . actually he didn't, but there seems to be a couple of unresolved issues."

"I know about the issues, but I don't live in Virginia so I wouldn't be able to vote for the senator anyway." Christopher started walking toward Zecori again, but had taken only a step or two when Walcott caught up with him.

"Axel told me you have a sense of humor, and this is good, but you see, the general doesn't."

Walcott's anxiety seemed to have gone up a notch or two in the last few seconds. He had turned where he was facing him squarely, and Christopher could see his right eye had the same appalling condition as the one on his left.

"Very few generals join the Vaudeville circuit after they retire," Christopher said, helpfully.

Walcott laughed, with each little ha-ha identical, and slightly off key, as if he was reading from a sheet of music and didn't know what a treble clef was. He adjusted his tie as if his collar had suddenly grown tight. "You have a rather droll way of putting that."

"I have a suggestion to make."

"I think I understand what you are getting at, but Axel suggested we should try to arrive at some understanding before the general becomes offended."

"Why don't you let me handle this, and if the general objects, you can carry him back to Washington and park him in his bunker." Christopher started walking again, leaving Walcott standing beside the path.

As Christopher approached the spot where the two men were waiting, the guard finished his summation of the excavation site with a sweeping two-handed flourish like an orchestra conductor reaching the end of the *1812 Overture*. The general didn't look as if he was impressed.

"Dr. Christopher," Zecori said, extending his hand. Christopher was relieved the general was not wearing his uniform. This was always a problem where military personnel came together, negotiations sometimes becoming deadlocked while they tried to figure out who outranked whom and how to handle the seating arrangement.

Christopher released his hand and pointed toward the tent a few yards to their left. Zecori's forehead was damp with sweat and there was a fine layer of dust on the spit-shined leather of his shoes. He could not help wondering if it was Walcott's job to make sure they passed inspection each morning, scurrying around with a can of shoe polish and a nervous tic under his eye.

The flaps were up on the tent, but the air inside wasn't much cooler. Christopher gestured toward a metal water cooler standing on a nearby table, but Zecori gave a negative shake of his head. The general's hair was gray, swept back close to his head like the feathers on an eagle. His eyes were the same color as his suit, and Christopher could not decide if this was an accident, or if he had selected this particular shade of blue to give himself some kind of tactical advantage. If memory served him correctly, this was the same suit he had worn on his daily appearances on TV during the Iraqi invasion, only this time he didn't have his pointer or a map to show the location of the problem areas.

"I'm not going to mince words with you," Zecori said, fixing him with an ominous glower. "I am going to expect daily reports from you as to the progress you have made, and I am going to give you a list of directives and a time frame in which I expect you to implement them."

Christopher tried to keep his surprise from showing, and could not help wondering if Zecori was not aware he was no longer serving as chief negotiator.

"I appreciate your comments, General, and I will convey them to my superiors at the Vatican. I am sure they will be interested as well."

"Whatever you think is appropriate, but I want you to understand that this delegation will be operating under orders coming from the White House and they will pass directly through me."

Abraham's Bones

When Christopher smiled without making any comment, Zecori's features became as stiff and unyielding as the face on a statue. Only his eyes remained alive.

"I have brought a Mobile Communications Unit with me and they are in the process of contacting Senator Cauldfield's office. I suggest we go immediately to the parking lot and talk with him. Do you understand the conditions under which we will be conduction this operation?"

"Oh, yes. Absolutely," Christopher said in a companionable tone.

Zecori hesitated for several seconds as if he was waiting for a belated 'sir', but when Christopher did not say anything, Zecori made a sweeping motion toward the gate. As they came out into the sunlight again, Walcott gave him a searching look and a self-conscious smile. Zecori ignored both of them as they marched down the walkway to the lower gate.

Zecori's Mobile Communications Unit was a white van with a satellite dish mounted on the roof. There was a soldier inside with a set of earphones clamped to his head. He looked up as they entered.

"I have Senator Cauldfield's office on the line," he said, pointing to a red telephone attached to an equipment panel. Zecori spoke into it for a minute and then flicked a toggle switch.

"I'm placing the senator on the speaker in case we need to address some other issues while we have him on the line. Just speak in a conversational voice."

Christopher smiled as he settled in the seat, swiveling it slightly where he could look Zecori directly in the eye.

"Good morning, Amos," he said and saw the quick stiffening of Zecori's body. Walcott was standing just inside the door. He placed his hands on the back of the passenger seat and closed his eyes.

"John!" the gruff voice sounded from the speaker. "I've had the devil's own time trying to get in touch with you. Tobin tells me it will be later in the day before you get your equipment set up."

"It could be tomorrow. They are having an electronics expert flown in from Rome. It looks like something was damaged when they airlifted it in."

"Then you might want to keep the general and his unit in your area until everything gets sorted out. There are a couple of things we need to kick around. The press is having a field day over Nick Danville's disappearance. I have a stack of reports three feet high from every agency in the government, but no two of them agree. This is making the president look bad, and I wouldn't care, if it wasn't making me look bad, too."

"The media coverage should run its course by the end of the week. If the other thing you want is for me to vote for you, I've already explained it to Tobin."

Cauldfield gave a hearty laugh. "I haven't gotten over the part you played when they roasted me at my birthday party a couple of years ago. The last thing I need is for you to start meddling in politics. What I really want is information about an organization called Shiva. It is on our watch-list but no one seems to know anything about it. Someone has put a little pressure on the government over there, and the Prime Minister has asked us to turn off our spy satellites when they pass over Israel."

"Did this request come through the State Department?"

"The request came from the White House. This is how Julia got involved in this little project in the first place. The president sent her over to get everything rushed up and I drafted her to help us. It did not seem important at first, but now I am becoming increasingly concerned. Something strange is going on and I don't know what it is. I thought the two of you might be able to sort it out."

"I was under the impression Israel had a highly developed satellite program of their own."

"Their system is called the Ofek-6. Their launch system has had a number of catastrophic failures. I seem to recall them having four or five operational satellites."

"What would it accomplish if we turned ours off?"

"International politics doesn't have to make sense."

"I'll make a few discreet inquiries."

"There is another thing bothering me. Sanura is an excellent reporter, and she has helped me on dozens of occasions when I needed to know how things look from the Arab's prospective. Julia seems to think she is a bit too radical to be involved in any of this. There are a number of our people who agree."

"Radical isn't the word I would use. I have asked her advice on numerous occasions, and she gives me her opinion when she can. If she feels she can't give an honest answer, she simply refuses to reply. She has been hired by Erlich Publications to help Dr. Siedman on a novel she is writing."

There was a short pause and then Cauldfield said, "I don't mean to be indelicate, but I talked with Keith Maitland over the telephone. He even faxed the front page of a tabloid containing a story he had written. The information seems to indicate your relationship with her goes far beyond friendship."

When Christopher hesitated, Cauldfield spoke up again, his voice sounding gruff and haunted from the tiny speaker directly over their heads. "I want to speak with you in private. I'm sure Walcott and the general will benefit from a short walk while we discuss this."

Almost immediately, the two men rolled their chairs back and stepped outside. Christopher picked up the headset and clicked the speaker switch to the off position. He sat in silence for a few seconds, and then explained the problem to Cauldfield, detailing his own involvement and Sanura's stubborn refusal to listen to reason. He explained it all, including his own anxieties, leaving nothing out. When he had finished, there was a faint sound over the telephone that could have been a sigh, and then a pecking noise Christopher realized was the tapping of a pencil against some hard surface.

"I have a feeling you aren't helping matters by putting this off, John. Brian Siedman was one of my oldest friends, and his granddaughter made a favorable impression on me when she was here in my office. They need to hear this from you before they find out from some other source. This could be devastating, not only to the peace process, but to your personal relationships. You don't want them to learn of this from one of Maitland's articles."

"I really don't think it is very likely," Christopher began, but Cauldfield's strong voice overrode his protest.

"I wouldn't be too sure of if I were you. Maitland probably knows some of the details, considering the contacts he has around the world. This is likely to blow up in your face when you least expect it. We can't have something like this derailing the peace process."

Christopher thought about the enormity of the situation and the reaction he was likely to receive from Julia and Daniella. "Just give me a couple of days and then I'll tell them."

"Another detail has me puzzled, John. Do you know a doctor named Hershel Shanklen?

"Yes, Johns Hopkins Hospital."

"We were fraternity brothers in college. He was the one who diagnosed Dr. Siedman's condition. According to him, her mind comes and goes. Not your classic case of Alzheimer's. I cannot remember what he called her condition, but he did say something interesting. He says there is no way on earth she could be writing a novel."

"There are some days when she is completely lucid. It's possible he didn't see her on one of her good days."

"Shanklen said her memory is compartmentalized. It isn't the word he used, but you get the picture. Even when she is sharper than the proverbial tack, she wouldn't be able to write a book. There are a half dozen little worlds she is moving between and she isn't staying long enough in any one of them to get the job done."

"I'm more than aware of her limitations, but this is the part Sanura is going to play. Her job will involve collecting and editing what she does produce."

"There is also the possibility she is ghostwriting the whole thing. Julia made a remark about Erlich's treatment of the documentary and it got me to thinking. She believes he has taken credit for things when he shouldn't have."

"I agree, but I don't think there was any damage done. The whole world knows what Dr. Siedman accomplished during the last 40 years, and no amount of effort on Erlich's part will change the facts. Julia was overreacting and I told her so at the time."

"You've written several books, John. Is Dr. Siedman capable of producing a marketable novel?"

"I've read the first chapter and there doesn't seem to be any problem. However it turns out, I think it will be good therapy."

"A third of a million is a lot of therapy. Erlich is Jewish, but there were a number of charges made against his family during the Nazi era. If his father hadn't died at the end of the war, he would have faced trial at Nuremberg."

Abraham's Bones

"My only contact with Erlich was during the time he was producing the documentary. I went on television to help promote Dr. Siedman's work. It was done for her sake and not for his."

"Old men meddle in other people's affairs, and I guess I'm doing it now. It bothers me when I listen to Julia's accusations, then do a little investigating and find some substance to her complaints. The more I look at this, the less I like what I see. Some of the people setting on the other side of the aisle are trying to crucify me. These peace negotiations are crucial, John, and something stinks to high heaven. See what you can find out and get back to me. There is going to be quite a battle between the delegates before this is over. You might see some improvement if you got everyone together in a social setting as soon as possible. No one is as good as you are at soothing injured feelings."

"I'm going to be doing something next week."

"Do it sooner, if possible. Include everyone involved and especially the more radical elements. Let them vent a little. It would be a lot better if they let off their steam at a dinner party, rather than in the press."

"I'll see what I can do."

"Keep Zecori around in case you need him and don't let him forget you and Julia are running this show. If it becomes necessary, I will have Julia bumped up a job or two where she can outrank him. Take care, my friend, and don't get hurt any more than you have to. At this point we are only seeing the tip of the iceberg. I have spoken with the president and this is one thing in which we agree. You and your mission are going to be in our prayers, John."

Cauldfield broke the connection without waiting for his reply. Christopher placed the telephone back on the cradle and stepped out in the sunlight.

There were more than a few inconsistencies, as Cauldfield had suggested. As he thought about it for a few seconds, he realized this was the thing that had been bothering him from the very beginning.

Chapter 24

Julia finished reading the second chapter of her grandmother's manuscript, then slowly lifted her eyes and gazed sightlessly through the window. There was only one person with whom she could share this information, but it would be painfully embarrassing. Jeannie Carson had been her friend and roommate for over a year, and one of the most supportive persons she had ever known. The telephone was setting on the table beside her chair, but she realized it would be hours before Jeannie would be at her desk.

She pressed the back of her hand against her forehead, trying to decide what she should do next. *How many copies of the manuscript existed?* John had received the first two chapters, but it was unlikely he had read them, considering his busy schedule.

She turned in a complete circle, looking at the manuscript and her comfortable chair without gaining any inspiration. Canceling the contract seemed to be the safest option. She could plead illness and say her grandmother was unable to complete the task in her present condition. This would also solve the problem of Sanura Hamada.

Julia sensed movement behind her and whirled around to face the person standing in the doorway no more than ten feet away. She had left strict orders at the gate and the household staff was aware of her instructions.

Who had let her into the house?

Abraham's Bones

Julia's eyes darted toward the telephone, but when she hesitated, Sanura moved in her direction and came to a stop directly in front of her, studying her with an almost frightening intensity.

Although she had watched her countless times on television, Julia was surprised to discover Sanura was actually smaller than she appeared on camera, her body fashionably slender, but with the healthy appearance of an athlete. When she was on assignment, she always wore what appeared to be military issue of some indeterminate origin, but now had on a fashionable skirt and a silk blouse that made her hair look radiant in the light.

"May I help you?" she tried to say, but only managed to produce a dry whisper. When Sanura spoke, it was not what she expected.

"You're even more attractive than I would have imagined from just seeing your picture."

Ordinarily, a personal remark from a stranger would have annoyed her, but this was so unexpected she was strangely amused. She had been deliberately rude in not allowing Sanura to come into her home, and considering the fact she was an Arab, this was especially offensive. Every Arab she had known had always been polite to strangers, even when they did not particularly like them. It was a part of their culture, a natural outgrowth of living for untold centuries under harsh conditions in inhospitable places.

"Where have you seen my photograph?" she asked, suddenly realizing the significance of what Sanura had said.

"Oh, I have it on my dresser in Paris. John gave it to me."

Julia realized she was probably referring to one of the group photographs various news teams had made at the excavation site. During the last few years, her grandmother had stubbornly refused to allow anyone to photograph her unless she, Daniella, and John were in the picture.

"Thank you," Julia said. "It was a very nice compliment." She had a million questions she would have liked to ask, but before she had time to gather her thoughts, Sanura had moved past her, examining the room and its furnishings as if she was completely at ease.

"You have such a lovely home," Sanura said as she stopped in front of the two small paintings she had bought in Paris the previous year.

Julia knew she had seen something similar on another occasion, and then she suddenly realized what had given her an uncomfortable feeling of déjà vu. The previous year Sanura had interviewed Queen Rania of Jordan. She had started the interview by commenting on the richly furnished palace, and then moved to stand before a grouping of pictures on the wall. For the next thirty minutes, they had chatted as if they were two friends meeting in a favorite cafe.

"I bought those in Paris," she explained, feeling strangely out of place in her own bedroom. Sanura turned slowly away as if she was reluctant to abandon the meticulous examination of the paintings.

"I am familiar with the gallery. Would you believe I almost bought those? I decided at the last minute it was a foolish extravagance when I really don't spend much time in Paris. I think I bought a camera instead."

Julia reached up, self-consciously, and pushed her hair away from her face. She had meant to have it cut, but there hadn't been time. During the last half-century, there had been many women who had set fashion trends, some of them unintentionally. She had always wondered if they were amused or flattered when they ran into someone imitating their clothing or hairstyle. When she saw the careful way in which Sanura was watching her, she remembered something she had almost forgotten.

Watching the newscast on Al Jazeera one morning as she was combing her hair, she had tried to reproduce Sanura's unique smile. Daniella's face had suddenly appeared beside hers in the mirror and she had mimed her with complete perfection. When she had stared back at her in astonishment, she suddenly remembered Daniella had played the part of Sanura in a drama presentation at the university, amazing everyone with her ability to reproduce every gesture and even the nuance of her speech. Her sister had gone to the work site early. Was this Sanura's way of letting her know she was wise to Daniella's tricks and had a few of her own?

John had never explained his relationship with Sanura, despite her subtle hints. She knew they had met years before when he was in school, but there was some unfathomable mystery to this relationship she had never been able to understand. A few weeks after their breakup, she had caught a glimpse of them at a political function in Washington. This had been a celebrity night, with most of the top government officials in attendance and many well-known personalities from Hollywood. As they crossed the expanse of red carpet at the entrance, she could see cameras in the press gallery aimed in their direction.

"What is your relationship with John? He's never taken the trouble of explaining it to me," Julia demanded, and then stopped abruptly, astonished she had actually uttered her thoughts aloud.

"He's one of my dearest friends," she said, but her explanation failed to clarify anything Julia did not already know. She had started to look away when she saw Sanura's smile change subtly. It was like a playful jab in the ribs by some thoughtless adolescent.

Julia spoke up quickly, hoping she could hide what she was really feeling.

"I'm terribly sorry. It isn't any of my business, but John and I have known each other for such a long time I was naturally concerned."

"You shouldn't be concerned. It only adds to his mystique." Sanura's mouth widened, and this time it was not the subdued smile she used on camera. It lit up her whole face.

"Mystique?"

"Washington's most trusted negotiator involved with a woman who is caught up in every terrorist plot in the Middle East."

Regardless of Sanura's other failings, she obviously had a sense of humor. She had evidently been reading Maitland's articles in the tabloids. Julia spoke up quickly to hide her embarrassment and realized she was almost babbling.

"John and I are just friends now. We broke off our engagement more than a year ago."

"Yes, he told me."

Julia could not believe John had been discussing the intimate details of their relationship with this woman. She had considered, briefly, asking Andre to arrange a discrete investigation to determine what lay beneath her innocuous image. After she had considered the implications, she had been too embarrassed to broach the subject.

"Andre mentioned to me . . ." she began, then suddenly stopped when she saw the brilliant smile fade.

"Surely you don't mean Andre Havran?"

Julia was surprised, but also puzzled by the preemptive tone of Sanura's voice, almost as if she was a parent forbidding contact between two wayward adolescents.

"Do you know him?" Julia thought she was not going to answer, and when she did, her voice was cool and dismissive.

"Yes, I do know him as a matter of fact."

When Julia had explained the problem concerning the part Sanura had played in the production of Erlich's documentary, Andre had listened attentively but had not said anything about knowing her.

"How on earth . . ." she began, but Sanura brushed her question aside with a brisk wave of her hand.

"Marshall Wurman has been involved in almost everything in the Middle East in the last few years. I certainly hope Andre won't be staying here with us."

For a moment, Julia was unable to find her voice.

"With *us*," she said, a little more sharply than she had intended. "What on earth do you mean?"

"Your sister brought me here at John's suggestion. I am in the room at the far end of the hallway. All I need is a table for my computer and a bed to sleep on. I can take my meals elsewhere."

Having already made her objections known to John, she could not believe he had dismissed them so lightly. Before he left the house, he had said . . .

But what had he said? Had she only been hearing what she had wanted to hear? She did not want this woman in her house. It was an insult from someone she had thought she could trust with her life, and now he had heaped this indignity on her with no thought of her feelings.

She suddenly realized what Sanura had said about the small bedroom. It was not a bedroom, actually, but a storage room for unused household items. It was hardly suitable for a guest—even an unwelcome one like Sanura. John would assume she was the one who had made the arrangements. This was like the story of Cinderella and she did not intend to play the role of the wicked stepsister. For an instant, she wondered what part Daniella had played in this. This was the kind of childish prank college students were capable of inflicting on their roommates.

Abraham's Bones

"The small bedroom is hardly suitable," she said. "The one at the head of the stairs is not being used at the present time."

Sanura spoke up quickly in protest. "Oh, I really wouldn't want to impose. The small bedroom is quite adequate."

Of all the games people played, this was the one Julia liked the least. At any social event there was always a guest or two making elaborate efforts to demean themselves. This was an act maiden aunts often polished to perfection.

"Nonsense," Julia said. "It is hardly bigger than a closet. I don't think there are any electrical receptacles and you will need them for your computer."

Julia turned abruptly toward the hallway before Sanura could protest any further. She went briskly past the closed door of Daniella's room without stopping and opened the door leading into what they had always called the corner bedroom. This was the largest one in the house, a suite actually, with a child's bedroom in an alcove behind the bath.

Sanura had followed her rather hesitantly, her gaze traveling around the room to examine the lavish furnishings and the large four-poster bed. She stopped under the chandelier with her hands clasped demurely behind her back.

A study in shyness, Julia thought, as she glanced at her from the corner of her eye. *Spare me!*

Julia threw open the doors of the walk-in closet, quickly checking the storage cabinets, then flicked on the light in the bathroom. Everything seemed to be in order, she decided as she crossed to the door leading into the small bedroom.

"You may use this room for an office," she said. "I will ask the household staff to remove the bed and bring up a desk from one of the rooms below."

Without giving Sanura a chance to protest, she went to the opposite wall and threw open the doors leading into Daniella's bedroom.

There will be plenty of time for the whip and thumbscrew, she promised herself.

She had started to close and lock the doors, but instead, pushed both of them back against the wall. "This is Daniella's room," she said. "You may want to leave the doors open where you can visit back and forth—just like sisters."

"This is terribly kind of you," Sanura said, ignoring the sarcasm.

Julia could not read the quick, fleeting expression as she turned quickly away. "I'm sure you will find it adequate, and if you should need anything further, you only have to ask."

"There is one more thing," Sanura said. "I wish to have a copy of your grandmother's manuscript as soon as possible. There's a great deal of work to be done and I am already behind schedule."

Julia thought of several answers, but realized the strategy she had mapped out before Sanura's arrival was the best way to handle this impossible situation.

"Grandmother is quite ill and I am going to cancel the contract," she said, waiting for her objection.

"You cannot cancel the contract. I have letters from all of her doctors. I know as much about the state of her health as you do."

"Her medical records are privileged information. How on earth did you obtain copies of them?"

"It was a condition of Dr. Erlich's contract. He arranged for a physical exam before she signed the papers."

"And you think this is reason enough to meddle in her private affairs?"

"Her private affairs became the concern of Erlich Publications when she signed the contract. If you haven't read it, I would suggest you do so. Some of the issues concern you as well as your grandmother. One of them is the manuscript itself. I insist that you turn it over to me immediately."

"This is out of the question."

"Then I will speak to John," Sanura said and turned toward the telephone. Julia shot out a hand, but instead of catching her elbow as she intended, she caught the loose fabric of her sleeve, pulling it up to reveal a pattern of dark bruises encircling the upper part of her arm. Seeing the direction of her gaze, Sanura jerked her sleeve back down, looking unsure of herself for the first time.

"What on earth happened to you?" Julia asked, without taking time to realize the inappropriateness of her question.

"Well . . . you might say it was an accident. You see, John and I had a discussion and things got out of hand."

Julia's eyes narrowed suspiciously. "If you are going to suggest he struck you, I'm going to have to say I don't believe you."

Abraham's Bones

Sanura looked startled for a second, and then made a sound in her throat that turned into a surprised laugh.

"Nothing dramatic, I'm afraid. The last time I saw him in Paris we had a disagreement of sorts, but we worked it all out this morning. He kept me from getting in more trouble than I was already in."

Julia took a quick step away from her, but it was not fast enough. Sanura's eyes blinked closed, but it did not hide the pleased smile. Julia focused her attention on the sunlit strip of beach visible through the window. She suddenly remembered something she had almost forgotten.

A photograph in a newsmagazine had shown Sanura standing at the foot of an elaborate staircase in what was probably a presidential palace in Baghdad. Saddam Hussein's youngest son had been standing behind her, his cruelly handsome face smiling into the camera. Both of them had looked radiantly happy. *There was a certain type of person who enjoyed dangerous situations and despicable people. Perhaps she had provoked John into some traumatic situation.*

Julia shrugged the thought aside and turned away from the window. "You still can't have the manuscript. There are reasons I can't go into at the moment."

"I think you owe me an explanation. This matter concerns me as well."

Julia hesitated. "I cannot explain this now. I will talk to John tonight and let him decide."

In all of Julia's life, even as a child, she had never had the luxury of being able to give an open display of her displeasure. Now, in full adulthood, she was tempted to have the mother of all fits. She did not argue any further, but waited for only a second or two before sailing past her into the hallway. She could not allow herself to act out any of her fantasies. One child in this house was enough, and Daniella is overdue for a lesson in maturity.

It would take only a few minutes to run the manuscript through the paper shredder and then she would deal with the computer files. She would erase everything and then she would call the publisher's office in New York.

Chapter 25

His heart was pounding and he realized he should have stayed on the hard surface of the roadway rather than running along the sand at the edge of the surf. He had never run on a beach before. Rather than being the perfect place to exercise, as it appeared in the movies, he had found that running through soft sand stopped just short of torture. It had been three days since he had been able to run, and his legs felt stiff and weak. The wind was hot and there was no breeze, although it was obvious there had been a storm at sea. The waves were crashing hard against the blocks of stone along the edge of the surf, and occasionally surging several feet higher, foaming among the rocks. An unexpected wave had caught him, soaking his jogging shoes and filling them with sand. Several feet ahead was a block of stone shaped oddly like a footstool. He trudged through the soft sand and dropped wearily on the top of the rock when he saw the woman coming toward him. When he saw the mane of dark hair and the confident way in which she was walking, he thought at first that it was Julia, and then realized this person was slightly older, probably in her mid thirties. She had altered her course slightly and was now coming directly toward him.

"You're Gary Maser," she said as she stopped a few feet away, appraising him. One hand was in the pocket of her skirt, while the other held a pair of sandals hooked over her index finger. Her accent was British, although it was not the language of the typical

Abraham's Bones

Londoner, with the dropped consonants, and the sound coming from the back of the throat. This was Oxford English with a lilting intonation he could not identify—something wonderful and melodious. He wondered is she was a singer.

"Guilty as charged," he said and saw her mouth widen. Glancing past her shoulder, he saw a path leading up the hillside from the beach, and realized the large house on the crest of the ridge was Dr. Siedman's residence where he had been earlier in the day. He had not seen her until he had stopped, and he wondered if she had come down the path from the house.

"I have some very good news for you, Mr. Maser. We have heard from Congressman Danville's kidnappers only a few minutes ago."

"We?" he said wondering if Julia had sent her.

"They sent a note, actually. Daniella called and asked me to stop you and give you the message."

He looked down the beach in the direction of the hotel and realized it was more than a mile away. Normally he ran three miles each morning, but he was exhausted from running on the soft sand in the oppressive heat.

"Oh, no," she said as she saw the direction of his gaze. "It isn't necessary for you to run back. A car is waiting in the access road at the back of the house. I've been asked to bring you up."

She had pointed to a path a hundred yards or so down the beach, but the other path went directly toward a wrought iron gate inset into the stuccoed wall. A call to Washington was an absolute necessity, and it was important for him to contact the local authorities as well. He had not thought any of this through because he had not expected to make the exchange himself. The kidnappers had insisted on a wire transfer, but there was some kind of procedure for doing that. He could feel his anxiety rising steadily.

"It's not necessary for you to make any preparations," she said when she saw his hesitation. "All of the arrangements have already been made."

She had already turned away, motioning for him to follow. He pointed at the nearer path, but she was moving purposefully down the beach. The house would have a phone and he desperately need to make a call. He hesitated for a few seconds and then ran to catch up with her.

"You didn't tell me your name. Are you connected with Julia's family?"

"I'm a cousin, actually," she said, as if making this admission somehow amused her. My name is Chandra."

She had said a car was waiting for him. Perhaps someone in the car had a phone. The path was steep but she was going steadily upward without any apparent difficulty. It was hotter than he had imagined and the run through the sand had exhausted him. A short stop to rest would have been nice, but he did not want to reveal his weakness in front of someone who could climb like a mountain goat. His breath was coming harder and he could feel the sweat running down his back and pooling at the tight band of his shorts. The trail appeared to level out a few feet above them, and as they came up in front of a grouping of low-growing bushes, he saw the top of a car gleaming in the sunlight. He could see two men standing beside the car. Both of the front doors were open. The driver was standing with his elbows resting on the top of the door, while the other man was looking toward the high, windowless wall surrounding the back of the compound. Chandra continued to climb effortlessly, while he stumbled along watching for patches of loose gravel. The man standing at the driver's door had a short black beard. As he glanced across the top of the car, his eyes widened in surprise.

"Hello!" he called, feeling the last of his anxiety turn to relief. "Chandra didn't tell me who I was to meet." He quickened his pace as he started around the rear bumper, his hand outstretched. The driver of the car had turned, facing him, and he caught a glimpse of his face for the first time.

They had shown this picture to him in Washington.

For a brief second, he felt an almost overpowering fear, and then he swung wildly around, leaping across the loose stones and plunging down the narrow pathway. He heard a faint sound near his ear, and saw sand kick up some distance away.

A silencer! They were using a silencer.

There was no way he could run a zigzag course as he had seen people do in the movies. Sharp rocks lined the path and it would be impossible to run through the loose sand. He tried to speed up but the pathway was treacherous. Another bullet passed his ear with the same fluffing sound, this time kicking up sand near the edge of the

Abraham's Bones

surf. He did not look back, but he was aware of someone above him, descending rapidly along the pathway. He was almost to the beach. Taking his eyes away from the trail long enough to take a quick look in each direction, he realized the beach was completely deserted.

I will run into the water, he decided. He had been on the swim team at Yale. *If he could just reach the water, he would be able to escape.*

A hard blow in the lower part of his back made him stumble, but he was almost to the surf. Strangely, he could feel no pain and he wondered if the bullet could have struck his kidney. The person chasing him was gaining steadily, but he was still almost a hundred feet ahead. He hit the first wave and ploughed through, taking a quick look over his shoulder.

She had cast her dress aside and was running, dressed in only a bra and a pair of low rise briefs, running with her forearms extended slightly for balance like an Olympic sprinter. At first, he thought she did not have a weapon, and then he saw the light reflect from the surface of the knife held between her teeth. He was past the surf now into deeper water and he began to stroke hard. A hot searing pain had replaced the numbness in his lower back and he decided it was probably the effects of the salt water. He was bleeding and he could feel himself weakening. Were there sharks in the Mediterranean? He did not know, but he realized there probably were, for the Straits of Gibraltar connected it to the ocean. He felt something touch his shoulder and realized she was upon him. He shook her hand loose and dived underneath the next wave. He had held his breath once for four minutes. The water closed around him and he was suddenly aware of an overpowering sense of dizziness. Shooting upward through the water, he thrust his head into the blinding sunlight and took a deep gulp of air, just as he had done thousands of times in the Olympic sized pool at the university. He sensed movement behind him, but it was too late to turn, for she was upon him again, her arm locked around his neck. He tried to twist away as the sharp blade bit deeply into his side.

The most difficult problem in any strange country was not the inability to speak or understand the language, Maitland had discovered early in his career. There was always someone around who could speak English, even in the most remote corners of the world. He fished around in the pocket and counted another bill into the outstretched hand as he watched the cab driver's face. The angry expression altered somewhat, although the tip he had given to him was not large enough to earn a smile or a word of thanks. His arm hurt from the tips of his fingers all the way to his shoulder. He was lucky that nothing had been broken. The doctor had said to take one of the pills every four hours, and he was counting down the minutes until it was time to take another. The nurse had wanted to put his arm in a sling, but he had refused, finding that he was more comfortable holding it across his abdomen with his thumb thrust down behind the buckle of his belt.

Glancing up and down the street, he saw a hand-lettered sign in the window of a shop that said 'Internet Cafe' with a larger sign above it that he assumed was the same message in Hebrew. He had not eaten since early morning and he felt weak, but he did not know if it would be possible to keep anything on his stomach. A cup of hot coffee . . . or perhaps he needed something cold and soothing. Since his accident, his stomach felt alarmingly queasy, probably the effects of the medication, or perhaps from some internal injury the hasty exam had not uncovered. He crossed the street at the intersection, forcing himself to keep up with the rushing crowd, while keeping a wary eye on the erratically moving traffic. He hurried along a little faster as the light changed, and had started to step up on the curb when the heel of his shoe caught on the edge of the pavement, causing him to stumble forward while fighting to regain his balance. A man standing directly in front of him grabbed his forearm—the injured one—and clamped down hard. When he let out a little howl of pain, the man looked at him in alarm, then thumped him between the shoulder blades with the heal of his hand.

"My son has asthma, too. Verrrrry bad," the man said in broken English, giving the throbbing muscles of his shoulder a reassuring squeeze before turning away.

"Think you," Maitland managed, grimacing with pain.

"No prob'be'leeem!" the man assured him as he went rushing toward the street crossing.

Maitland stood for another moment with his good hand braced against the rough surface of the wall, then slowly made his way toward the door of the Internet Cafe. He had to send an email, and it would be foolhardy to do so from his hotel room. This would take no more than a few minutes. He could handle that. A few more feet and he would be safely inside and seated in front of a keyboard.

His steps slowed and he came to an abrupt halt, swaying unsteadily. For some unaccountable reason, he could not shake the feeling that he was being followed—someone with a gun, a knife, or some kind of deadly poison to slip into his drink. He ran a shaking hand across his forehead and discovered that he was feverish. A few more steps, he thought, just a few more steps, as he went inching toward the door.

He whispered to himself as he realized something he had not suspected before, but now he could see it with a surprising amount of clarity. *John Christopher is trying to kill me!* he decided, and gave a loud and creaky laugh. He had started to turn, to look behind him when the sidewalk tilted sharply toward his face.

Benji seemed to be studying the dregs in the bottom of the cup as if he was thinking he might find his future written there. "How well do you know Sanura?" he asked.

During the years when Sanura had been one of the top seeded tennis players, sports reporters had approached him at almost every tournament he had attended. He had always refused to comment. "We have been friends for many years."

"You're familiar with her past?"

Christopher hesitated a little longer this time, wondering if Benji actually knew something or if this was a fishing expedition. "You're asking about her career, I assume."

"Actually, I'm asking about her family. I understand you had some trouble crossing the border from Xinjiang last month."

He had crossed the border into China at Beijing's request to evaluate some recently discovered ruins along the route of the ancient Silk Road. He had been traveling with an army detachment when they had came under fire from a local warlord.

"All of the problems were worked out with a few phone calls," he answered evasively.

Benji did not say anything for almost a full minute. "I'm not trying to pry into your personal affairs, but these problems are causing some concerns between our respective governments. The border region has a rather large Muslim population. A number of extremists have taken refuge there. Our information seems to suggest bin Laden was among the expatriates for a while. We searched Maitland's room and discovered a rather detailed file in his possession. We are not sure if he has put all of the information together correctly, but he has everything he needs to reach some devastating conclusions."

"Do you happen to know if Maitland has Julia or Daniella under surveillance?" Christopher asked cautiously.

"Actually, he has focused his attention on Daniella from the moment of his arrival. One of our agents spotted him in a restaurant when she was there with a young man named Gideon. I understand Maitland left the restaurant immediately after they did. He was observed picking up the drinking cup she had used."

Suddenly, Christopher's mind was racing. "For what purpose? Her fingerprints?"

We have a spy in the top level of our government with access to the Prime Minister's daily briefings. That is when we made our request to Washington to turn off the spy satellites. You are in danger, and I think you understand this situations well enough to realize it could involve something serious."

"There is certain amount of danger in serving in any government position," Christopher said.

"We have reason to believe Julia, Daniella, and Sanura are vulnerable as well."

He thought for a moment, wondering how this information might tie in with what Sanura had told him earlier. "Julia and Sanura would react rather strongly to any security measures, while Daniella would be likely to stage an outright revolt."

"We are especially concerned about Daniella," Benji said.

Christopher set his cup on the table and looked up at Benji's worried expression. "In what way?" he asked cautiously.

"There is an investigation underway. Our concerns have been increasing by the hour."

"Could you be more specific?"

"At this time, no, but I think you ought to be aware there is some interest here as well as in Washington. I'm sorry but I can't go into the details at this time."

"Then what do you suggest?"

"Putting the proper security procedures in place would be the best solution, but an alternative would be to get Daniella and Sanura involved in the peace process. She is running errands for the excavation staff, so it would be easy to include her in this without arousing any suspicion. You might also want to get her involved in the editing of Dr. Siedman's manuscript as well."

"To what end?"

"In elementary school, it is called the buddy system. They force children on an outing to stay with the same friend. Sexual predators are not likely to approach two kids on a playground, but a child alone is fair game. We tend to forget it works for adults as well. If they stay together it will minimize the danger."

"This would be a lot more difficult to arrange than you might imagine. There are certain personality issues involved."

Abraham's Bones

window overlooking the harbor and ordered coffee. Benji was silent until they had been served and the waiter had moved away to attend a group of tourists at another table.

"Now," Christopher said as he examined the guarded expression on Benji's face. "What's this all about?"

"As I told you earlier, I'm with Special Forces."

"I assume you are referring to Mossad."

Benji was studying a freighter making its way up the coast in the direction of Tel Aviv.

"Ordinarily, I would make a strong denial, but Leora assured me I can trust you explicitly. Actually, I am with Aman. There are a number of matters we need to discuss, but it is more important for me to make you aware of the seriousness of your situation."

When Christopher did not ask the expected question, Benji sighed and opened the pouch he had placed at his elbow. He extracted a report printed on thin sheets of glossy blue paper and extended it across the table. Near the bottom of the page was a short underlined statement: *Subject examined under extreme prejudice,* which he recognized as a euphemism for torture.

"I'm not sure I understand the significance of this."

"Are you aware you have been under surveillance for the last few weeks?"

"It was brought to my attention, although I don't believe there is any cause for alarm."

"Our sources are very reliable, Dr. Christopher, and we have confirmed our suspicions through information we have received from several independent sources. The question naturally comes to mind as to why they were following you even before your appointment was announced."

Christopher hesitated. "I'm assuming all of your information didn't come from one interrogation session."

"We have received intelligence from several sources, but you can thank a reporter named Keith Maitland for bringing some of these matters to our attention."

When Christopher started to interrupt, Benji gave a humorless laugh. "Maitland's accusations were ridiculous, but several of his comments made us realize while he had interpreted the facts incorrectly, there was some substance in what he was suggesting. Under the circumstances, there was only one conclusion we could reach.

Joe Prentis

Chapter 26

Christopher did not immediately recognize the soldier waiting in the hallway outside the door of his office, but when he turned, he realized it was Benji, the young man he had met when Leora had picked him up at the airport.

"Benjamin Zivie," the soldier said and offered his hand. He opened a diplomatic pouch and produced an officious looking document with a seal of red wax affixed to the flap. "I believe this is a bit out of the ordinary, but my government has requested I serve as consular representative until someone else becomes available. I'll try not to be too much of a nuisance."

"I'm sure there won't be any problem," Christopher said, but before he could open the door, Benji made a gesture toward the far end of the hallway.

"I'm wondering if I could buy you a cup of coffee."

Christopher had started to decline the offer when he realized Benji was not simply trying to be sociable.

"Sure," Christopher agreed. "Just let me put this inside." Crossing to his file cabinet, he locked the envelope in the top drawer. Benji had stepped inside and was carefully inspecting the cramped workspace. When Christopher started to speak, he touched his upper lip with the tip of his finger. Christopher led the way out of the office, making casual conversation about the weather and the work at the excavation site. They found a table near the

"We thought so, initially, but our operative happened to notice he was making an effort to keep his fingers away from the rim. We have been monitoring his computer and discovered he has sent a package to an Internet site that checks DNA samples for litigation purposes."

When Christopher started to scoot his chair away from the table, Benji held up a cautionary hand. "This may be nothing more than a fishing expedition. At least we found nothing in his notes to make us think otherwise. He checks every detail of his investigations. This is how he brought Senator Leland Wilkins down. A sample of DNA he had obtained matched the DNA of Wilkins' missing intern. Just as a precaution, we have contacted the company who will be doing the DNA testing. They have agreed to send the report to us. We might alter the results if we think it is in the national interest to do so."

"Who knows about this?"

"Only a few of my superiors on a need-to-know basis. They have told me this was not your first excursion into Xinjiang."

Christopher lifted his coffee cup to his lips, trying to decide how he should reply, when he saw the careful way in which Benji was watching him.

"That was a long time ago," he said. "It is not something I want to remember."

"We all have things we had rather not recall, but it is important to remember that there are others who will never forget."

Christopher shrugged the statement aside. "I would assume you have made a thorough search of Maitland's papers."

"What we found in his room was too elaborate and detailed for him to have thrown it together in a matter of days. I think it is more likely someone passed the information along to him for a reason, or reasons unknown. There were no government documents in his possession, but we did find some meticulously detailed reports. "

"I appreciate the information," Christopher said, thinking of the far-reaching implications of what Benji had told him.

"What about the Gnome Project? I understand you were approached in Rome."

Christopher was surprised at this particular question. He wondered if Werner's contact with radical political groups had aroused their interest, or if it was something else.

"Werner seemed to think certain right-wind elements in the military might try to gain possession of the Temple Mount," Christopher said. "I think he was only rehashing some old concerns."

"My superiors aren't so sure. The name itself has raised concern with some of our security advisors."

"I'm not sure I understand what you are suggesting."

"A gnome is a mischievous creature that lives underground. They are said to wreck havoc with the plans of any unsuspecting person who crosses their path."

"I understanding it is a DNA project," Christopher said. "They hope to trace the development of the various cultures across the face of the ancient world."

"You are thinking of the Human Genome Project. It is highly unlikely they would spend the kind of money required just to cover the same ground some other organization has already covered. I'm not a scientist, Dr. Christopher, but over the last few days, they have obtained DNA samples from 63 persons and none of them are Jewish. Some of our best scientists are going over their findings, but they haven't been able to draw any conclusions. I wonder if you have an opinion as to what this could mean."

"I'm sorry, but I have no idea."

"My superiors are also concerned about a posible link between Angus McLeish and radical extremist in the military."

"McLeish has the reputation of being more of a showman than anything else. I'm not aware of any political interest."

"I understand he has the reputation of making some remarkable discoveries during the last decade."

Christopher paused before he answered. "It is more than just a reputation. Some of his discoveries have been nothing short of miraculous."

"In what way?"

"Archeological work is anything but spectacular. Progress comes slowly and usually after years of unproductive work. It is almost as if he has some psychic ability to know where something will turn up next. A few have accused him of planting artifacts only to discover them later. They refer to this dishonest practice as 'salting a dig.' Gold miners used to do the something similar by planting a few gold nuggets in a mine shaft and selling it to some unsuspecting businessman."

"I will pass your information along to my superiors. I think they will be interested. Our people will be investigating around the clock. It should not take more than a few days to complete our investigation. In the meantime, I'm going to stick with you like glue."

"Won't this be a little too obvious? If people are watching me, they are likely to become suspicious, not to mention the reactions of some of the representatives from the Arab states. They aren't likely to overlook an Israeli soldier following me around full time."

"A number of persons in my government have already commented on your relationship with Miss Hamada. At the very least, they might make some accusations of unfairness or bias. I'm sure you are more than aware of how this can occur at the smallest suggestion."

"Sanura is Muslim, Julia is a devout Christian, and Daniella considers herself to be a Jew. Any suggestion of bias would be ridiculous."

"Where religion is concerned, few people worry about the ridiculous nature of an accusation. I do not have to remind you of Sanura's importance in the Arab world. I shudder to think of what might occur if something was to happen to her because of these negotiations. I am a very good actor, Dr. Christopher. At one time, I even considered going on the stage. I'm going to attend to your needs in the same way the Secret Service attends to your president."

"I'm becoming nauseous already," Christopher said.

"Better nauseous than dead," Benji countered as he watched Christopher across the top of his cup. Christopher started to argue, but as he considered the many problems he would be facing in the days to come, he gave a reluctant nod of agreement.

Chapter 27

Daniella tried to stifle the little sound of surprise when she realized someone had stopped beside her chair. She had been so absorbed in her work that she had completely lost track of time. Looking at the clock, she saw that almost two hours had passed since she had taken a break. She had made a great deal of progress, although there was still a lot of work remaining before she would be ready to make a printout and have everything ready for the student workers who would be arriving over the weekend.

"May I help you?" she asked when the woman did not say anything. She looked somewhat familiar, although she could not place her.

"I'm Rachel Richardson," the woman said after a few more seconds of uncomfortable silence, then produced a leather folder with a laminated ID identifying her as a FBI agent. Daniella remembered that she had seen her earlier in the day. There had been some kind of disagreement between her and Julia, something to do with a security issue if she remembered correctly. Richardson continued to stare down at her for a few more seconds, her eyes tracing a path from the crown of her head all the way to the soles of her sandals.

"You looking surprisingly like your sister," she said.

Daniella did not know what to make of this inane comment, but realized that what she was experiencing was irritation rather than amusement. She did not have time to waste on guessing games, but evidently Richardson was waiting for some kind of response, or was it a confession? *What exactly did she want?*

"You are going to have to give me a vowel, Vanna. I have no idea what you are asking."

"Don't get flippant with me, young lady. You would do well to remember who I am."

"Look..."

"No, you look! I am a federal agent and I have some questions to ask."

"You are an *American* federal agent, and this is not American. You are a guest in my country and not the other way around." Daniella was pleased to see that her statement had momentarily stopped her, but the small victory was short lived. Digging into the jetsam in the bottom of her purse, Richardson snatched a photograph from among the contents and presented it with a flourish. It was a picture of her standing at the service line on a tennis court. Examining the signs in the background, she realized someone had made this photograph the previous spring, and judging from the angle of the camera, they had made it from the top of the stands with a telephoto lens. There was nothing remarkable about this, for half of the people who attended tennis games were carrying a camera. She glanced up and realized she was still looking at her in the same disapproving manner.

"Do you know where that picture came from?" Richardson demanded.

"I have no idea."

"This was in the possession of an American tourist who was transported to the hospital a short time ago. He has been unconscious since arriving and there was no identification. One of the doctors recognized this picture of you, but the medical personnel have no idea who he is or what might have happened to him."

Daniella glanced from the picture to the disapproving expression on Richardson's face. "I am sorry, but I can't help you."

"I would like for you to go with me to the hospital to see if you can identify him."

"I'm sorry, but that is out of the question. If there is a problem, you might want to talk to John Christopher or Dr. De Silva. If you will excuse me, I must get back to what I was doing."

Abraham's Bones

"Look," Richardson began in a more reasonable tone. "No one is accusing you of anything. This man was seriously injured and I would suppose he would like to have your help. Having this picture in his pocket leads me to assume he knows who you are. Forget about what I said just a moment ago. Helping him is the decent thing to do."

"The decent thing is to complete what I am doing now—but I will go to the hospital."

"Thank you," Rachel said, tucking the photograph into her purse. "My car is outside."

"I can get to the hospital without your help," Daniella said as she dropped the pen beside her notepad. Rachel looked as if she was prepared to say more, but when Daniella turned toward the doorway, she nodded in agreement.

Herzi was convinced the man was innocent, despite the continuing suspicion of the two officers who had brought him in. There had not been sufficient time to run a comparison on the blood smear on the left front fender, but the small swatch of cloth caught in the bumper was enough to convince anyone that Kadmiel's car had been used in the commission of this crime. He did not think, however, that Kadmiel had been the driver.

"Tell me once more about your keys," Herzi said. "This is the part of you story I do not understand."

"I swear on the name of my forefathers I did nothing!"

"I do not want you to swear on anything," Herzi said, his voice hardening slightly. "What I want is the truth."

"And I have given you the truth!" Kadmiel said. His hands were open in supplication, but they were trembling. Herzi's fellow officers were watching their suspect carefully, and he knew they were convinced this uncontrollable trembling was evidence of his guilt. He wasn't so sure. In more than thirty years as a police officer, he had heard almost every lie conceived by man, but this bizarre story had the ring of truth.

"Tell me once again," Herzi said.

"I was asleep," Kadmiel said, his voice taking on a wheedling tone. "I worked the night shift and I had been home no more than an hour when I went to bed. I swear on the name of my forefathers I am telling you the truth!"

"Please," Herzi said holding up his hand for silence. This much of the story was true, but this was where it started to sound suspicious. Kadmiel had gone to bed with the doors securely locked, and his car keys in the pocket of his trousers. He had awakened an hour later with the keys missing and his car gone. The front door had shown some indications someone had attempted to pick the lock, but there was no evidence it had occurred recently. His officers had accepted the story at first, until they found 'Thank You' written on the bathroom mirror with lipstick.

"Someone used your car in a murder attempt, yet you claim to know nothing. I find this very hard to believe. I have no choice except to lock you up until you are willing to talk."

"I have a job," Kadmiel said. "A very good job! If I miss work they will fire me."

"If I do not find the person who was driving your car, I might lose my job. I am afraid you leave me no choice."

"No, wait! Please listen. There was a girl. A very pretty girl. I brought her to the apartment with me because she said she had nowhere else to go. I was only trying to protect her."

"And what did this mysterious guest of your look like?"

"Very pretty. She had long dark hair reaching to her shoulders. Her clothes were very nice. They were the kind of clothes a rich girl might wear while attending some expensive school in America."

"So you are an authority on what rich girls wear while attending expensive schools?" Herzi said, taking a quick look at the worn and wrinkled clothes Kadmiel was wearing.

"Please, you must believe me. I lived in America for three years. I was a maintenance worker at a school called Brown University. It is in Rhode Island."

"And what does this have to do with the rest of your story?"

"All of the girls were from rich families. They are different. Very different from the American tourist you see on the street."

"And how do you know the American tourist you see on the street are not from Brown University?" Herzi asked.

"This is so confusing," Kadmiel said. His hopefulness of a moment before had now turned into despair.

Abraham's Bones

"It *is* very confusing," Herzi agreed. "Over the years I have learned the truth is usually simple."

"I have remembered something else," Kadmiel said, suddenly, his eyes darting around the room.

"And what have you remembered?"

"I remembered where I saw her before. It was no more than a few days ago. She was jogging beside the roadway near the beach. There was a young boy following her on a bicycle. I think he was an Arab."

Herzi continued to stare at Kadmiel until he began to shrink back into the seat. "Lock him up for the moment. I have someone I must talk to."

"But my job!"

Herzi turned away, not bothering to answer.

"I've taken my break an hour early so I can drive you to the hospital," Kevin complained. "What do I get out of this?"

Seeing his expectant expression, she could not suppress a grin. "I was thinking in terms of a veggie burger."

"And if I want more?"

"Do you want fries with that?"

"I was going to suggest a date," Kevin said, his voice rising slightly.

"Are you sick?" Daniella asked, frowning at him in mock horror. "That would be like dating my brother. I've known you since . . ."

"You've known me since you were a skinny kid of ten and I wouldn't give you the time of day. Correct me if I'm wrong, but this looks suspiciously like payback time."

"It's a scheduling problem. I will put you in my date book and let you work your way up."

"Date book!" he said, wrapping his arms around the steering wheel and leaning his head sideways to look at her. "Is this a hunk list or what?"

She pointed toward the windshield as the car started to drift into another lane. He jerked the steering wheel, and frowned at her again.

"Actually, the list is on my computer. I have all the names, the date I met them, and all of their personality qualities. This is so I won't forget anyone, or maybe make some kind of stupid mistake when I can't remember their name."

Kevin took his eyes away from the busy street and focused on her face again. "Whenever I try to talk to you, I have to lean around this Gideon dude. Is he your bodyguard or what?"

"He is just a friend."

"Then you must be his only friend. No one else likes him."

"He's just lonely."

"He shouldn't be. He hangs around your neck like an Orangutan. And what about Romeo you went strolling off with early this morning."

"Are you jealous?"

"Yes!"

"Good!"

"I'm serious," he said after a moment. "I have waited two years for you to grow up and now you are telling me that I am going to have to wait *longer*. What about this person we are going to the hospital to meet. Has he been chasing you so long his heart gave out?"

"I have already told you I don't know him."

"Maybe you should check on your computer under misplaced hunks. He was carrying a picture of you. Did they find it next his heart?"

"I was *told* he was carrying a picture of me. I don't even know if that is the truth. This grim, angry woman from the FBI . . ."

"Rachel Richardson, Kevin said, rolling his eyes. "She makes everyone go ballistic." He whipped the car to the right, tailgating a truck for a hundred yards, then turned into the entrance of the hospital. He made a rapid circle of the parking lot and found a place near the walk. "I am going to wait for you here. I don't think I could stand to see you doing the final scene from Romeo and Juliet if this guy turns out to be some long lost boyfriend."

"That is a possibility," she mused, watching his face. "I understand the picture was covered with drool."

"Just go," he said waving his fingers at her. "Just don't come back here with a broken heart."

She studied his profile for a few seconds while he continued to look straight ahead, then jerked the door release and bounced from the seat. "You can kiss the back of my hand when I get back."

"Now you're breaking *my* heart."

She blew him a kiss as she went up the walk toward the entrance. The doors hissed open and she saw the nurses glance up as she went toward the desk. She recognized a couple of them but could not remember their names.

"You're here to see if you can identify our mystery patient," one of them said before she could ask her question.

"He's not . . ."

"If you are wondering if he is dead, dangerous, or deranged, the answer is no to any of the above. Actually, he is kind of cute," she said coming around the end of the desk. "He reminds me of that singer—I can never remember his name—but the one who is always singing about his broken heart. Did I tell you that he is major, seriously cute? If you don't want to take him home with you, I would like to have a go at him myself."

Watching the nurse from the corner of her eye, Daniella could not decide if she was joking. As they turned a corner in the hallway, she felt a strange feeling of misgiving that she had not felt since her first day at boarding school.

"Don't worry," the nurse said. "I'll be right here with you. I won't allow you to steal him away without a fight."

The nurse's one-sided monologue had been amusing, but as they passed through the doorway, this was no longer funny. The man was lying motionless on the bed. If it had not been for the movement in the drip attached to his right arm, she would have thought him to be dead. She would have guessed him to be in his middle thirties, and very handsome, despite the bandages covering the right side of his face. "Is he going to be all right?"

"I think so. We haven't found any serious injuries and there are no broken bones."

"Do you know what happened to him?"

"By looking at the bruises and abrasions, I would say a car struck him. We don't have any record of this, which means he was probably treated at some doctor's office. We have contacted the police, but they haven't sent anyone around to make an identification. We were hoping you could help us with that."

"I'm afraid I won't be able to help you. I have never seen him before."

"Are you sure?"

She had moved closer, looking down at his face. "I'm positive. When do you think he might awaken?"

"There is no way to know. It might be today or tomorrow. The sound of a familiar voice will sometimes do the trick. After seeing the picture, I thought you might be the answer to our prayers."

Daniella touched the back of his hand hesitantly with her fingertips, and then sat down slowly on the edge of the mattress.

"Maybe it would help if you would talk to him," the nurse suggested.

"What would I talk to him about?" Daniella asked. Physical contact with him was not as uncomfortable as she would have imagined. Glancing at the clock, she saw she had been gone from the lab for no more than fifteen minutes. *I will stay for an hour*, she decided, though she had no idea what she should say. She closed her eyes for a moment and then looked back at the still face.

"When I was a little girl I wanted to be an astronaut . . ." she began, watching his face carefully for any reaction. Behind her, she heard the faint squeak of rubber soles as the nurse turned and went quietly from the room.

Chapter 28

From where he was sitting near the front windows of the restaurant, Christopher had an unobstructed view of the harbor where ocean going yachts were tied up along the length of the marina. Further out to sea, he could see the taut canvas of a 65-foot sailing yacht billowing in the breeze. He had often wondered why someone would pay the immense sums required to maintain a boat of that size, when a motorized yacht was far less expensive. As the helmsman spun the wheel and the ketch heeled sharply in the wind, he felt a tingling of excitement and an intense longing for a time when he was less encumbered with the cares of the world.

He tore his eyes away from the window, writing a note to remind himself of some unfinished items of business, then flipped the notepad closed and placed it in the pocket of his sun bleached khaki shirt. Looking toward the reservationist's desk, he saw a young, fashionably dressed woman moving toward the archway, but did not immediately realize that it was Sanura until she turned down the long expanse of carpeted aisle toward the table where he was seated. He buttoned the pocket of his shirt and frowned thoughtfully, trying to remember exactly what he had said when he suggested getting together at the restaurant. He could not imagine how anyone could have misunderstood this simple invitation. When Sanura was on assignment, she was always dressed in military apparel, as she had been when he had seen her only a few hours before.

Since then, she had changed into a sequin-trimmed dress that fit her like a glove. Her diamond earrings caught the light from the lamps in the high ceiling, surrounding her with a magical aura. He wondered if they were the ones he had given to her on her birthday.

And then he saw Julia and Daniella, trailing along several paces behind her, all three of them having the appearance of runway models at some prestigious fashion show. As they moved closer, he could see that Daniella was wearing a pair of high-heeled thongs, making her almost as tall as the other two women. For some unfathomable reason, they had turned a simple meal into a gala event. He ran his hand across the stubble on his chin as he slid Sanura's chair out.

At a nearby table, a group of American tourists looked up from their plates. "Such beautiful sisters," one of the women commented. Daniella's head swung toward their table, and then she looked away in sulky silence.

As Daniella folded her lithe body into her chair, Sanura moved hers slightly to the right, crowding in against her in a deliberately provocative manner. Daniella compressed her lips tightly together and gave her a narrow-eyed look. When there was no reaction from Sanura, her hair swung in the opposite direction and she subsided into a sullen, watchful silence. Seeing the studied indifference on each of their faces, he could not help wondering how much trouble they were going to cause him.

Christopher placed his order while the three of them took their time examining each entrée without being able to make up their minds. When Julia lifted her shoulders and inclined her head in his direction, he ordered for her as well. Sanura made her request in Arabic, which the young man wrote down without any hesitation. She presented the menu to Daniella with a flourish and she ordered in Arabic as well, watching Sanura all the while from the corner of her eye. The young man thanked them in Russian, and then in flawless Farsi, asked if there was anything else. When Daniella told him, "No," in rather subdued English, he gave them an elaborate bow and marched away in the direction of the kitchen.

Leaning back in his chair, Christopher was unable to suppress a smile. "If we've concluded our celebration of the United Nation's Language Hour, I suggest we get down to business. I am short on time as it is and I have a meeting scheduled. Some rather serious problems have occurred and I need your help."

"Does this concern the announcement Maitland made early this morning?" Sanura asked. "I heard it on the radio just a few minutes ago."

"What announcement?" Julia said, turning her head slightly in Sanura's direction, although she was making no effort to meet her steady gaze.

"It's about your grandmother's manuscript," Christopher said,

Julia was staring back at him in astonishment. "How could he know anything about the manuscript? There are only three chapters, and no one has seen it except the four of us."

"Maitland claims Dr. Siedman plagiarized portions of it from a previously published book. After dropping this little bombshell, no one has been able to reach him for comment."

Julia tossed her head in annoyance while Daniella's eyes became round and unblinking. Julia was the first to recover.

"What a vile, wicked thing to say! He is only doing this to get back at mother. He has always suspected she had something to do with his problems at the network. I'll call our lawyer and threaten him with a lawsuit unless he makes a retraction."

"Suing a newsman is usually an exercise in futility, especially if the person involved is as well known as your grandmother."

"There's only one way he could have known anything about the contents of the manuscript," Julia said, darting a brief, angry glance in Sanura's direction.

Sanura's shoulders moved like the languid stretching of a cat. "You gave me a copy of the first three chapters no more than an hour ago. Having this article in today's newspaper suggests he had the information since yesterday, if not before. Writers sometimes send portions of their manuscript to trusted friends to get their reaction. There is also the possibility she could have sent an outline of the book to Dr Erlich. Maybe this is what Maitland is talking about."

"She sent a short synopses but it was only one page in length," Julia said. "I have a copy and I really don't see how anyone could have drawn any conclusions after reading it. Her proposal was rather vague and little more than a formality. "

Sanura was quick to disagree. "Surely there must have been some detailed information, when you consider the amount involved in the contract. In her documentary . . ."

"In *your* documentary," Julia corrected, propping her elbows on the edge of the table and leaning toward Sanura. "What you did is unforgivable. You allowed Erlich to take credit for everything, while she was made to look like some pathetic hanger-on trying to grab some of the headlines."

"I did no such thing! Have you read the contract?"

"I haven't, but I can imagine what it must contain if you were the one who drafted it."

Sanura's eyes blinked closed and then she was looking at her again. "I owe you an apology for what I allowed to happen, and I am so sorry. There was almost five hours of narration. I had control of everything except the editing. Erlich edited it down to fifty minutes. I did not see the final cut until it was in the hands of the network. They took several statements out of context. In the present contract I drafted six restrictions to keep any of this from happening again."

"Then maybe you should have drafted a seventh because he appears it *has* happened again despite your virtuous intent."

"There is also the possibility that Maitland is lying. I have spent most of the day trying to find him, but he seems to have disappeared from the face of the earth."

"There is also the possibility that you are lying as well."

"I don't think a cat fight will solve any of this," Christopher said, causing both of them to immediately lean back in their chairs, even though their bodies were still poised like two boxers being forced to retreat to neutral corners. "We need to put our heads together and find out how this could have happened rather than trying to assign blame. I had not intended to meet with anyone before the first of the month, but this unfortunate publicity has made it necessary for us to make some changes in our plans. Some of the Palestinians have already accused us of bias, and I expect that we will hear the same thing from the Israelis in short order."

Julia's attention was fastened on her hands, clasped tightly together in front of her, but the small lateral movement of her pupils made him aware that the smallest provocation would cause her to renew her quarrel with Sanura.

"How do we prove him wrong?" she asked.

"I don't think it's a matter of proving him wrong. He has played hard and loose with the truth for a great number of years. This time he seems determined to inflict some catastrophic damage. His accusations about the manuscript are only the tip of the iceberg. Send a request to Cauldfield's office for them to check with the CIA and see if he can obtain a list of people Maitland has met with in the last few days. I am sure someone in the intelligence community has him under surveillance. I want the three of you to work together on this. We need some answers and we need them in a hurry."

"Surely you aren't suggesting that Sanura and Daniella become involved in the peace process?" Julia said, aiming a puzzled frown in his direction.

"And why not?"

"Well, for one thing, neither of them has a security clearance."

When Christopher did not respond, she said, "It's out of the question. You would never get permission from Washington or from the Vatican."

"Our first priority is the manuscript. If we don't come up with some reasonable explanation, there might not be a negotiation. Maitland evidently intends to use the same black magic he used when he forced Leland Wilkins to step down. Contact Erlich Publications and get a list of everything they have received. Contact the news services and ask to see copies of any evidence they have pertaining to Dr. Siedman's book. I don't think there would be anything to gain from a lawsuit, but you probably need to contact your lawyer. Pursue any avenues that might produce results. We won't be discussing anything of a confidential nature in the next few days. This arrangement could move things along nicely for a number of reasons. Sanura is known and respected throughout the Muslim world. Her involvement will help us gain the trust of some of the more reluctant delegates. Daniella knows more about a computer than anyone we could possibly hire. There's going to be a lot of research to conduct in the next few weeks."

"That's not fair," Daniella complained. "I have a few more days of work to do at the office and then I want to join the others at the excavation site. I wasn't here last year and I want to do something meaningful instead of wasting my whole summer setting behind a desk."

Daniella continued to look hopeful, but when she realized he wasn't going to give in to her request, her eyes slid away, looking hurt and rejected. Christopher suddenly realized Julia was studying her sister carefully, although he was thankful she was keeping her thoughts to herself. When Daniella looked back at him again, he saw the pleading look in her eye.

"If I go into archeology as a career, I will need the experience," she argued, her face coloring slightly.

"I didn't know you had decided to become an archeologist," he said.

"Well . . . I have. I just decided in the last few weeks," she added when she became aware of the skeptical gaze that Julia had aimed in her direction.

"I'll probably be going to Egypt sometime in the next two weeks. You can go with me. If you are genuinely interested in archeology, visiting the ruins at Thebes and Tel el Amarna would be a tremendous experience for you."

Daniella still was not convinced. "Why couldn't your secretary do the research?"

"Because you have the necessary experience and she doesn't."

"Leora needs my help," Daniella insisted stubbornly.

"I'm sure Leora can find someone else to help her," Julia murmured, giving him some belated support, although there was not much conviction in her voice.

"I wouldn't ordinarily impose on you, but we desperately need the kind of help you can give us," he said.

"Couldn't they send someone out from Washington?"

"It would take months to train someone. There is a scarcity of people in government service who speak Middle Eastern languages, while you speak all of them fluently. That is the reason Julia and I was approached by recruiters from the State Department four years ago. They wanted someone with our language skills."

"I don't want to be tied up with this all summer. I have some plans of my own." Her elbows were propped on the edge of the table and she was peering at him through her fingers as if she was looking through the bars of a cage. He could scarcely bring himself to make his next request.

"I also want you to help Sanura with the editing of your grandmother's manuscript."

He heard the sudden, explosive sound of her breath, and then she straightened in her chair as if someone had prodded her from underneath the table. "I don't want to *do* this!" she cried. "Why couldn't I work at the excavation site and do the office work at night?"

"I would like for you to remain here where the three of you can work together."

She stared back at him, while her expression ran the full range of emotions from shock to denial. He knew he would have to tell her more than he had intended in order to gain her compliance, but this would have to come later. "I'm sorry, but there are security issues involved. I want you to stay with Sanura night and day for your mutual safety. I don't want you slipping off by yourself."

"But I have a social life, I have friends, I have things I want to *do*."

"No one is saying you can't do the things you usually do when you are here. I am simply saying you need someone with you in order to be safe."

"You mean like having her tagging along on a date? Are you *serious*? She is old enough to be my mother."

"Daniella . . ."

"John, *please*!" Daniella cried, swinging her head toward the exit as if she might flee at any moment. He covered her hand with his and she gripped it like a mountain climber clinging to the safety of a narrow ledge. He leaned forward, but before he could say anything further, Julia interrupted.

"I think we could solve most of our problems if we destroyed the manuscript and claim that grandmother hasn't actually written anything," Julia said. "It would provide the best defense and there's no way anyone could prove us wrong."

"Would you want to testify in court that the manuscript never existed?" Christopher asked. Daniella had withdrawn her hand and was setting with her head bowed, looking down at the table.

Julia gave a weary sigh. "When you put it that way, I suppose I wouldn't. This seems so unfair. It's like someone saying you can't have your own private thoughts."

"There's a contract for a third of a million," Christopher reminded her. "Erlich might choose to argue the point."

"No money has changed hands. If she is unable to finish the manuscript, Erlich won't have incurred any expense. I don't see how there could be any liability on our part."

"That's not exactly true," Sanura said. "There has been some expense. He has some of his people working on an extensive publicity campaign. These things have to be done months in advance, and there is the matter of my salary. At this point, it is not a substantial amount, but I am not prepared to return what they have paid me. I have living and travel expenses."

"I don't see a problem concerning your expenses," Julia replied in a dismissive tone without waiting until she had finished. "I would be willing to cover the full amount. You could forget the book and go on with your life instead of being tied up here for the entire summer."

"It still wouldn't solve the problem," Christopher said. "If Erlich wanted to sue, this would become a larger issue from a legal standpoint. Potential profits in a contract are sometimes treated as if they are already in the hands of the recipient. He could sue you for the entire amount."

Julia paused thoughtfully, considering the possibilities. "If the manuscript was withdrawn and we explained my grandmother's medical condition, I am sure everyone would understand. People have faith in the quality of her scholarship. It is not as if some unknown novelist was attempting to foster a hoax on the public. What proof could they have?"

"Maitland says he can prove his copy of the manuscript was written on your grandmother's computer."

"That's impossible," Julia said, "and how could he prove it came from her computer?"

"A text file contains the author's identity," Daniella said when Christopher only shrugged.

"You're joking," Julia said. "How could something like that possibly work?"

Daniella looked for a moment as if she could not believe her sister was serious, and then, as if she was explaining to a child, she said, "When you install software on your computer, the installation programs prompts you for a name. From then on when you save

Abraham's Bones

something on your drive, it places an identity stamp in the file containing the author's name, the date, and the time it was saved to the disk."

"So what are you suggesting? Someone stole a copy of one of her disk?"

"It's not even necessary to do that," Daniella said. "There is a program called a key-clicker. It is like a computer virus. If you put it on someone's computer, you can read every key as it is pressed. People use this program to steal credit card numbers and banking information. It this instance, they would be able to see the text as it appears on her monitor."

"They would have to have access to her computer to do something like that," Julia argued. "The house is secure. It is almost like a fortress."

"You don't have to have access to her computer. You could do it from anywhere in the world. You only need an Internet connection. Half of the kids in junior high have done this to their friends."

"You knew there was some problem with the manuscript before this occurred," Sanura said, "I have a right to know what this is all about."

"I knew nothing of the sort!" Julia said.

"I'm sorry, but I don't believe you."

Julia opened her mouth to continue the argument, then closed it without saying anything else. When Christopher continued to study her carefully guarded expression, she looked away, avoiding his eyes.

"If Maitland can prove his accusations, it will reflect unfavorably on everything we have done at the excavation site over the years and on my credibility as well. I don't have to remind you of what is at stake."

Julia sighed heavily. "I will do whatever you think is best, but it doesn't make any sense that Maitland would make a ridiculous charge like this when there's no way he can prove it. He's going to look like a fool in front of the whole world."

"Maitland has some evidence or he wouldn't be making these charges. I want the three of you to spend the evening examining every possible scenario and try to determine how this could have happened. See if Dr. Siedman's computer is on the Internet. Find out if it has been in the shop for repairs. Speak to Miriam and make a list of everyone that has been in the house in recent weeks. It could have been a repairman or someone there under false pretense. There has to be an explanation and we have to find out what it is."

Christopher knew all three of them were on the brink of rebellion. Julia seemed ready to walk out when Sanura broke the uneasy silence.

"I have contractual obligations with Dr. Siedman's publisher, and a tremendous amount of work to do in the next few weeks. I must talk to Dr. Siedman as soon as possible."

Julia's head swung in Sanura's direction and she was now bristling with anger. "I do not want you talking to my grandmother!"

"Then how can we possibly work together if we have no basis for trust?"

Julia did not say anything for a few seconds, then lifted her chin and spoke as if the words hurt her mouth.

"I will give you a copy of everything she has written."

"But I want to examine the computer to see what is really on the disk. That might require carrying it to an expert. You are being deceptive, and I want to get to the bottom of this."

"That's ridiculous," Julia said, trying to force some indignation into her voice.

"And after I have examined the computer, I want to speak privately with Dr. Siedman."

"You may not, under any circumstances, speak with my grandmother in private."

"You raise these ridiculous objections because you are hiding something. You think you have me fooled, but I have proof that will substantiate everything I suspect."

Sanura had dropped her bombshell and it was now time for Julia to either deny the accusations or explain her actions. Christopher waited for a moment, and when Julia saw how carefully he was watching her, she dropped her hands in her lap.

"Whatever," Julia said, as if she could not see why there was a problem in the first place.

If Christopher had not been watching so carefully, he would not have seen the almost imperceptible signal that passed between Julia and Daniella. Daniella had been a computer guru since she was in grade school. If there was something on Dr. Siedman's computer they did not want Sanura to see, it was obvious it was not there now. No amount of electronic sleuthing would be able to uncover it. He knew he must pursue these matters carefully or Julia would accuse him of taking sides with Sanura just as Daniella had.

"As soon as Erlich Publishing is made aware of Maitland's accusations, they will be demanding answers. We must to be in a position to answer their questions. I do not have to remind you of the consequences if we discover that Maitland is right. If it becomes necessary to explain the problem to your grandmother, then that is what we will have to do."

Julia was still working on her indignation but was not succeeding very well. "Sanura may meet with her under my supervision. I will not have her talking to her unless I am present."

"Then that is settled," he said with a casualness he did not feel. He was relieved that Sanura did not look triumphant over this small victory.

Chapter 29

Maitland awoke with a start. When he heard a commotion outside the thick door, he knew that he had probably shouted something in his sleep as he came tumbling out of a nightmare.

Where am I?

His realized with a growing sense of horror that his right arm was secured by a strap, but when he swung his head in the opposite direction, he saw a clear plastic bag suspended over the side of the bed. *I am in a hospital!*

The door opened abruptly and a nurse filled the opening, looking at him in a questioning way. A large man, who was obviously a policeman, was peering past her shoulder. The nurse came quickly toward the bed and pushed him back to a reclining position and started fussing with the drip. His vision was blurred, and he drew back in alarm as she suddenly bent toward his face, lifting his eyelid. The bright light hurt as she shined it in his pupil, and then repeated the procedure on the other side.

The policeman was standing very close to the head of the bed and Maitland found himself looking up at the soft underside of his chin. "Do you think it would be all right if I were to ask him a few questions?" he asked.

"You may question him if you keep it brief. I have to go and fetch the doctor."

Abraham's Bones

Maitland's mind was racing and he could feel the panic building as he considered his predicament and wondered if he might be in legal trouble. Where was he? This was obviously a hospital and the man looking down at him had the features of someone from the Middle East. Could he be in Iraq, Iran . . . surely this was not Afghanistan . . . no, it probably wasn't, for he could not remember going there, but then he suddenly realized that he couldn't remember anything. His name . . . What was his name? His vision had cleared, somewhat, and he saw a nametag over the pocket of the man's shirt. He could not read it, but the lettering was obviously Hebrew. That meant that he had to be in Israel, but why was he here? He had no idea.

"I assume that you are an American, for the nurse has told me that you were speaking English with an American accident. Is this correct?"

"Water," he whispered. His mouth felt as if it was packed with cotton wool, and he knew that he did not want to answer any questions until he had time to think everything through. He had obviously been talking in his sleep. The policeman hesitated, taking a quick look around the room.

"I'm not sure that I should offer you water. The doctor will be here in a moment. I will let him decide."

The man had no more than spoken when the door bumped and a large, serious looking man dressed in surgical scrubs was peering down at him. "How do you feel, Mr. Maitland?"

Maitland hesitated before he answered. He had not known his name, but somehow this sounded right. What was he doing in this hospital? Then he remembered a car rushing toward him, and the driver spinning the wheel at the last moment. This had not been an accident.

"I am a little confused," he said, and had started to repeat his request for water when the nurse placed her arm behind his head and lifted it slight as she fitted a straw between his lips. He sucked hard, almost convulsively, and felt the cold liquid hit the back of his mouth.

"Easy," the nurse said, and pulled the straw back a couple of inches. "You need to take your time. All of it could come back up if you aren't careful."

"How long have I been here?" he asked. It was easier to talk now, although his throat still felt parched.

"You have been here for a couple of days. We only learned who you were no more than an hour ago. You had no identification on your person when you arrived and this is one of the things that has been bothering us."

"Am I under arrest?"

The policeman glanced at the nurse. "No charges have been filed against you, but we would like to conduct a more thorough interview before you are released from the hospital."

"It won't be until late tomorrow," the doctor said. "It will depend on his condition and if he has anyone who can care for him."

"I have no one. I am here on a business trip. I am . . . was staying at a hotel."

"Very well," the doctor said. "I am going to suggest you get your rest and I will see you in the morning. In the meantime, I believe any further questions can wait until then."

Maitland saw the policeman give a reluctant nod of agreement, then follow the others out of the room. He lay back, thinking. Everything seemed to be falling into place, although the accident itself wasn't completely clear.

Then he had another thought. Who was the girl who had sat at his bedside reading to him? He could remember the touch of her hand and the soft, sympathetic voice, although he had been unable to respond. She had read to him, and part of the time she had just talked, telling him things about herself. He knew instinctively that she was not a part of the hospital personnel, for she had leaned forward and kissed him softly on the forehead before she had left.

He glanced toward the window and saw it was dark outside. He saw movement from the corner of his eye and realized the door was opening cautiously, and then he saw her standing there, looking toward the bed.

"They told me at the desk you were awake," she said, the words coming in a rush, and then, suddenly, she came floating toward the bed.

Daniella Siedman! he realized, and for a moment he could not breathe. She seated herself on the side of the bed with a little bounce, taking his free hand between both of hers. He could remember the soft touch and the warmness of her fingers. She had

Abraham's Bones

seemed like an angel to him. He wondered what her reaction would be when she learned who he was, and the terrible secrets he had discovered.

As Christopher came around the edge of the unloading area in front of the hotel, he saw a group of tourists queuing up at the steps of a tour bus, while a man with an ill fitting suit was checking their name tags against a list on his clipboard.

Walking rapidly toward the entrance, Christopher saw an array of cameras aimed in his direction, but as he circled the end of the queue, he realized the cameramen were not focusing on the tour group, but were rushing with predatory intensity to intercept him. He wondered if there had been some word from Danville's captors, but realized his secretary would have contacted him if there had been any news. There was a confused mingling of voices as they stepped in front of their cameras, speaking rapidly into the microphones, then turned and extended them in his direction. There were several familiar faces in the group. Brittany Boxter from CNN was the senior reporter and she asked the first question.

"Do you have any comment concerning Keith Maitland's unfortunate accident?"

This question was so completely unexpected he did not immediately reply. "When did this happen," he asked, "I haven't heard."

"It came over the wire about an hour ago."

Brittany was one of the good ones, but as she leaned toward him, he could not help noticing the little gleam of satisfaction in her eye. He had met her shortly after arriving in Washington to work for the State Department, and had carried her out to lunch on a couple of occasions. He had always enjoyed her company, but this was business and he knew she would not let friendship stand in the way of a good story.

Maitland had covered the political scene in Washington before his banishment to the European bureau of the network. Being two thousand miles away had done little to alter the situation, except he was no longer able to pursue his quarry up the steps of the Capitol Building. Few officials had been prepared for his questions, and the results had brought about some historical moments. Maitland had few friends among the press corps, but reporters had a reputation for defending one of their own. He knew something was expected of him, and as he examined their eager expressions, he decided to keep it simple.

"As soon as I return to my office I will contact someone in government," he said. "I'm sure they already have a full investigation underway and I will assist them in every way possible."

Brittany's eyebrows lifted a fraction of an inch. "We have already contacted someone in government, but the investigation has taken a surprising twist. We have located a witness who claims an automobile struck him at a street crossing. He claims to have heard him make an accusation implicating you."

"There must be some misunderstanding," Christopher said. "As soon as I've had time to investigate this, I will report back to you. I'm sure the Israeli government will be cooperative as well."

"In a story Mr. Maitland filed shortly before he disappeared, he mentioned an additional problem. This one involves Dr. Siedman's research materials."

Ordinarily, he would have brushed such a ridiculous question aside, but coming from a responsible reporter like Brittany, he knew there was something afoot. "No one has seen her research materials. I can't imagine where that came from."

"It has to do with DNA. I have spoken with Mr. Werner and Professor Rosen and they are rather noncommittal. I understand you met with them in Rome?"

"Our discussion had nothing to do with Dr. Siedman's manuscript."

"But you haven't answered my question. Did it have anything to do with her research materials?"

"Her manuscript is a historical novel."

"I understand she has a number of documents in her possession that seem to have originated from SISMI headquarters. In case you are not familiar with the acronym, it refers to the Italian bureau of military intelligence."

"I'm familiar with the organization in general terms, but I can't conceive of any set of circumstances that would have caused Dr. Siedman to consult with a covert organization. She has, on some occasions, consulted with some specialists in the field of history or archeology, but nothing she has written has any connection with espionage or government."

"Do you have any information about an organization called Propaganda Due. It is my understanding they . . ."

"I believe they are involved in some of the conspiracy theorists latest revelations. They have also been linked with the Masons, the Rosicurians and al-Qaeda," Christopher said in a casual way without placing any of the blame where it belonged. He immediately knew he had failed to ease any of Brittany's suspicion when she continued as if she had not heard.

"My investigation seems to indicate there is some substance to each of these allegations. Our New York bureau is checking with Erlich Publications, and they have also contacted someone in Homeland Security."

Brittany was a good reporter and usually followed her story wherever it led, and these disjointed questions were different from what he had come to expect of her. There was a certain element here—an irrational paranoia—making this seem to be part of a script from a late night suspense movie.

"It's time for my coffee break," he said, stalling for time. "Why don't we go inside to the conference room?"

"We're already set up out here!" one of the cameramen complained as if the suggestion was a personal affront. Brittany lowered her microphone and spoke briefly to the man behind her, and then with a swirl of blonde hair she did an about-face and frowned up at him.

"I think we've just been outvoted," she said. "It would take too long to shift the equipment inside."

Another reporter had inched her way to the front of the group and extended her microphone. "Would you like to comment on Senator Erlich's investigation?" she asked, watching his face carefully for any reaction.

When Brittany swung her head in the young woman's direction, Christopher knew his initial suspicions had been correct. Brittany had been prepared to lure him into making some damaging admission before she sprang her trap. This young woman had evidently ruined the surprise, whatever it was.

"I'm not familiar with Senator Erlich's investigation," he said.

During the previous year, Erlich had used every method at his disposal to prevent Senator Cauldfield's election as Senate Majority Leader after Leland Wilkens had stepped down. Cauldfield had intended to start an investigation of campaign contributions to several members of the senate. He seemed to recall Erlich having come up for discussion.

"Senator Erlich has some questions about your appointment," Brittany said. "Would you care to comment?"

"I was appointed by Cardinal Mason. You might want to direct your questions to the Public Relations Office at the Vatican."

"Senator Erlich has three areas of concern. Your lack of fairness toward the Israelis, the connections you are alleged to have with terrorists, and problems you seem to have with members of the opposite sex."

"Let me know if he turns that into a book. I'll want an autographed copy."

"If you are called to testify before a senate subcommittee, will you claim diplomatic immunity?"

Christopher paused for a moment, aiming a smile directly into the lens of the camera. "I hardly think it is likely, seeing I have no knowledge of what is going on in Washington beyond what I have seen on your newscast."

"I think you are evading the question, Dr. Christopher!" someone called out from the rear of the group.

"If asked to testify, I will reveal everything I know about each of you," he said, winking into the camera as he stepped past Brittany and headed toward the door leading into the lobby of the hotel. He had taken only a couple of steps when he realized Brittany was still at his side. Her cameraman was scurrying along with a sideways movement like a garden spider going after an ill-fated bug.

"Do you think Senator Erlich's investigation is motivated by personal reasons?"

"I don't think I'm following you."

"I'm referring to his daughter. Do you think he is trying to get back at you?"

"I don't know Senator Erlich or any member of his family."

"His brother is Richard Erlich, the head of Erlich Publications."

"I have met Dr. Erlich, briefly, but I was not aware he and the senator were brothers."

"I understand you had a personal relationship with Senator Erlich's daughter."

"I'm afraid not, and now if you will excuse me, I have some important business to take care of."

"Jeannie Carson. Does that refresh your memory?"

When Christopher stopped abruptly, the cameraman bumped into Brittany. She ran her hand across the back of her head and grimaced, but her attention did not waver.

"I can't say I know Miss Carson. I've only met her once."

"There are allegations about a personal relationship."

"I can't imagine how you arrived at that conclusion."

Brittany reached inside her equipment bag and produced a computer printout. Christopher could see a long column of numbers and a jumble of notes written in the margin.

"This is a copy of her phone records indicating you made numerous calls to her apartment over a two month period early last year."

"My fiancée was her roommate."

"Your *former* fiancée, Dr. Christopher. The records indicate these phone calls were made over a period of weeks after you broke off your engagement. Keith Maitland has a transcript of some of the messages you left on her answering machine and he sent a copy along to me. Some of them were . . . rather descriptive, I understand."

Christopher thought back, trying to remember. He had left several messages on Julia's answering machine. In all of the messages he had asked her to return his calls, and on two occasions he had asked her to meet him at one of their favorite restaurants. He could not recall anything of a personal nature, and certainly nothing suggestive.

"You will have to excuse me," he said, looking at his watch. "I have an important meeting."

Brittany's hand closed on his forearm while she waved her cameraman off. He immediately turned away, reaching for the power switch on the side of the camera.

"I'm sorry about the hard time I've been giving you, but a story is a story. You have always been fair with me so I am going to level with you. I received this information about Jeannie Carson in an envelope delivered to the desk at my hotel. There wasn't a note or anything in the package. I checked it out as well as I could, but something about this doesn't feel right. I am going to hold this thing about Carson, but the rest of it is on the record. I would like to get together with you later in the day to discuss some of the details."

"Tomorrow perhaps, but the rest of my day is already scheduled. Surely you didn't come all the way from Tel Aviv just to investigate some rumors."

"This isn't just rumors, John, and this going to stop with some article buried on the fifth page of some newspaper. More than likely, there will be a full senate investigation, and you will be called to testify."

Glancing toward the group of reporters at the front walk before he spoke, he lowered his voice where he could not be overheard. "Just off the record, what do you think all of this is about?"

"We have received some information from Congressman Danville's captors," Brittany said, ignoring the question. "Would you care to comment?"

"I don't think I have anything to contribute," he said when he realized she was not going to answer his question. He had hoped she would be more cooperative after his assurances that he would get back to her after he had time to check on the investigation of Maitland's disappearance. Evidently, this was not going to be the case.

"I thought Danville's release was an intricate part of your mission."

"My mission is to do everything I can to promote world peace. If it involves Congressman Danville's release, then I will be glad to assist the authorities in any way I can. I'll even sing at your wedding if it advances our cause."

"I understand André Havran has arrived. Is this the reason for his involvement?"

"To attend your wedding?"

The look Brittany gave him was a mixture of amusement and annoyance. "I was thinking of the peace mission. Is there a connection?"

"We have mutual friends. Mr. Havran is here on a visit."

Abraham's Bones

"I'm not trying to jerk you around, but I think it would be better for everyone involved if you discussed this on camera. You were with the State Department long enough to know the routine. Nothing creates more suspicion than trying to avoid the issues."

"I'm not trying to avoid the issues, but I won't have anything to contribute before tomorrow. I'm sorry."

"One more question, Dr. Christopher. Since your arrival in Israel, your name has being mentioned with increased frequency by al-Qaeda."

"So you are one of Keith Maitland's fans."

The look she gave him was stubborn but determined. "There seems to be a factual basis in some of these accusations."

"If you will excuse me, I have a meeting scheduled and I've kept my friends waiting too long."

Brittany took a step away from him, pausing as she looked at the group of reporters standing near the edge of the parking lot, and then turned her attention back to him. He could see the curiosity in her level stare as well as a look of determination. This was not going to be easy, he told himself as he pushed his way through the entrance. The group of men waiting for him had retreated to the far side of the lobby where they were trying to hide inconspicuously away from the cameras. As soon as this meeting was over, he would have his secretary contact the police. The cause for world peace was too important to have it sidetracked by unfounded accusations in the press.

Then he thought of his earlier conversation with Julia. He could not think of a reasonable explanation for Jennie Carson's behavior, unless it was jealously. Thinking back, he tried to remember how Julia and Jennie had initially met. Julia had never mentioned Jennie's family, and he wondered if she was aware Senator Erlich was her father. It was not beyond the realm of possibility for there to be a connection between Jennie and Maitland's never-ending crusade against the present administration in Washington. As he thought about this for a few seconds, he realized Maitland's interest in him had gone back several weeks before he had accepted his current position. He could not think of a reasonable explanation.

Joe Prentis

Chapter 30

The air coming off the sea was colder than Daniella had expected, but she knew it would take only a minute for her body to warm up once she had reached the firm sand near the edge of the water. The air felt icy on the exposed skin between the bottom of her jog bra and the top of her low-slung pants. After arriving in Israel, she had slept well and had assumed she was over the effects of jet lag, but suddenly it was back with a vengeance. One moment she had been sleeping soundly, and in the next, she had found herself wide-awake as if it was the middle of the day. Exercise always relaxed her and a hard run along the beach was probably all she needed to get back to sleep. She could not see her watch, but she guessed it was around 2 a.m. The beach was dark and deserted, with the only illumination coming from the distant lights on the public beach.

At the university, she had always been an early riser, awakening hours before any of her roommates were out of bed. Before it was daylight, she would be jogging along the streets near the sorority house, seldom encountering anyone as she made a long circle through the center of the campus. The campus police had cautioned her on several occasions, suggesting this pre-dawn activity could be dangerous. Instead of filing a report as they had threatened to do, she would find a patrol car idling in front of the sorority house each morning as she came down the steps. They would pull away from the curb as she turned into the darkened street and follow her at a safe distance until she had completed her run. On several occasions, these two young men had asked her for a date and had even offered to buy her breakfast. She usually chatted away at them in a mixture of Hebrew and Farsi, leaving them confused and unable to determine the language she was speaking. On one occasion they had recorded her voice without her being aware and had carried it all over the campus trying to find someone who could identify the language. They had questioned several of her sorority sisters and all of them had gone along with the gag, inventing elaborate stories to conceal her identity.

Only it was not entirely a joke, Daniella decided. Her mother had sidestepped every question she had asked about their past, and her grandmother had tried to appear open and honest, although she could not hide the troubled look when she had questioned her on a number of occasions.

Our family immigrated to Israel after the war. Your father and mother divorced before you were born and I adopted you and Julia. What else is there to know?

She had never had the courage to ask her sister or to question John. She had developed more than her share of childhood fantasies over the years, even going so far as to tell some of her classmates on Family Day that John was her father. She had cried herself to sleep when they had not believed her. She had never been able to accept the fact that uncaring parents had abandoned her and her sister into the custody of an elderly grandmother. She had been foolish enough on one occasion to discuss this with her roommate, but had vowed never to make this mistake again.

"Do any of these repressed memories involve that school at Hogwarts?" Hollis asked, and then leaning her head sideways, she had said, "You've been reading too many Harry Potter novels. I think you are definitely a muggles."

Hollis had stopped abruptly and apologized, but despite the apology, she had suffered weeks of torment from some of the older students. Someone had written Platform 9¾ on the door of her gym locker, and some of the students called her Hermione for the rest of the term. Unanswered questions had continued to torment her in her sleep. Tonight had been one of those nights and she had awakened suddenly, knowing she had dreamed something disturbing. As she tried to remember, her dream had faded into nothingness. When she had been unable to go back to sleep, she had slipped quietly downstairs and made her way to the beach. She did not want to think about her dreams, and was determined to relax and enjoy her run. Suddenly, she slowed her pace and came to an abrupt halt. The shifting shapes she had seen in her dreams had never made any sense before, but suddenly they did. For some unexplainable reason, she could remember a succession of small details.

The hut where they had slept was cold and she remembered the frigid air on her exposed skin as she was quickly bundled into her clothes. Someone extinguished the smoldering fire and the darkness closed around her. The door creaked loudly as she stumbled through the opening with someone holding tightly to her hand. A strong wind tugged at her clothes as she looked around trying to locate the source of the stench. Dead bodies were stacked in front of a ruined building. Most of them were men, but there were a number of women and children as well. These bodies were stiff and lifeless, their clothes encrusted with blood.

Daniella was suddenly aware of another detail from her dream she had never been aware of before. The man in her dream was speaking Farsi!

"You must go now. You must go quickly! They are coming just over the hill."

The girl had pulled her along until she could walk no more, and then picked her up and ran toward an open gate where a small truck had been idling. Unseen hands had reached down for her, but the girl had swung away and held her tightly for a moment.

You must never forget I love you, she said, then lifted her high over her head and passed her to the waiting hands in the back of the truck. The small convoy had speeded quickly away and she had caught one last glimpse of the girl standing on the crest of the hill. She remembered crossing a high range of mountains where a man had zipped her inside his coat against the warmness of his body. *Where are we going?* she had whispered to him. *I am carrying you to your family, where there will be someone to love you,* he said.

It had been a disturbing dream, but she had no idea of what any of it meant.

Then she realized something else she had never thought about before. Miriam had taught her to speak Arabic when she was very young, but no one had ever taught her to speak Farsi. Were these disturbing events repressed memories, or was this part of a dream?

She stopped when she reached the edge of the water and removed her shoes, dumping the sand, and then laced them up again. Looking in both directions, she started a slow run toward the distant glow of lights at the public beach. She increased her speed gradually and fell into a long stride. It was good to be safely home after the events of the previous weekend. She had received an invitation to spend the weekend at a beach house on Long Island with a group of friends from the university. Taking a jog just before daylight, someone had suddenly appeared out of the darkness and chased her along the deserted seashore. She had barely been able to stay ahead of the dim shadow in the darkness, and each time she looked back, he was still there. Reaching one of the access roads where the surface was firmer, she had run as fast as she could and had finally been able to outdistance him. The police had found no one fitting the description she had given. It had left her shaken, her nerves on edge.

Her breathing had steadied and she knew she had run more than a mile, although she could see none of the landmarks around her. She decided she would go on for at least another half-mile or so before she turned back.

Ahead of her was a level area of hard packed sand used as a launching ramp by some of the local fishermen. Several small buildings faced into the parking lot above. She decided she would circle this paved area so she would not have to break stride as she turned back. The ramp had a rough surface and she could feel the muscles in her calves straining as she ran steeply uphill. She considered continuing down the lane between the buildings, but realized the dark surface of the pavement would make it impossible to see the surface of the roadway. She did not want to risk turning an ankle by stepping into an unseen pothole. Reaching the top of the incline, she ran behind the nearer building and made a long circle through the parking lot before she returned to the beach. She had started to sweat now and the cold air touching the dampness along her ribcage was invigorating.

Her eyes had adjusted somewhat to the darkness but it was still difficult to see. When she reached the hard packed sand just above the water line, she could see an occasional footprint, but little else.

A thin sliver of moonlight peeked from behind the thick clouds for an instant and she saw there were two sets of footprints near the edge of the water. The smaller shoes were obviously hers, but the others were larger and broad across the instep. She could not remember having seen any tracks as she had crossed this expanse of beach only a moment before. Ahead of her was the place where she had jumped an unexpected wave and had left a deep imprint in the sand. As she approached the place, she could see one of the broad footprints had landed squarely on top of hers.

Oh, please, God! Don't let this happen to me again.

She decided she would not look back, but increased her pace instead. The rush and hiss of the waves drowned out any sounds. Risking a quick peek over her shoulder, she saw nothing but an empty seascape dimly illuminated by a thin ray of moonlight. In less than ten minutes, she would be back at the house and safely in her room. Although she was sure there was no one there, she realized she needed to get off the beach. She angled away from the waves and started up the rise toward the safety of the buildings above. It was darker away from the dim fluorescence of the surf, and she had to move much slower through the soft sand. She chanced a look over her shoulder again and felt the tiny hairs lift along the nape of her neck. A stooped figure was jogging along a hundred yards behind her, bent at the waist where he could follow her footprints in the darkness. She increased her speed, tripped on something, and went down hard. She rolled and was on her feet again almost instantly.

He's gaining. Move!

Another quick look over her shoulder made her aware he was closing the distance. Her throat constricted painfully when she saw the baseball cap and the dark jacket unzipped halfway down his broad chest.

This same man had chased her along the beach on Long Island!

She turned her head around and ran for her life.

Chapter 31

Maitland did not know who had screamed until he heard the hard pounding on the thin wall directly behind the headboard of his bed. His heart was racing at an impossible rate, and he could feel pain—a sharp, searing pang in the center of his chest leaving him breathless and frightened. He lowered himself cautiously until he was lying down again, being especially careful not make any sudden movements that would cause him any additional discomfort.

Relax—I need to relax. Taking inventory of the rest of his body, he determined rather quickly that he did not have anything that did not hurt. For some unknown reason, this seemed remarkably amusing and he found himself laughing, his body shaking painfully. *Not only do I hurt,* he decided with a growing sense of horror. *I have gone crazy as well!*

The doctor had given him some pain medication when they had discharged him from the hospital, but he could not remember if he had taken one of the pills recently. As he thought about this, he could not remember for sure if he had taken one at all. His stomach felt queasy and his head was pounding with vile insistence, almost as if someone was beating on the outside of the door.

Then he realized the pounding noise was, indeed, coming from the hallway and he cringed back against his pillow and reached for the sheet with his good arm.

"Open the door or we will kick it down!"

Rolling his body away from the edge of the bed, he tried to maneuver his elbow underneath his right side where he could raise himself into a setting position, but it was too painful. He called out to the person on the opposite side of the door, as a jagged crack appeared across the face of the panel, and then with another kick, the whole door splintered and came crashing down on the floor just missing the end of the bed.

"Get up!" the man demanded as he kicked the wreckage aside and came toward the bed, his large hands flexing as if he was prepared to fasten them around his neck.

"No, please! I cannot get up. I have been in an accident and I think I have just had a heart attack. I need a doctor."

Maitland suddenly realized the man standing beside the bed had on a police officer's uniform, and the two others he could see through the opened doorway, were police officers as well.

"You must come with us. Get dressed quickly or be prepared to come as you are," the man threatened.

He had gone to bed wearing nothing but his underpants, but he did not know if he could get dressed without help. When he did not immediately move, the big police officer reached for his arm. He shrank back, trying to move his arm out of the way, but the man grabbed it with a tight grip and jerked him erect, placing him on his feet. He stood there swaying with dizziness and pain.

"That is the way he screamed before," someone complained from the hallway. "He is crazy, that one. Take him away and take his things with him, for he won't be returning to this hotel."

A thin wail was still emanating from his tortured throat, but like someone trying to find the off-switch on some unknown piece of audio equipment, he did not know how to make himself stop.

"Shut up!" the police officer demanded. Leaning toward his face, he placed an enormous fist against his nose with so much force he staggered backwards, and for an instant, he thought he was going to fall across the bed. Suddenly, he heard a commotion from the hallway, and then someone came rushing toward him despite the protest from the two police officers at the door.

"What are you *doing* to him? Are you crazy?"

Maitland could understand nothing else they were saying, for both of them had switched to Hebrew. The girl—he suddenly realized it was Daniella—had shoved the man's arm aside and forced herself into the narrow space between them. He had no idea of what she was saying, but the police officer had now taken a step backwards while she continued to shout at him, motioning all the while toward the hallway. Finally, with an open-armed gesture—as if he was disavowing any responsibility—the policeman turned toward the doorway, herding his fellow officers along in front of him.

"But who will pay for my door?" a short man asked in a querulous tone from the hallway.

"I will pay for your door," she said. "Now go and stop your pathetic whining!"

When the man started to object again, Daniella dug into the pocket of her jeans and removed a folded wad of currency. She peeled off a couple of notes and pressed them into the man's hands. Someone else came into the room, and Maitland saw it was a young man, probably in his late teens. He looked around at the wreckage and gave a low whistle between his teeth.

"Help him get dressed," Daniella commanded.

"I am *not* going to help him . . ."

"Kevin," she warned in a low voice and the young man immediately sprang to life. She had thrown his suitcase open on the end of the bed and was folding his clothes neatly inside. Maitland sucked in his breath with a little cry as he started moving painfully toward the bathroom. He did not know what was happening, but he could feel his relief turning into laughter again.

I really am crazy! he decided, but the knowledge did not give him any comfort.

Herzi settled his lean frame into the chair in front of Christopher's desk, thumbing slowly through the pages of a small notebook. "This is very confusing, Dr. Christopher, but my investigation has turned up several items of information I find to be very disturbing."

Christopher glanced at the growing pile of papers on his desk. In the past hour, his office had received dozens of messages from world leaders around the globe. In Washington, Senator Erlich had continued to put pressure on the administration to protest to the Vatican about his appointment, but so far, Cauldfield had remained firm. He had received three urgent messages from Brittany demanding an immediate meeting, but he did not thank it was wise to speak with her until he received a reply to the message he had sent to Cardinal Mason. He had been trying to reach Havran when this policeman had appeared at his door.

"How may I help you?" Christopher asked, wondering if this had anything to do with Maitland's disappearance, or was it something else to add to his list of worries.

"We have found the body of a young American named Gary Maser. I am afraid he was murdered."

Christopher's preoccupations with his own worries made him suspect he had not heard Herzi correctly. "When did this happen?" he asked cautiously.

"A trawler picked him only an hour ago. The time of death has not been determined. I've come here to speak with Daniella Siedman. I understand she has been running errands for the excavation staff."

"And what connection does Daniella have with this?" he asked, cautiously. "I am afraid I don't understand."

"I understand she was the last person to see him alive. There have also been some other disturbing developments. We have been able to trace the car that attempted to run over Mr. Maitland to its owner. While we believe him to be innocent, we have learned he was in the company of a young woman who fits Miss Siedman's description. I would like to ask her some questions."

"I can assure you she had nothing to do with any of this," Christopher said.

"Nevertheless, I think you are aware of police procedure and the necessity to follow our information wherever it leads us."

Christopher's first reaction was to refuse the request, but he realized delaying the inevitable would serve no useful purpose. "I will have my secretary send for her," he said as he crossed to the connecting door of the offices.

"I have already taken the liberty of contacting her," Herzi said. "I have also asked Mr. Maitland to join us. I could have asked you to come to the police station, but I thought it would be better to do this informally. I am sure we only need to clear up a few details."

There was a soft knock at the outer door, but before Christopher could move, Daniella had pushed it open, looking at him in a questioning way. Seeing Herzi seated in front of the desk, she hesitated for a few seconds, and then came inside and pushed the door closed.

"Did you send for me," she asked, glancing at Herzi before she directed her attention at him again.

"Actually, I did," Herzi said. My name is Herzi and I am with the police. Two of my officers have told me you were involved in an altercation at a hotel this morning. I understand a door was broken down."

Daniella hesitated for a few seconds, and before Christopher could caution her, she had thrust her hands into the back pockets of her denim shorts and was looking at Herzi in icy silence. "Did your officers tell you they were the ones who broke the door down?" she asked. "It happened as my friend and I were coming down the hallway."

"I believe the item of information is in my report. I also understand you paid for the damage to the door."

"I had little choice in the matter. The hotel manager complained, and I thought it was the best way to avoid any additional problems."

"Ah, I see. I am sure Mr. Maitland was very grateful for your help. I understand you went to the hospital to see him a short time after he was injured."

Christopher felt a little stirring of uneasiness, as he wondered why she had not mentioned any of this to him.

"I see I have asked a question you do not want to answer," Herzi said, watching her expression carefully. "Why did you go to the hospital initially? I understand there was a young man with you on both occasions."

"Kevin Krishnan."

"So you do remember."

Christopher saw her eyes dart in his direction, and then she was looking at Herzi again.

"You also knew a young man named Gideon Wellhausen, I understand."

Daniella was frowning at him again. "Do I have to answer these questions?" she asked. Before Christopher could reply, Herzi was suddenly on his feet, looking down at her along the length of his nose.

"I am afraid you have no choice. I could have had you brought to the police station, but out of respect for you grandmother and for Dr. Christopher, I chose to question you here. Why are you so hesitant in answering my questions? They seem simple enough."

"What happened to Gideon?" she demanded.

"And why do you think something has happened to him?"

"You spoke of him in the past tense as if he is dead."

"Which is the reason I am asking these questions," Herzi said. "He was killed an hour ago in a terrorists incident in Jerusalem."

Daniella made an involuntary sound of fright and placed her hand across her mouth. Christopher had started toward her when Herzi waved him away. He stopped five feet from her, but he was close enough to hear the sound of her breath caught high in her throat.

"There are several other things that trouble me," Herzi said. We have a picture in our possession showing you participating in a tennis tournament in Boston last year. Our technicians were able to enhance a section of the background and we were able to identify Gideon peering through the fence. Can you offer an explanation for this?"

"I did not know him until a week ago when he showed up here. I am sure there must be a mistake. He is from a small university in Hungary."

"I understand this was the impression you tried to leave on everyone, but our evidence suggest otherwise."

"There is a mistake."

"We also have documentation showing him at a pool party you attended late last fall. We also have a photograph to substantiate this."

"Is there a purpose for these questions?" Christopher asked.

"I was coming to the point, Dr. Christopher.

Daniella jumped as the door behind her suddenly opened and Pierce and Havran appeared in the doorway. "We've been trying to reach you," Havran said as he glanced in Herzi's direction. "We have been checking a few things since we spoke with you on the phone. I think we can clear everything up."

"If you have an explanation that would explain all of this, I would very much like to hear it," Herzi replied.

"There are some security matters involved," Pierce said. "I think you need to excuse the young lady."

"Very well, but don't go too far," Herzi cautioned. "I might want to speak with you again."

The door leading into the hallway opened and Maitland looked uncertainly at the group, and then his eyes fell on Daniella as she turned away. She hesitated for a moment, giving Maitland an icy glare, and then she turned and ran wildly from the room.

Chapter 32

Daniella ran up the rear stairs and turned down the hallway toward her room. Her shirt was wet with sweat, her hair disheveled. She rounded the corner and headed toward her computer. Bringing up the file where she stored her emails, she selected all of them, hit the delete key, and sat back with a sigh of relief as the cursor swept upward and the files disappeared. Taking a deep breath, she covered her face with her hands and realized she was trembling.

A shower, she decided. *I must take a shower and then I will get my passport.*

She ran to her closet and grabbed a bra and panties from the top of the drawer, then wheeled around, wondering if she had forgotten anything.

Last week she had copied all of the files on her computer so she could bring them with her. What had she done with the CD?

Retracing her steps to the computer she grabbed her CD travel case and began to flip through the files. She had encrypted everything and had put a label on the front identifying it as her lesson plans for her last semester. Turning the case around, she flipped the catch and ran quickly through the other sleeves, frowning thoughtfully to herself. Where was it? She had seen it the night before when she had received an email from Jared. It had to be here somewhere.

"Is this what you are looking for?"

She jumped, making a little sound of fright and then swiveled around in her chair. Sanura was standing just inside the connecting door between their bedrooms with a CD dangling between her fingers. She had encrypted all of her files with the latest version of the Fortress Program. No one outside the NSA had been successful in cracking the code. Seeing Sanura standing there with the CD—her CD—enraged her. Why had she been going through her things?

Suddenly, without being aware she had moved, she found herself on her feet. "How dare you go through my things!" she shouted. "I want that back!"

Sanura pushed herself away from the doorjamb and came slowly toward her, her face flushed, her eyes narrowed and angry. "I want to know what you have been doing, you little idiot."

"How *dare* you," Daniella said, and suddenly she was rushing toward her, her hands closed into fist. She grabbed at the CD, but Sanura sidestepped her assault and shoved her toward the bed. Grabbing the post at the foot, Daniella launched herself in her direction again. Sanura grabbed her arm and turned her around, then lifted her in the air and slammed her down on the bed, penning her effortlessly to the mattress.

"I hate you!" Daniella screamed. "I hate you, I hate you . . ."

Sanura's hand covered her mouth, but she was so enraged she could not stop struggling until she seized her by the throat. "I want you to stop or I will choke you," Sanura threatened.

Daniella had freed one hand and she was reaching for her hair. Sanura grabbed her wrist and jerked it down, but the hand holding her throat did not loosen. Daniella looked into the angry eyes, only an inch from her own, and suddenly stopped struggling. When Sanura loosened her grip on her throat, she suddenly burst into tears, covering her face with her hands, while uncontrollable sobs wracked her body. "I want you to turn me loose. I'm leaving and I will never be back."

"I also have your passport. You're not going anywhere."

"Why are you doing this?" Daniella demanded.

"I'm trying to protect you. They took me to the police station and they stripped me and they searched me. Then they came here to search my room. Andre turned them away at the gate. I think what they were looking for is on this CD. I have been able to recover part of it, and eventually I will be able to recover the rest. I want to know what you have been doing."

Daniella tried to answer her, but her rage had turned to fear.

"What are you doing?" Julia cried from the direction of the doorway. Sanura shifted her weight and Daniella was dimly aware of Sanura waving her sister away. Julia remained where she was for a moment, but when Sanura rolled on her back and gather her in her arms, Julia turned and left the room, pulling the door firmly closed behind her.

"I am sorry," Daniella said, her voice muffled against Sanura's blouse. "I am *so* sorry."

"I want you to tell me what you have been doing," Sanura said softly. "I want to try to fix it, and we might not have very much time. If they don't get the answers they are wanting from John and Andre, they will be back."

Daniella wiped her eyes with the back of her hand, and then she lifted her head and looked at her. "I have been trying to find my father."

"Oh, dear God," Sanura whispered as she looked down at her face. "What have you done?"

"I have been very careful," Daniella said.

"Not careful enough. Maitland has records of contacts you have made, as well as copies of airline schedules and travel reservations. What you have done has been very dangerous. Andre is going to try to fix it, but you must promise me that you will never do anything like this again."

"All I wanted to do was see him. For all of my life they have told me he left before I was born. No one knew where he was, and then I found out he was still alive."

When Daniella started to lift her head, Sanura pulled her against her again, tucking her face against her shoulder. She tried to pull back for an instant, and then overcome with nervous exhaustion, she relaxed her body and was instantly asleep. Sanura continued to hold her, staring at the darkening ceiling.

Maitland shoved his way through the door of his hotel room, and then came to a halt looking toward his suitcase setting on a table against the wall. He moved slowly toward it, examining its posi-

Abraham's Bones

tion in relation with the wall and the other objects in the room. He went to his camera case and jerked the zipper. Turning the camera on, he checked the exposure total as he started to scan slowly through the pictures, comparing them with what he could see in the room. There could be no doubt, he decided. Someone had carefully searched the room, but had not placed everything back as they had found it. He reached for the cell phone hanging on his belt, then paused, knowing it would be dangerous to make a call from the room. It was important to talk to Senator Erlich, but he decided he would go to one of the public phones along the street.

He locked the door behind him and went quickly down the corridor. The lobby was quiet, but there were still some tourist wandering around in the parking lot outside. He turned quickly toward the street, remembering he had seen a phone booth on the next block. Walking rapidly along, he was relieved to find most of the shops still open and the street well lighted. Feeling inside his jacket, he found his address book and ran his finger down the page until he found the number of Erlich's office. When he reached the booth, he wasted no time in dialing the number. It rang for the third time before someone answered. Wedging his shoulder into the corner, he shifted the receiver to his other hand as he took a quick scan of the street. A couple of tourists were strolling slowly along the opposite side of the street carrying a small child. A man was looking through the window of a small shop. Suddenly the man turned away from the display he had been examining and looked toward the phone booth. Maitland felt his breath catch in his throat.

He had seen this same man in Rome when he was talking to Sangallo. Maser was dead and he had received a report from a trusted informant that Congressman Danville was dead also, despite the optimistic bulletins the government had continued to issue by the hour. He wondered how this man had found him on this side street. Somehow, he had made a serious mistake in allowing them to follow him here.

He wondered what other mistakes he had made.

Christopher was almost to his car when he saw a van with military markings coming rapidly around the outside of the parking lot. Underneath the grill, blue lights were flashing. The van slid to a stop and the window came whirring down. Pierce swung the door open and moved over to make room in the back seat. He was in the act of closing the door when the car started up again with a lurch, swinging in a tight circle toward the street.

"Sorry I couldn't give you any advance warning, but I only got word a few minutes ago. We have located the house where they are holding Congressman Danville. Some of our people are already in place. We have to hurry."

Christopher fastened his seatbelt as Pierce shuffled through some papers he had taken from a wrinkled envelope and passed two of them across. The first was a printout from a computer showing the close-up of an auto license plate, and the other was the front of a run-down house with tree leaning toward a narrow porch.

"We have every reason to believe Congressman Danville is being held in this house." Pierce removed another photo from the envelope and handed it to Christopher. He glanced down at a picture of a tall man standing inside a chain link fence at the rear of the house. He appeared to be feeding a dog. The picture was grainy and indistinct, but there could be no doubt this was the man he had seen in the photo in the embassy meeting in Rome, the man Stoltz had thought was the leader of Shiva.

"Are you sure they are still there?" Christopher asked.

"We are certain. One of our people made these photographs only a few minutes ago. They are prepared to make an assault on the house as soon as we arrive."

Christopher felt a little stirring of uneasiness. An assault on a house where hostages were involved was seldom successful. This was usually a last ditch effort where there was no other alternatives. "What about Danville?" he asked.

Pierce gave a little shake of his head. "We will do everything we can to assure Congressman Danville's safety. We believe we have a very good chance of getting him out alive."

Christopher had not paid much attention to their whereabouts, but as he looked at the houses rushing by, he realized the area looked familiar. The houses were becoming more scattered and there were several weed-grown lots. Pierce reached inside his jacket and lifted his phone to his ear. Christopher could hear the terse commands and was aware that Pierce was looking at him again.

"They decided to make a run for it. Our men had no choice but to open fire."

In the distance, a helicopter was lifting into the air, rapidly gaining altitude. He could see a plume of smoke rising from the end of the street.

Chapter 33

"Dr. Christopher! Dr. Christopher," one of the reporters shouted as they passed through the hotel entrance and approached the speaker stand at the edge of the parking lot. He realized it was Brittany standing in front of the little mob of reporters, waving a notepad frantically in the air. Arav had forced them to set up their equipment well away from the entrance of the hotel, and as they waited impatiently in the sweltering heat, their displeasure was evident. They obviously considered this to be an act of harassment or a personal insult. In the absence of any hard news, they had aired their grievances over the networks, speculating on who was to blame.

As Christopher and the group of government officials moved down the walkway, a detachment of soldiers pushed a curious crowd of tourists back. The camera crews were jockeying for position, hoping to angle their cameras where they could catch the side of the news vans, with their satellite dishes and the name of the news services printed along the side. He ignored the shouting as they walked to the table where a forest of microphones rested in front of the podium. He did not know what was on the other side of the hastily draped tablecloth, but he saw several cameras dip toward it briefly, then focus again on his face. When he came to a halt facing the crowd of reporters, Arav was on his left, while Pierce was on the opposite side, staring into the crowd.

Abraham's Bones

"General Arav and Colonel Pierce have statements to read regarding the joint operation to rescue Congressman Danville," Christopher said. "I think all of you already know it was not completely successful." He stepped back as Arav moved toward the microphones, the lines of his face standing out in stark relief in the bright sunlight.

Christopher swept the crowd with his gaze as Arav described the investigation and the events leading up to the attempted rescue. He was surprised Maitland was absent. He was only half listening to what could have been a campaign speech the world over. Arav expressed his appreciation to unknown officials and faceless individuals who had served in various ways, emphasizing the joint nature of the operation. In the presence of the heavily armed cadre of troops, the reporters were subdued, but he was aware of their eyes fastened on him. They were not buying this version of what had happened, but were waiting for him to return to the microphones. As Arav droned on, he saw Brittany reach for her cell phone and frown into the middle distance as she listened, but seemed to becoming increasingly frustrated as she tried unsuccessfully to interrupt whoever was on the other end. When she had completed the call, she frowned down at the phone for a minute, and then looked up at him, her face filled with resentment. He was suddenly aware of some of the other reporters speaking into their phones, and were having the same reaction as Brittany.

When Pierce had finished with a speech that would have been appropriate at a war college, he walked back to the podium, braced for the barrage of questions he knew was coming. Brittany had already lifted her microphone, but he saw her hesitate as someone leaned toward her ear, whispering, and then she was looking at him again.

"On behalf of all of the news services, we would like to thank you for keeping us informed," Brittany said, "and we look forward to your continued cooperation as the negotiations move forward." Her eyes blinked closed for a second, and then she was looking back at him. As he studied her enraged expression and her strained smile, he knew this was not over.

Christopher walked to the window of his office, looking out at the darkened parking lot. The hotel staff had removed the barriers where the news teams had parked their vans during the last three days, and he could see strips of yellow plastic tape fluttering in the breeze. A small civil disturbance in Jerusalem had drawn most of them away, while others were in route to America, Paris, and Rome to await the next international crisis. He had spent the remainder of the afternoon trying to reach Brittany. She had refused to accept his calls, although the desk had assured him she had not checked out of her room.

He had reserved a table in the restaurant for dinner, but had canceled the reservations when he discovered Daniella was still sulking in her room, angry and hurt over his inability to prevent Herzi from questioning her. Sanura had to meet with a friend in Tel Aviv and had informed him she would not be returning before the next day. Julia had claimed she was not hungry. His secretary had placed a stack of reports on the corner of his desk before leaving. He decided he would read hastily through them, and then make plans to meet with the excavation staff and the IAA the following week. He picked up the newspaper from the corner of his desk and glanced at the headline.

International Conspiracy Crushed

He ran his eye down the column, reading about Congressman Danville's death, while unable to understand why the press had treated the ones involved in this unfortunate event so kindly. He frowned when he saw a separate paragraph detailing the heroic effort of the emergency team to save Danville's life, and the difficult decision by the surgical team to withdraw life support.

He had seen the body and there could be no doubt Sanura had been correct. Danville had been dead for at least forty-eight hours before they had stormed the house. There was a picture of the Sheikh, the same one he had seen in Rome, and also another of him in the morgue with a single bullet hole through the center of his forehead. This article speculated on the location of the bullet, and wondered if it had been suicide. The final story was much longer, explaining Shiva in great detail and hinting there might have been one or two members in midlevel positions in the government, and possibly as many as a dozen in various post in the military. The power of Shiva was destroyed, if indeed it had ever had any power, the reporter said with a great deal of enthusiastic patriotism. He did not know Sean Everly, who had written the article, and he wondered at the sources Everly had quoted. He mentioned Dr. Siedman's upcoming novel, suggesting it would be aimed at a young audience who was awaiting its arrival with the same breathless expectation their younger siblings experienced while waiting for the latest issue of Harry Potter. According to the article, Maitland had released the first three chapters on the Internet and Erlich Publications was threatening to sue. Several of New York's largest publishers were bidding in an effort to buy the contract from Erlich. Mifflin had offered an undisclosed amount reaching into the lower six figures, with the promise they would have eight million copies in their first printing. This was the most incredible thing he had ever read, and it made no sense whatsoever. He could not believe this reporter had written this account voluntary, which raised an equally puzzling question. How had they forced any of them to concoct these outrageous stories?

Christopher was suddenly aware someone had stopped in the doorway behind him. He lowered the newspaper and turned quickly around, experiencing a sudden feeling of alarm as he saw the anxious expression and the rumpled clothing.

"I wonder if I might speak with you for a moment," Angus McLeish said, his eyes darting around the room.

"I was about to grab a sandwich," Christopher said, as he saw his eyes dart toward the ceiling, examining the tile and the ductwork. "I wonder if you would like to join me?"

"I would," McLeish said, running his hand into the inside pocket of his coat, as if to assure himself that whatever he was searching for was still there. When he continued to stand as if he was in a trance, Christopher gestured toward the doorway. McLeish nodded his head as if he was suddenly coming awake.

The hallway was almost empty, and when they reached the restaurant, he could see most of the guests sitting near the front windows. When the waiter gestured in that direction, McLeish pointed toward the far corner of the dinning room where the light had already been dimmed. When the waiter glanced at him with a puzzled expression, McLeish replied with a humorless laugh.

"We have some pressing business," he said. "We wouldn't want to disturb your other guests."

The waiter gave a good-natured nod and changed directions, leading them to a side window offering a spectacular view of the harbor.

"What is this all about?" Christopher asked when the waiter had taken their order and moved away to seat some other late arriving guests.

"I see you have been reading the newspaper," McLeish said.

"Yes," he admitted when McLeish kept staring into his eyes, waiting for his answer.

"I am going to trust you," McLeish said after a moment. "I really have no choice."

"I am not sure what you just said was a complement," Christopher said. McLeish gave a brief flicker of a smile and then he was staring back at him again.

"I obtained a copy of the first three chapters of Dr. Siedman's novel from an Internet site," he said.

"I am aware it has been illegally posted."

"I was quite shocked when I read through it, and then saw the accounts in the newspaper."

His hand had closed around Christopher's wrist and for a moment he found himself staring into a pair of half-mad eyes.

"I'm not sure I understand," Christopher said, attempting to free his hand.

McLeish seemed to come alive all at once, reaching for his inside pocket. He produced a wrinkled envelope containing a dozen sheets of paper. Flipping quickly through them, he selected a sheet and slapped it down on the table, keeping his hand on top of it for a moment.

"This is a copy of one of the photographs you received from Father Sangallo in Rome. Notice the small drawing in the left hand margin. I haven't been able to make any sense out of the other symbols, but after I carefully examined the sketch, I realized this line represented the western wall of the city. I believe the symbol in the margin represents a signal tower on the hill above the city. I hiked up there yesterday and dug down a couple of feet into the soil. I found a few of the foundation stones. I believe a portion of this represents a map, and these symbols represent geographic features. I talked with one of Father Ricci's associates. He hasn't been able to make much progress with a translation, but he has been able to determine the meaning of a few words. This one is the name, Simon."

Christopher turned the photograph toward the light and began to examine the text, not immediately understanding the reason for his excitement. The letters were poorly formed, some of them crowded together in uneven lines. He had seen something similar on a facsimile of what had become known as the Copper Scrolls, one of the artifacts discovered in the caves near Qumran on the northwestern shore of the Dead Sea. There had been 900 scrolls in the collection, inscribed in ink on animal skins and papyrus. Only two of them had been engraved on a thick copper sheet. The team of translators had initially been puzzled, but had eventually decided the inscription gave the location of over 60 sites where treasure had been hidden away before the Romans had destroyed the temple complex in Jerusalem. The text on the copper scrolls had been poorly drawn, and the conclusion they had reached suggested they had employed scribes who could not read, guaranteeing the secrets contained in the inscription would not become known. McLeish would have a difficult battle in trying to prove this was somewhat similar, if indeed, that was what he was suggesting.

"There is also a brief mention of a signal tower in Dr. Siedman's manuscript," McLeish said, "but no one knew the signal tower existed until I read this, then dug down a few feet and discovered the foundation stones."

When Christopher stared back at him, not completely sure he understood what he was suggesting, McLeish leaned forward and spoke in a fierce whisper. "Many years ago, Father Sangallo's artifacts were in the possession of Dr. Siedman's family. I believe these tablets are in a language many thousands of years old, and I strongly suspect she has been able to make a translation. It is quite possible the story in her novel is accurate. This could be the key to a very valuable storehouse of artifacts. The temple treasure described in the Copper Scroll was never found, but here we have benchmarks to start in our search. This could be the archeological find of the ages, and there is also this. "I received it no more than an hour ago. It is a report from a lab in Tel Aviv." He hesitated for another moment, and then lifted his hand revealing a note scrawled across the surface of the page.

Blood type does not match!

When Christopher looked up, McLeish was leaning toward him, poised as if he might take flight at any moment. Christopher wondered if he was going to spring some surprise he was intending to develop into an over-blown story about the Middle East. What would it be this time? A drop of blood from the crucifixion cross, proving the man crucified was not really Jesus of Nazareth. Several novelists had already done something similar. The shock value of these stories was wearing hopelessly thin. Before he could speculate any further, McLeish tapped the sheet with the tip of his finger.

"This document proves the man killed yesterday was not the Sheikh," McLeish whispered.

Christopher took his time answering, his mind racing at the possibilities. "How could you possibly prove that?" he asked cautiously. "Do you have a sample of his DNA?"

"I don't, but it wasn't necessary. The man who was killed was a European. Dr. Rosen ran the test for me. There is no doubt that he was not of Middle Eastern extraction. Perhaps when you have seen this, you will not doubt the accuracy of my information." He thumbed quickly through the other sheets and placed one of them in front of him.

Christopher's eyes darted around the sheet of paper.

"Don't you understand the significance," McLeish whispered. "The man killed on the raid was an impostor, a double perhaps, in the fashion of many of our world leaders over the last few decades. Winston Churchill had a double, as did Stalin and more than one of the American presidents. I not only have the medical reports I obtained from someone in the medical examiner's office, I also have this."

McLeish pulled a small package from his pocket and unwrapped the tissue paper. Christopher saw a necklace, and as McLeish turned it toward the light, he saw the emblem he had seen for the first time on Sangallo's photographs. The pendant was made of alabaster, with two winged figures and a shield, and at the bottom was the two bird-like figures constructed of seven straight lines.

"I did not know the significance at first," McLeish explained, "but I discovered this is the emblem of Shiva. Anyone wearing this would be a family member or someone in the inner circle of leadership. The man killed earlier today did not have this pendant. He was an imposter, some poor fool, perhaps, who had been hired for the purpose of protecting the identity of the Sheikh. Our intelligence services have been chasing their tails for the last decade trying to locate him, and they have failed again."

Christopher saw movement from the corner of his eye. When he turned his head toward the archway, he saw Daniella coming rapidly across the floor toward their table. She had dressed for the occasion in a short skirt and a sleeveless blouse, her hair full and loose on her shoulders. When she saw him looking, her smile became radiant, in sharp contrast to the strained, unhappy expression he had witnessed over the past few days. He climbed to his feet and held a chair for her. On the opposite side of the table, McLeish had closed his hand, concealing the necklace, and had made a small, involuntary sound of surprise. Darting a glance in his direction, he realized McLeish had focused his attention on the pendent suspended around Daniella's neck on a small gold chain. The overhead lights were subdued, but there was enough illumination for him to recognize the small oval with two bird-like figures composed of seven straight lines. It was identical to the one McLeish was concealing in his hand.

Christopher closed his eyes, remembering the cold, darkened village and the icy wind. Dead bodies were stacked in front of a ruined building. Most of them were men, but there were a number of women and children as well. These bodies were stiff and lifeless, their clothes encrusted with blood. The tall, bearded figure had approached him and placed his hand on his shoulder. "This is my youngest daughter. You must return her to her grandmother where she will be safe," he had commanded, placing a small child in his arms. When he looked up, the man was gone, having vanished into the darkness.

McLeish had leaned toward Daniella. "That emblem," he said cautiously. "Are you aware of the legend surrounding it?"

"Yes," Daniella said, lifting it between her thumb and forefinger where she could look down at the design for a minute before aiming her smile in his direction again. "They call it the emblem of Abraham. My father sent it to me. Everyone thought he was dead, but they were wrong. This is the most wonderful thing in my whole life. It is going to change everything!"

Christopher felt a cold tremor of fear as he examined her innocent expression and realized how wrong he had been, and then a second thought occurred to him, even more frightening. How far did this conspiracy extend into the Israeli government, and were there secret supporters in Washington as well. Everything in the last few days had been too easy for any of it to be an accident. *This is going to change everything*, Daniella had said. Ambassador Stoltz had warned of Armageddon.

He was terribly afraid that both of them were right.

Printed in Great Britain
by Amazon